THE BLOODY LEGIONNAIRES

Geoffrey Davison

SAPERE
BOOKS

THE BLOODY LEGIONNAIRES

Published by Sapere Books.

20 Windermere Drive, Leeds, England, LS17 7UZ,
United Kingdom

saperebooks.com

ISBN: 978-1-80055-021-6

Farewell, Monsieur Traveller: look you lisp and wear strange suits, disable all the benefits of your own country, be out of love with your nativity and almost chide God for making you that countenance you are, or I will scarce think you have swam in a gondola.
— William Shakespeare

Chapter One

It was approaching one a.m. on the morning of 13th March. The man stood in the dark shadows, in a dimly lit street in the old quarter of Budapest and watched the building opposite him. On the top floor of the building was a light at a small window.

The man glanced at his illuminated watch dial and gripped his bulky briefcase. A gust of wind blew a cloud of dust into his face. He felt no physical discomfort. All his faculties were concentrated on watching the light from the window and listening for any sign of danger.

The light at the window flickered. It was the signal that he had been waiting for. His eyes searched the darkness around him, and his ears strained to pick up any sound of danger. He saw and heard nothing. He left his cover and quickly crossed the street and entered the building. A night light gave a dull, blue glow, but the man knew the staircase and the treads to step on warily. He quickly climbed to the top floor landing and came to an apartment door. On the door was a printed card. It read — 'Madame Zena, Astrologer and Clairvoyant. Consultations by appointment.'

The man knocked gently on the door.

A woman's voice called out, 'Come in. My door is always open.'

The man opened the door and stepped into the apartment. The room was lit by a small table lamp close to the window where Madame Zena was sitting in front of heavily draped curtains, at her table and crystal ball. She had a dark face with grey hair. Over her shoulders was a colourful shawl. The man took a seat facing her at the table. He held his leather briefcase on his knees.

Madame Zena's dark brown, spidery fingers gripped her crystal ball. 'There has been no change,' she whispered. 'The time is not right. The signs are not in your favour. The paths of two major planets are moving closer to each other. It is dangerous for any minor star to get too close to them. When their paths move away from each other again, then the time will be right. You must be patient.'

'It is too late,' the man said. 'It is too late!'

Madame Zena continued to stare into her crystal.

'You must stay clear of the two planets.'

'I had to move!' There was desperation in the man's voice. 'I had to! I will pay for my protection. I have made arrangements to leave the country. I need help.'

Madame Zena looked up from her crystal ball. She saw the urgency reflected in the man's eyes.

'You must remain undercover,' she whispered. 'There are negotiations taking place. You must wait…'

She stopped abruptly. The still of the night had suddenly been shattered by a motor car. It had entered the street, and it was in a hurry. The man's eyes flashed nervously, and his cheek muscles went taut. He gripped his briefcase.

There was a screeching of tyres as the car came to an abrupt halt outside the apartment. The man instantly got to his feet.

Madame Zena remained seated.

'Behind the curtain is a bedroom. There is a window that opens onto the roof. There is a path over the roof. Take it.'

'Where do I go?' the man pleaded.

'You must stay undercover until you can be protected. You must make for Zurich. I will contact Zurich. If they can help you, you will be informed. Otherwise, stay undercover. Use the local press. You know the codes?'

'Yes.'

'Then go.'

The man needed no urging. He disappeared through the dark velvet curtains that screened the bedroom.

Madame Zena remained seated at her table. She heard footsteps on the staircase getting closer. Suddenly, her entrance door burst open and two men entered the room. They had revolvers in their hands.

'Good evening, Comrades,' Madame Zena said.

The men ignored her and rushed into the other rooms of the apartment, including the bedroom.

A third man entered the apartment. He was tall, hatless and wearing a dark overcoat. He walked into the middle of the room and glanced about him, with a superior expression on his face. The two men spoke to him in Russian. He snapped out an order. They hurried out of the apartment and down the staircase.

The man slowly removed his gloves and took the seat facing Madame Zena.

'Good evening, Comrade,' Madame Zena said. 'I wasn't aware that we had an appointment.'

The man gave a faint smile of amusement.

'We have now, Madame,' he said. 'Look into your crystal ball, and look hard.'

Madame Zena again gripped her crystal ball with her spidery fingers.

'Tell me, Madame, where is Visinsky?'

'Visinsky, Comrade? Who is it that I look for?'

'He is a man from my department, Madame, and he has been concerned about his future.'

Madame Zena put her head nearer to the crystal. She studied it thoughtfully, then looked up at the man.

'The crystal tells me nothing about such a man, Comrade.'

The smile left the man's face. In its place came a look of anger. Suddenly he lashed his hand across the table and sent the crystal and its stand flying across the room.

Madame Zena fell back in her chair. The man produced a revolver and pointed it at her.

'Study this, Madame,' he hissed, 'and not your crystal ball.' He leaned forward. 'This man has been consulting you about his future, Madame.' He spoke coldly and his eyes had narrowed. 'Now where is Visinsky? Tell me!' Madame Zena had recovered her composure.

'I do not know the whereabouts of such a man, Comrade,' she said. 'He has not consulted me.'

'And if such a man should consult you, Madame. What would you tell him?'

'I would tell him that I could not help him. The signs are not favourable.'

The man sat back.

'The signs are not favourable,' he said. He continued to eye her coldly. He knew the signs that she was referring to, and he understood what she was saying. He looked into her dark face and squeezed the trigger of his revolver twice, in quick succession. There was a sharp *crack! crack!* and two bullets smashed into Madame Zena's heart, killing her instantly.

The man stood up. He still held his revolver in his right hand. His left hand smacked the table angrily.

'Visinsky,' he hissed. 'Visinsky, we will find you. We will find you and kill you. You are a dead man.'

Visinsky had heard the two revolver shots. They had been faint, but unmistakeable, and they had sent a cold chill down his spine. He knew what had happened and he knew what he was now up against. He was on his own and there was no turning back.

Chapter Two

Giuseppe Garibaldi Bassito was the undisputed head of the Bassito family of Naples. He was Papa, Grandpapa, Uncle, Brother, and Cousin. His wife worshipped him; his sons admired and feared him; his daughter loved him, and his brothers, cousins and half cousins looked upon him as their leader, protector, and benefactor.

Bassito owned and ran an export and import business with connections that spread into the various cities of Europe. He also operated an undercover organisation for providing his legitimate company with all the necessary cash that it ever needed. He had friends in many quarters. He also had enemies, but no one would dare betray him, and no one would ever dare to utter the word *Mafia*, but it was always a thought. Bassito was his own Caesar, and his family, his business and his friends were his own Mafia.

When Bassito's daughter — his beloved Maria — brought her boyfriend, Nico Minchello, to ask permission to marry, Bassito was particularly delighted, because, not only was his daughter obviously happy, but also because the Minchello family was a highly respected family of bankers. The marriage would give Bassito's business interest further respectability. Bassito gave his blessing to the marriage, and decided that the announcement of their betrothal should be made at a gathering of the two families at Bassito's villa. Signora Bassito and the women of the household set about making the lavish preparations for the occasion, and Bassito enjoyed himself just watching his bulging wife commanding her flock of helpers, and the radiant happiness of his daughter.

In between watching the delights of his family, Bassito also enjoyed himself downtown, in the company of a particularly attractive and shapely mistress called Gena. Gena was one of Bassito's delights as much as his family was, but with Gena, Bassito had a different relationship and different surroundings. His family lived in a comfortable villa overlooking the Bay of Naples. It had its family heirlooms and family portraits, and a distinct gloomy air of family respectability. Gena, however, was provided with a modern luxury flat and all the necessary modern conveniences. She demanded luxury, and she could have got it elsewhere if Bassito had not been prepared to give it to her. But then Bassito was a wealthy man who had no qualms about spending money — so long as he got value for it, and so long as he was not double-crossed. Bassito was kind, generous, benevolent, and even at times humorous. He was also shrewd, ruthless, and at times merciless.

It was on the thirteenth of March that Bassito selected for his daughter's party to announce her betrothal. It was a quiet night for his operations. There was nothing planned, and every preparation was made for Bassito to spend a peaceful evening with his family in their villa.

The party started according to plan. The guests arrived punctually. The wine flowed liberally. The compliments and the emotional outbursts of love and affection for Bassito were liberally bestowed upon him, and not too modestly accepted. The meal was noisy and lavish. Bassito sat back and gave an approving nod of his head to his grey haired, robust wife who had long since been condemned to wearing black robes. She gave a grateful smile of thanks for his acknowledgement, little knowing that his thoughts were elsewhere, with the curvaceous and delectable Gena.

All was going well until one of Bassito's office 'assistants' — a smartly dressed, dark-suited young man — came and whispered into Bassito's ear. Bassito's face instantly clouded over, but he was immediately able to put on the mask of the benevolent patriarch again.

'You must excuse me,' he announced to the gathering. A hush fell over the room. 'A slight matter of business to attend to. I shall only be a few minutes. Please…' He waved his arms in a grand gesture of benevolence. 'Please enjoy yourselves.'

His daughter looked at him appealingly. 'Papa, the speeches?'

'Only a few minutes, my angel.'

He kissed her and his wife, and left the room followed by his sons Antonio and Carlos. As soon as the double doors to the large dining room were closed behind him, Bassito cast off his look of calm benevolence. His face became stern, his eyes cold.

'How dare the Inspector come to my house on such an occasion?' he demanded. 'How dare he?'

His assistant didn't answer him. He stood to one side. Bassito stormed into his study. Inspector Paledo and his assistant, Sergeant Grazzelli, stood waiting for him. They saw the look of annoyance on Bassito's face, but the Inspector was not overawed. He had long since suspected the benevolent Bassito and his organisation of other activities. Now he had found a possible lead into those other activities. He welcomed the opportunity of crossing swords with Bassito, but he was cautioned by the knowledge that the Chief of Police was also a friend of Bassito's and a potential guest at Bassito's daughter's forthcoming wedding.

'Good evening, Signor Bassito,' the Inspector said. 'I do apologise for having to disturb you on such an evening.' He gave a look of regret for his intrusion.

'I trust it is not a trivial matter,' Bassito replied. His two sons and his office assistant stood behind him.

'That is for you to decide, Signor,' the Inspector replied. 'There has been a break-in at your office and warehouse.'

Bassito's face turned to thunder. That somebody should dare to attempt to break into his warehouse!

'The guard was very observant,' the Inspector went on. 'In fact, he shot one of the men — dead!'

Bassito had picked his guards carefully.

'The dead man?'

'He was one of your employees — Benito Garcini. I do believe he drove one of your vehicles.'

Bassito knew Garcini. He knew all his employees. Garcini had been one of his couriers. He had been one of his drivers who had journeyed regularly into France and Switzerland.

'There can be no mistake?' he hissed. 'Garcini was one of the gang?'

'He was. They wore stockings, of course, and did a very neat job. Except for the quick reaction of your guard, they would have all got away.'

'He will be rewarded,' Bassito said, tight-lipped. 'How many others were there?'

'Possibly two or three. I think only two.'

'They will be found.'

'We have, naturally, put out all the necessary alerts and warned the border authorities, but until we check further…'

Bassito had not been thinking of the police finding the two robbers, he had been thinking of his own organisation. His own men and his own links. His organisation would find them, but they would not be brought back for punishment. They would not live!

Bassito looked up from his dark thoughts of revenge.

'What damage? What was taken?' he demanded.

'It would appear that there is little damage to your property. Perhaps the guard interrupted them before they had time to — shall we say, help themselves?' The Inspector gave a faint smile. 'There were some explosives found. Obviously they were on intent on blowing the safes. It could be that they didn't find it necessary.'

Bassito scowled. He was thinking of one of his safes in particular.

'Did the guard recognise anything about the other two men?'

'Unfortunately not. They wore black stockings and black clothing. They were professionals. One was perhaps smaller and slimmer than the other. Both fit men.'

Bassito relaxed his features.

'Well, Inspector, it would appear that we have one dead, crooked employee, two accomplices on the run, and very little stolen or damaged. For that we must be thankful.'

Bassito's sons and assistant relaxed their features. Papa Bassito was smiling again.

The Inspector frowned.

'There is just one small matter, Signor,' he said.

Bassito raised his eyebrows.

'There were some articles of jewellery found on Garcini.'

Bassito's guts turned hard and ice cold.

'Did you have any jewellery in your safe?' the Inspector asked.

Bassito looked at the Inspector and the two men knew each other's thoughts. Bassito had indeed been safeguarding some very special jewellery.

'Any jewellery I possess,' Bassito hissed, 'is in the bank vaults, or in my wife's safe. Not in my office.'

'As I thought,' the Inspector lied. 'You see it would appear that this jewellery — this small amount found on Garcini — matches the description of some of the pieces that were stolen from the home of the Austrian millionairess, Contessa Vallego at La Villa della Rosa on Lake Maggiore, four months ago. The total value of her missing jewellery was insured for one thousand million lire. Naturally both we, and I am sure, the Insurance Company, will be very interested.'

Bassito's face looked black and he felt pangs of fear that he had never felt before. The jewellery was a special shipment to the States that had been organised by a powerful syndicate in the States. Bassito had only been brought in as a link in their chain. All the arrangements had been made to handle it, and the men who had made the arrangements were men who did not like being let down or double-crossed. They were men with underground connections that could rock the foundations of any Government, never mind Bassito's business and family. Bassito could see that his own empire was in danger, but he controlled his feelings.

'Inspector,' he hissed, 'I run a legitimate business, as your Chief of Police will vouch. You can search my business premises and warehouses at any time. I know nothing about the Contessa's jewellery, or the side-lines of my employees.' He gave the Inspector a softer look. 'This is the night my daughter celebrates her betrothal. Please, Inspector.' He opened his arms appealingly. 'I do not like being upset on such a night.'

The Inspector gave a look of understanding.

'Signor, I appreciate your feelings. I offer you my humble apologies. It is most regrettable that I have had to disturb you. A policeman's lot is not a pleasant one.'

'I shall be most grateful if you will continue with your enquiries elsewhere, or at another time, Inspector.'

The Inspector had the faintest suspicion that Bassito's remark was intended as a promise of a reward. He saw the look on Bassito's face and knew that it was either a promise of a reward, or of retribution. Either way, the Inspector was not influenced. He had a foot in Bassito's door, something that he had been trying to get for a long time. He would be back to open the door wider.

'Goodnight, Signor,' he said politely, 'and my congratulations and good wishes to Signor Minchello. He is certainly marrying into a remarkable family.'

Bassito nodded his head and gave a wave of the hand. Antonio, Bassito's eldest son, escorted the Inspector and the Sergeant from their premises. When he returned, he closed the study door. The atmosphere in the room was charged.

'Garcini,' Bassito spat. 'The traitor!' He looked wildly at his two sons and his heavy man. 'Who were those other two men?' he asked. 'Who would dare to do such a thing?'

'None of our own men, Papa,' Antonio said, daring to speak although his father was in such a mood. 'Nobody would dare cross you. Garcini must have made contacts when he travelled abroad.'

Bassito let fling a string of oaths that damned Garcini's soul to hell and his two accomplices to a fate worse than death. Then his shrewd, calculating brain began to tick again.

'Spread the word around,' he ordered. 'Get the men scurrying into every gutter and corner of Naples. Contact Rome, Milan, Genoa, Zurich, Marseilles. Spread the net far and wide. Spend money — offer large rewards. Wherever they are, they will not escape.'

He snapped out a further string of orders on how to deal with the local police enquiries, and the functions of his office.

His two sons immediately set about implementing his orders. Bassito and his bodyguard returned to the festivities.

'Papa!' Maria exclaimed. 'You have been so long.'

'Oh, my Maria!' Bassito embraced his daughter. 'Come!' he called out. 'More wine. We must celebrate.'

Inspector Paledo and the Sergeant drove back to the police headquarters.

'Bassito was upset,' the Sergeant warned.

'Yes, wasn't he? It is going to be very interesting.'

'Interesting?' the Sergeant asked.

'There are going to be so many people looking for those two men — Police, Insurance Detectives, and Bassito's men. I almost feel sorry for them. After all, they have not committed a crime against the State in its truest sense — only against Bassito.'

'You think Bassito's organisation stole that jewellery?'

'They are linked with whoever did.'

They drove in silence until they reached the police station.

'I wonder who will find those two men first?' the Sergeant asked, as they entered the building.

'I only hope it is not Bassito's men,' the Inspector replied. 'For their sake.'

Chapter Three

For Lieutenant Simon Ducan, March thirteenth began with all the signs of another ordinary, routine day at his desk in the Russian section of the Department of Military Intelligence. Even at the end of the day, in the evening, if he had reflected on the day, he would have agreed with the original signs, with the possible exception of an interview with a Monsieur Marcel Poujet of the Department of 'Service de Documentation et de Contre Espionage'. An interview that had been abruptly cut short by a telephone call to Monsieur Poujet. Both of which were to later make that day a day of great significance for Simon Ducan.

Ducan had given the interview a certain amount of thought. It had made him curious. It had also amused him, but he had cast it aside as another example of the bureaucracy that had enveloped him and was strangling the real work that he had hoped to achieve. So to Simon Ducan, March 13th had just been another one of those boring days that he had come to expect since being commissioned into the army.

Ducan had been encouraged to join the army by the trustees of his family's affairs, who had thought it time that the young adventurer had his wings clipped, and set upon a career that would both serve France and Ducan. It had been suggested that the Department of Military Intelligence would be an ideal posting for him. He had the necessary qualifications. He could speak several languages fluently, and in particular Russian, which he had learned from his family, who were of Russian descent. The first Ducan had been a Russian emigre called Canvynsky, who had fled to Paris in the early part of the nineteenth century. He had been the son of a wealthy Russian banker in Moscow, but had fallen foul of the establishment because of his liberal politics and had been forced to flee the country. In Paris, Canvynsky had set up business as a banker, supported by his family still in Moscow. He had married the daughter of another Russian emigre who had changed their family name to Dupres. Canvynsky followed suit and adopted the name of Du-can. Subsequent generations of the family had dropped the hyphen from their name, but did not forget their Russian heritage, or knowledge of the Russian language, which had been passed on from father to son. The first Ducan had become a successful banker, and following generations had either been bankers or traders. Simon Ducan belonged to the branch of the family that had developed trading interests. His grandfather had set up and developed a thriving trading station in Djibouti, French Somaliland, providing the French colony with many of the essential luxuries from France, that helped to make life in the colony more bearable.

Simon Ducan had been born in Djibouti and had been brought up in the colony with intermittent periods in France. He had not achieved any academic successes in his studies in either France or Djibouti. Nor did he achieve any success in business, where he had shown no interest in the family's trading interests. Instead, he had travelled widely all over the world.

When the trustees had suggested a career in the army, Ducan had agreed. He had been attracted to the suggestion of a posting in military intelligence. The thought had sparked off his imagination with the promise of a career of unusual interest, and the opportunity to show initiative and originality. He had been badly mistaken. At St. Cyr, the Officer Training Academy, he had suffered the boredom of a regular routine which, coupled with the discipline, had offended his natural desire for freedom. He had clashed with the system and with the traditional thinking of the military academics. He had endured, but his results and reports had been varied. However, he had been accepted for the posting to military intelligence headquarters in Paris on a temporary basis. It was just as well, because the nature of his confidential reports would have made it difficult for him to have found a posting to one of the more select regiments, and a posting to some minor role would have soon resulted in him resigning his commission.

Ducan had joined the staff of Colonel Gourbet in Paris, and had set about his work with enthusiasm. But slowly his enthusiasm was being drained out of him. He found himself at a desk in a small office with a constant supply of papers in his in-tray for translation.

Occasionally he was given a glimpse of another world linked with his work in the department. Twice he had been asked to accompany Colonel Gourbet, Head of the Department, to a state function. One had been given at the Polish Embassy, and the other had been at a reception given by the French Government to a visiting delegation from Hungary. On both occasions, Ducan's role had been that of translator, which he had performed with enthusiasm and he had been complimented by the Colonel. There had also been vague suggestions that perhaps Ducan had a lot to offer the service.

What Ducan was not aware of was that the very slow process of vetting, watching, and checking back was taking place all the time that Ducan was serving his period of apprenticeship. There was a future for Ducan, but the French Government, and the French Intelligence Service, had to be one hundred per cent sure of him.

The job of checking out Ducan's past and loyalty had come to the attention of Monsieur Marcel Poujet, deputy to the Director of S.D.E.C.E. — 'Le Service de Documentation et de Contre Espionage' — the department that controlled and operated all of France's intelligence and counter-espionage services. Poujet was unique. He had a brilliant brain, with the analytical mind of a scientist, and the memory of a computer. He had taken a doctorate in Psychology at University. He had also studied politics and languages. He had been destined for the elite Diplomatic Corps, but a chance meeting with a former senior official of the Intelligence Department had side-tracked him into becoming part of France's spy machinery. That had been twenty-nine years earlier. Poujet was fifty-six years old with a wealth of experience. He had become the Director's right-hand man. The man who kept his eyes and ears close to the ground. He was the man in the shadows with fingers in many pies, including the military academy at St. Cyr. When a newly commissioned officer was posted to the Department of Military Intelligence, he heard about it. When that officer had a Russian background and a personal knowledge of East Africa, he was brought to Poujet's attention. The small French colony in East Africa was soon to be granted its independence. The territory was bordered by Somalia and Ethiopia — two countries where Russian Intelligence had established its networks. French Intelligence had a great need for the services of a man like Ducan who could speak the native language, but first Poujet had to be totally satisfied with him, and with Ducan, the reports from the Academy left a question mark. They described him as intelligent, unorthodox, and at times uncooperative — a man who was capable of giving excellent service if he was so inclined. It made him sound like a rebel without a cause.

Poujet decided to interview Ducan himself. Ducan was summoned and presented himself at Poujet's office. It was not the type of room that he had expected of a man of such high office. It was quite small and drab. One wall was covered with a large map of the world, the others were all bare and decorated in a dull green. There was a faded red carpet on the floor and a large desk in front of a small window. Poujet was seated at his desk with his back to the window when Ducan arrived. He stood up, and the two men greeted each other formally and silently studied one another. Poujet was a tall, ungainly, and untidy looking man, with a slightly bent posture. His hair was thick, wiry and greying, and made him look older than his years. His features were rather prominent but not striking, and he had one slightly lazy eye that always looked half closed. His build was broad but not bulky. He looked more like a schoolmaster from a small country school than an official of the Intelligence Department. Ducan felt immediately at ease in his company. There was something reassuring and comfortable about him in his crumpled dark suit. It was an image and impression that Poujet used to his advantage.

Poujet in turn was quickly appraising the Lieutenant, although it was not the first time that he had seen Ducan's face. A photograph was in the documents that Poujet had been studying. He had also seen Ducan at the two receptions that he had attended with Colonel Gourbet, but it was the first time that he had seen Ducan at close quarters. He noticed Ducan's fine, evenly tanned features that were the result of a very mixed pedigree, but he was looking for something else. He was looking for Ducan the rebel. Ducan didn't look like an angry young man, he thought. His appearance and dress were neat and conventional. He was conforming. His hair was short, his suit a dark grey, but in Ducan's eyes Poujet thought that perhaps he did see some of the rebel. The eyes were dark and seemed to have a glint of amusement about them.

'Please sit down, Monsieur,' Poujet said.

'Monsieur.'

Ducan took a seat and faced Poujet.

'I have asked you here, Monsieur,' Poujet said, 'so that we can complete certain formalities.'

He spoke slowly, in a soft, drawling accent, which also had the effect of putting a person at ease.

'Formalities, Monsieur?'

Poujet gave a shrug.

'We live in a society of bureaucracy. It is essential that our records and documents are fully up to date.'

'You have checked me for security, Monsieur?' Ducan asked with an impish smile, as if he was amused by the procedure.

'You are on the staff of a department concerned with the affairs of military secrets.'

'I was given a security check before I was accepted by St. Cyr, Monsieur, and again before I was posted to the department.'

'And again now that you are in the department. It is customary.'

Ducan sighed. 'It seems such an unnecessary waste of the taxpayers' money.'

'Why do you say that?'

'Because, Monsieur, I am not carrying out any work of national importance, nor do I have access to any such documents. I am a clerk, Monsieur, I am a translator. Either the country is short of clerks or it is short of translators.'

'You volunteered for the department. Why?'

'I thought I had something to offer my country. I also thought that it would be interesting and require both intelligence and initiative.'

'Perhaps it will in time.'

Ducan nodded his head in appreciation of the remark. 'In the meantime, I am a clerk.'

'In the meantime, you are a clerk,' Poujet agreed. He sat back. He recognised Ducan's impatience. He had also read it in Ducan's reports.

He changed tack and tried to establish the basis of the rebel in Ducan.

'You were expelled from your school in France, Monsieur,' he said.

'I was asked to leave,' Ducan smiled, 'which I agree was the same thing.'

'Why?'

'I didn't conform.'

'In what way?'

Ducan hesitated. 'I was a colonial. They were all from wealthy families in France.'

'A colonial?' Poujet asked. 'There were surely other colonials at the school?'

Ducan gave a patient smile.

'Monsieur Poujet,' he said, 'you are probably aware that in my family tree, we have introduced a variety of colourful blossoms. One of my uncles married a Hungarian dancer. Another married an Austrian opera singer. My grandfather married an Egyptian belly dancer — of great charm and beauty, I might add. Unfortunately, she died soon after my father was born. My grandfather rectified his sins and married the daughter of a respectable shopkeeper in Djibouti. Need I say more?'

So it was a colour problem that had made him rebel and not conform, Poujet thought. He was surprised. He thought Ducan was of stronger character.

'My breeding did not cause me concern,' Ducan said, as if reading Poujet's thoughts. 'It caused others concern.'

Poujet cast his lazy eye in Ducan's direction.

'Do you also read the sands?' he asked.

Ducan seemed to enjoy the remark. He gave a broad smile.

'There must be some of the native instinct in me,' he suggested, 'but I regret, Monsieur, I can neither read the sands nor produce chickens from my sleeve.'

It was Poujet's turn to smile.

'Times have changed now,' Ducan said, 'and also people's attitudes, Monsieur.'

'You still came very close to the bottom of your class at St. Cyr,' Poujet pointed out. 'Were you still being uncooperative?'

Ducan shook his head.

'I differed with the views of my tutors. I considered their views old-fashioned and not in keeping with the needs of the future army of France.'

'And what do you think they should be?'

'I think that soldiers should not be blindly led to obey without questions. I think they should be encouraged to think — to have initiative.'

'Surely the officers and the "*sous officiers*" are so encouraged.'

'After they have been drilled and driven into the system.'

'Obedience first and initiative second.'

'There is no reason why they cannot be managed simultaneously.'

'Perhaps. You have not served with a regiment?'

'Not yet, Monsieur.'

'Would you like to?'

'That would depend on the regiment and its role. Also my own duties. I think I should hate the drudgery of the regular routine of a base camp.'

Poujet smiled. 'Yes, I think you would.'

He glanced at Ducan's file, although he knew all the details.

'I cannot see any reference in your dossier to any particular success, Monsieur,' he said slowly, 'either in the academic field or the field of sport.'

Again he cast his lazy eye in Ducan's direction. For a brief moment he saw the sparkle disappear from Ducan's eyes, then it returned, but Poujet felt that his arrow had hit home.

'No, Monsieur,' Ducan sighed. 'I have not many successes to my credit.'

'Does it bother you?'

'No, Monsieur, and you?'

'Success indicates dedication. The ability to dedicate oneself to something shows strength of character. Would you agree?'

Ducan looked thoughtful. He gave a bland smile.

'Success, or dedication, needs a motive, Monsieur. There must be the need. Either a cause or a necessity. The necessity is often for economic or personal gain or even glory. I have not had the need to fight for either, nor have I been blessed with any particular gift that I have wanted to exploit.'

'Perhaps you would have found one if you had had the need.'

Ducan shrugged.

'I am sure if we were to pursue this discussion to its ultimate conclusion, we would find the problem was both related to my childhood and my wealthy family.'

'I am sure we would,' Poujet agreed. 'Would you have wished for other circumstances?'

Ducan shook his head.

'You forget, Monsieur, that I was brought up in French Somaliland. It is a barren, Godforsaken country. The Somalis believe that everything is Allah's will. Perhaps some of that has rubbed off on me, or perhaps it is because I have seen so many of the poor creatures living their meagre existence, that I do not worry about the past — or the future.' He gave Poujet a disarming smile again. 'Or about success, Monsieur,' he added.

Poujet grunted. The grunt was not significant. It was his way of passing on to another topic.

'You are not married? Do you have a mistress?'

'No, Monsieur.'

'Have you had any affairs?'

'Several, but I tired of them.'

'What do you do with your free time?'

'Play bridge, drink with my friends. Occasionally I have an affair. I read. I like the theatre. In winter I enjoy skiing. I assure you Monsieur, I am quite normal.'

Poujet rubbed his chin.

'Did you tire of being a playboy, Monsieur?'

Ducan shook his head.

'You are wrong, Monsieur. I was not a playboy. I travelled the world, but I worked my way. I certainly tired of the family trading business, and I also tired of travelling, but I suppose I got it out of my system.'

'What were you looking for, Monsieur, when you were travelling?'

'I was just looking, Monsieur, not searching.'

Poujet grunted again. He was beginning to suspect that Ducan was not a rebel without a cause, but just a young man who had been provided with everything, except a cause.

'You travelled in Russia?' he asked.

'Yes, Monsieur, I travelled across Russia twice. After all, it is part of my heritage.'

Poujet didn't look up, but his lazy eye was turning in Ducan's direction.

'And what was your impression, Monsieur?' he asked. 'Was it better, or worse, than living in Somaliland?'

'It is different,' Ducan replied. 'To understand it, one has to be aware of its vastness.'

Poujet saw sadness in Ducan's eyes.

'It is a soulless state,' Ducan said with feeling, 'which is a pity. The natives are a colourful people who have been painted grey. There is no religion — no freedom. I think I would prefer to live in the Somali Desert.'

Poujet looked thoughtfully at the file on his desk. Either Ducan was a very good liar, or a man of feeling.

'After all, Monsieur,' Ducan added cheerfully, 'at least seventy per cent of me is French. A Frenchman could not enjoy so much greyness in his life.'

Poujet thought he was a man of feeling. He had decided.

'When you were in Russia, did you travel into Siberia?'

Poujet was not looking at Ducan as he asked the question. His eyes were on his wall map and on a particular area of Siberia, and his thoughts were not of Ducan, they were of another Frenchman — Claude Bichante, a member of Poujet's department who had been arrested two years earlier in Moscow, by the Soviet Authorities, and sentenced to fifteen years hard labour for alleged spying activities.

Ducan sensed that Poujet had a particular reason for the question.

'I only travelled as far as Tomsk, Monsieur,' he said. 'It is on the fringe of the territory. It was a desert of snow and ice. Fortunately it was spring, and the ice was beginning to melt.

The winters are very long and severe, and the summers short. It is not a territory that I would wish to return to.'

Poujet nodded his head in silent agreement and put Bichante to the back of his mind. He would not forget about him — he could not, but the present was for Ducan.

'Why did you join the army?' he asked.

'I was tired of travelling. I wanted to be of service.'

'To your country?'

'To my country,' Ducan agreed, and shrugged, 'also to myself. I want to do something useful.'

Poujet's telephone rang. He excused himself and picked up the receiver. 'Yes,' he said.

He was given an important message. It told him that a French agent had been murdered in Budapest and that a defector from Russian Intelligence was at large. It was very grave news. Its implications and side-effects could be far reaching, but Poujet accepted the news without any trace of concern. He replaced the receiver carefully and looked at Ducan apologetically. 'I regret that I have other matters to attend to. Thank you for giving me a few minutes of your time. I do hope we will have an opportunity to pursue our conversation on some other occasion.'

He stood up and held out his large hand. Ducan also stood up. He was taken aback that the interview had ended so abruptly, and also disappointed. He had been enjoying the gentle cut and thrust of their discussion.

Chapter Four

For Jean-Pierre Pascal, March 13th also proved to be an eventful day in his life. Pascal was one of Poujet's protégés, and a man moulded in Poujet's ways, but Pascal operated in the field, and on March 13th, he was given an assignment that proved to be unlike any other that he had ever experienced. Fortunately for Pascal, the call came late in the evening — a fact for which he was later to be eternally grateful.

Pascal had not been expecting the call, but nevertheless he had arrived early at Catherine's apartment and he had been particularly pressing to make love to her. He lived from day to day. He had to take his pleasures whenever the opportunity arose. He soon had her resting her naked body next to his, and as she lay in his arms, he enjoyed the luxury of their surroundings and the delights of her young shapely body.

He would never tire of making love to her, he thought. She was sheer luxury, like her bedroom, and he had visited many bedrooms and slept with many women. He was content just to lie and absorb it all for a moment, but the girl was becoming eager. She pressed her youthful body to his, and his hands gently caressed her and excited her, and her kissing became more passionate. She struggled with her body to get closer. Wild youthful passion burned within them, and she clung to him.

The moment passed and she lay in his arms with her eyes closed. She would sleep now, he thought, and was glad that he had pleased her. He knew that soon he would have to leave on another assignment, but if she asked where he was going, or how long he would be away, he could not tell her. All that he could say was that he had to go away on business and would be back in a few days.

When the telephone rang, he quickly picked up the receiver. The girl stirred.

'Yes,' he said.

'This is the florists,' a man's voice replied.

Pascal looked at the girl lying naked on the bed. She was asleep again. He turned his back on her.

'I didn't order any flowers,' he said.

'There has been a delivery of black orchids.'

Black orchids! Pascal slipped out of the bed.

'The Fox has gone to ground. He is being hunted.'

'The Master of the Hounds?'

'She has had a fatal accident.' There was a brief pause, then came the order. 'Follow the hunt. Stay with it from behind. There is a plane leaving in one hour. Everything is arranged.'

The telephone went dead. Pascal gently replaced the receiver on its stand. He took a last look at the girl in the bed, and then at the furnishings in the room. He had a feeling that he was not going to see them again for quite some time. His face hardened. He quickly dressed and left the bedroom. He had started his mission.

Chapter Five

Madame Zena's death was not reported in the Paris press. She had not been French. She had been a Hungarian who had worked for several western intelligence agencies, including French Intelligence. In Budapest, her death had been reported as a motor accident, but French Intelligence knew otherwise.

In the departments of French Intelligence — the S.D.E.C.E. — there was anger and concern. Their anger would be satisfied. They would get their revenge. An agent of the Eastern block would be found dead in the Seine. Their concern, however, could not be so easily satisfied. Madame Zena's murder had left a delicate and uncertain situation.

A week before her death, Madame Zena had been approached by a man calling himself Andre Visinsky, who had claimed to be a newly trained agent of the K.G.B., sent to Budapest to be fed into the West. Visinsky had wanted to defect to France, and was prepared to pay for his protection with information. Madame Zena had sought advice from Paris. Visinsky had been given the code name *Le Renard* — the Fox, and his request had been considered by senior officials of the French Intelligence and members of the Government. There had been caution and suspicion. Visinsky was an unknown. French Intelligence needed time to check on him. There was uncertainty about his value to France, and there was Bichante in Russia. Bichante was a member of the S.D.E.C.E. and his return to France was important, both for the President and the department, and negotiations were taking place in Moscow for his release. That had influenced Poujet's recommendations.

There were also diplomatic moves afoot to pave the way for the French President to visit Moscow later that year. The French Government was seeking to safeguard its interest in East Africa when the small French territory was granted its independence. France needed a working relationship with the Russian Government, who had a strong foothold in that part of Africa. The French President also needed a good press. Bichante's release would bolster his image with the French public. Visinsky — the Fox, was not to be allowed to upset the delicacy of the detente that was developing, or to hinder Bichante's release and return to France. Madame Zena had been given strict instructions. The Fox was not acceptable at the present time. There was too much at stake. He was to stay in his own lair, until the time was opportune.

Suddenly, the situation had dramatically changed. The Fox had taken flight and the wrath of the K.G.B. had been incurred, and with Madame Zena's murder had gone the only means French Intelligence had of identifying their Fox. Only Madame Zena had made contact with him. That had been Visinsky's own doing to safeguard his position.

In Paris, Poujet and the other senior officials aware of the situation could only sit and await events.

The man Poujet consulted regularly was his superior — the Director of S.D.E.C.E. — Monsieur Henri Marchand. Marchand had been appointed to his position three years earlier by the President. He was a forceful man — a man who looked as if he had come from peasant stock, but in fact came from a family of wealthy landowners. He was large and bulky, with dark hair and a formidable face and moustache. He was a man of intelligence, and had the ability to direct and control any of the departments that the President might have offered him. He had been offered the department dealing with

France's intelligence services, and he was making a success of it. Marchand had been quick to assess Poujet's ability and had promoted him to his high office. He had made a wise choice. The two worked well together. Poujet was the Head of the Department and responsible to Marchand. Marchand was the link with the President and the Government.

The first move by the Russians was to abruptly terminate the negotiations taking place in Moscow for Bichante's release. The French Government suspected a change in Russian policy. Marchand and Poujet suspected that it was a K.G.B. reprisal for the Fox's activities. Their suspicions proved correct. Two days after the breakdown of the negotiations in Moscow, Marchand was called to the Foreign Office to join the French Foreign Minister at a meeting with the Russian Ambassador and a Russian Senior Attaché. The Russian Attaché was a Colonel in the K.G.B. and known to French Intelligence.

At the meeting, the Russian Ambassador expressed his regrets that the negotiations for Bichante's release had been suspended, but he assured the French Foreign Minister that the visit of the French President could still prove to be beneficial for both countries and perhaps Bichante's release could be a matter for the agenda during the visit. As a gesture of goodwill, it was proposed to bring Bichante back to Moscow where he would be imprisoned in less severe conditions than he was enjoying at the present.

The discussion between the Ambassador and the Foreign Minister was couched in diplomatic platitudes and jargon. The talks held separately between the Russian Colonel and Marchand were not so veiled. They spoke plainly to each other so that there would be no uncertainties.

The Colonel regretted the death of Madame Zena, who was known to be a friend of the French, but claimed that her death had been at the hand of a Russian traitor who had become a double agent, and the tool of certain western intelligence agencies, including the C.I.A. The Colonel even named him as Andre Visinsky. He claimed that Visinsky had murdered Madame Zena because she would not cooperate with him, and could expose him for what he really was. Visinsky had taken flight, but the K.G.B. intended to find him and bring him to justice. If the Russians could count on French cooperation in bringing this traitor to justice, then the Russians would see to it that the Frenchman, Bichante, was released during the French President's visit to Moscow.

It was a deal that held a loaded pistol at the head of Bichante. It was blackmail. It was also a licence for the K.G.B. to kill.

The discussions were reported to the President. There was relief in the Elysée Palace that the President's visit and Bichante's release could be safeguarded. The deal was agreed.

Later, Poujet was called into Marchand's office, where Marchand explained the situation.

When he had finished, Poujet shook his head sadly.

'So the Fox is more valuable than we realised, Monsieur,' he said.

'*Monsieur le President* is of the opinion that what we have not so far enjoyed, we will not miss. Bichante is more important.'

'Bichante is more important,' Poujet agreed, 'but how far do we cooperate?'

The Director lowered his head and looked grave.

'The Fox must not come knocking on our door, Marcel,' he said, 'or we hand him over. I have assured *Monsieur le President*.' He looked up at Poujet. 'He was told? He was left in no doubt?'

'He was told, Monsieur. He was not to make a move. He knew the danger.'

'*Bien*. Then he will take precautions to protect himself.'

'And as we do not know his identity, we cannot cooperate.'

'That is so, but the K.G.B. is a very powerful machine. He must be very desperate.'

'And desperate men find untapped resources of strength, Monsieur. He will have made preparations.'

'It will be a lonely trail.'

'Perhaps we could scent the trail, Monsieur…'

The Director sighed. He knew what was going through Poujet's mind. He didn't like having a pistol pointing at his head, and he felt sympathy for the Fox and Madame Zena.

Poujet confirmed the Director's thoughts.

'They want to exchange Bichante for the Fox, but there is still Madame Zena. The scales are tipped in their favour.'

'Except that they do have Bichante in prison and they know the identity of the Fox.'

Poujet muttered his agreement.

'That is our weakness, Monsieur.' He turned his head to face the Director and leaned forward. 'If it were possible, Monsieur?' he asked in a quiet voice. 'If we could perhaps…'

The two men looked hard at each other. The Director knew what Poujet was asking.

'I can be very discreet, Monsieur,' Poujet added.

The Director looked grave. 'Then be very discreet indeed.'

Poujet sat back and relaxed. He had got his answer.

'How?' the Director asked.

'There is Pascal, Monsieur. He knows the signs and the trails. He is a very patient huntsman. He will find him eventually. He has already picked up a scent in Vienna.'

The Director looked anxious.

'He knows the gravity of the situation?'

'He knows, Monsieur. Have no fear, he will follow from behind.'

The Director's features evened.

'Pascal in Vienna,' he said. 'Perhaps the Fox is making for Zurich.'

Poujet had also thought about Zurich.

'It is possible, Monsieur. It is very possible. Madame Zena might have instructed him to make for Zurich. It is the next link in her chain. She might have sent him to Russo.'

'Russo! Has he been informed?'

'He has, Monsieur. Russo is being watched night and day by Russian agents. So are many of our other agents and contacts. The Russians have been watching since the night of Madame Zena's murder. They are watching us, to see if we make a move. Russo put out his red alert the following morning. He will not be able to make personal contact with the Fox, if the Fox contacts him, but he will be able to pass on any necessary instructions.'

'To go into hiding?'

'Yes, Monsieur. To go into hiding.'

The Director sat back in his chair. He threw up his hands.

'Bichante! *Monsieur le President* and his visit to Moscow! All at risk. All because of one man. He must have something important to give us.' He gave a long sigh. 'It is a challenge, Marcel.'

Poujet gave the Director the benefit of his lazy eye and a knowing smile. 'It is a challenge that I will enjoy, Monsieur — to catch the Fox before the Bear kills it.'

The Director smiled. 'You are as cunning as a fox yourself, Marcel, but take care. It is not only the Russians. It is also the Americans.'

'The C.I.A.?' Poujet asked.

'Don't underestimate the Americans,' the Director warned. 'They're as devious as the Russians. Last night I was at the U.S. Embassy. Carson expressed his concern and regret at Madame's death. I have hunches now and then, Marcel. I'm suspicious of Carson and the C.I.A. They know more about this than we think. He even went as far as to offer us any help that we might need.'

'You refused?' Poujet asked immediately.

'Naturally.'

'Good, the C.I.A. could be looking for information. They know that Madame Zena was not murdered for some minor incident. They will want to know what it is all about, and they will also know that the Russians are watching our agents. We have a unique situation on our hands, Monsieur. We have the C.I.A. and the K.G.B. watching us very closely. I think, Monsieur, you will suddenly find yourself very popular.'

'Popular, perhaps, but I do not think I will be enjoying the next few months as you will be. Keep me informed, Marcel. I want to know every time your Pascal makes contact.'

'Yes, Monsieur.'

Poujet left the Director's office. He looked calm and unruffled. He smiled at his assistants who passed him in the corridor. In his own office, he spoke reassuringly to his staff, but when he was on his own he sat deep in thought. He was an expert angler, and to be expert at that sport required patience and guile — especially when the catch was a big one. The Fox had all the signs of being a very big catch indeed, and he wasn't going to lose him if it was within his powers to get a hook into him. He wanted the Fox for France, as well as Bichante's release and the President's visit to Moscow.

He rubbed his chin thoughtfully. The Fox had got to Vienna. If Madame Zena had given him any directions at all, it would have been to Zurich, and Poujet had a feeling about Zurich.

He picked up the telephone and got on to his deputy. 'Russo still red?' he asked.

'Yes, Monsieur,' came the reply.

'And the others?'

'Also red, Monsieur.'

'Get a message to Russo. Warn him that he might have a visitor from the East.'

He didn't wait for an answer. He replaced the receiver and turned his attention elsewhere.

Chapter Six

Poujet's feelings that the trail would lead to Zurich proved correct. Pascal's communications were by postcards to a florist in Paris. Through these cards, Poujet followed a trail from Vienna to Zurich, but from Zurich the trail suddenly turned south to Lugano, Milan and finally to Marseilles. In Marseilles, the flowers were pink carnations — Pascal was close, but not close enough to recommend a move.

Poujet didn't understand the trail. Something had gone wrong in Zurich. If the Fox had made for Zurich, he had done so on Madame Zena's instructions. Zurich was part of a chain that linked Vienna with Paris. After Zurich the move should have been into immediate hiding, not to Marseilles. Poujet was puzzled, but Russo was still red and not in direct contact. The Russians were still watching him.

'I want a meeting with Russo,' Poujet ordered, 'as soon as it is safe.'

'Yes, Monsieur.'

'And don't wait for Russo to tell us. Get someone to watch and report.'

Poujet waited patiently for more messages from Marseilles. None came. His other prediction proved correct. The Director was being courted by the Americans, the British and the Russians. He had suddenly become very popular, but he played it coolly and patiently.

So did Poujet, but after nothing had been heard from Pascal for two weeks, Poujet sent two of his assistants to Marseilles to enjoy a change of scenery. One of them became employed in the docks, the other in a downtown hotel. Again Poujet waited patiently, and his patience was rewarded. Pascal had indeed been in the Marseilles area, but more precisely he had been in Aubagne — in the headquarters of *la Légion Étrangère* — the Foreign Legion!

'Pascal is in the Legion!' Poujet exclaimed when he was told the news by Raphael, his senior assistant. 'The Legion! *Mon Dieu!*'

He went to his wall map.

'Vienna, Zurich, Milan, Marseilles. So that is why he was making for Marseilles.'

'How? When?' he asked.

'A section of about forty men left Marseilles four days ago for Ajaccio — Corsica. The Legion does its training in Corsica. Pascal was on the shipment, and the flowers are still pink.'

'Pink.' Poujet rubbed his chin thoughtfully. 'So he is still only sixty per cent sure,' he said, 'but he wouldn't have joined the Legion unless he was certain that the Fox had also joined.' He looked at his assistant. 'Not the Legion,' he said. '*Mon Dieu!* — poor Pascal — *la Légion Étrangère!*'

Poujet's assistant waited for his instructions. Poujet was thinking. The field had become narrower. The net was closing in on their quarry.

'The Fox is in the Legion,' he said aloud. 'The Fox, Pascal, and who else?' He raised his eyebrows questioningly, but did not expect an answer. He picked up his telephone and dialled a Marseilles number.

'Poujet here,' he said, when the caller came on the line. 'I need your help. A shipment of legionnaires sailed to Corsica from Marseilles a few days ago. It is absolutely necessary that I examine their files and documents.'

There was a pause as Poujet got his reply. His assistant saw his features harden.

'Then they will have to be made to change their rules,' he said. 'I do not want to be seen near their headquarters. This is important.' There was a further pause. 'I am not interested in what the Legion told any Inspector of the Naples Police,' he snapped. 'The Legion serves France. This is a matter of national security. Arrange an interview with whoever is in charge of the Legion's documents.' Another pause, then Poujet added, 'No, not in Marseilles, I can't stand the place. Somewhere quiet in the country.' A place was suggested. 'Chateau Surlin,' Poujet repeated. 'Tomorrow at one. Good. *Au revoir.*'

He replaced the telephone on its stand. He looked up at Raphael.

'The Legion does protect its own,' he said, and shook his head sadly. 'The Legion! That sacred cow!'

'The Fox has enlisted for safety,' Raphael remarked.

'So it would appear,' Poujet agreed, 'and by all accounts he is likely to get it. The Legion is not very forthcoming about its men. We have the Fox, Pascal and probably, no doubt, one of our Russian friends, all neatly tucked away in the Legion.'

'And the Legion will not cooperate?'

'If the Legion will not cooperate, we will have to make it cooperate.'

His chin dropped onto his chest as he contemplated the situation.

'Send Dupois to Marseilles immediately,' he ordered. 'Pascal and the Fox have been there long enough to leave a trail. I also want to know what has happened in those four weeks, and what the Fox can expect. He can also speak to the Marseilles police.'

'Do we fly to Marseilles, Monsieur?'

'No — we keep away from that place. I don't want to show too much interest. We fly to Lyon tomorrow, and drive to Aix-en-Provence. There is a chateau close by — Chateau Surlin. We meet Dupois there at midday. We meet Inspector Gaston of the Marseilles Sûreté and the Legion representative at one o'clock.'

Raphael left the room. Poujet reported the latest events to the Director. The Director was also taken aback and uncertain.

'See me when you return,' he said. 'If the Legion needs any persuasion, it can be arranged.'

'Yes, Monsieur.'

The following morning Poujet and Raphael flew to Lyons in a small, private aircraft. From the airport they drove to Aix-en-Provence and to the Chateau Surlin. The Chateau was old and tucked away in the wooded hillside on the outskirts of the town. It had long since been converted into a private hotel, and a number of cars were parked on its gravel driveway.

Dupois was waiting for them.

'Private apartments have been arranged for us, Monsieur,' he said, and led Poujet and Raphael to a room over the stables. There was some food and wine on a table. Poujet helped himself.

'Well?' Poujet asked, after he had satisfied his hunger.

'The previous shipment to Corsica was on March eighteenth,' Dupois reported. 'That means that Pascal and the Fox enlisted sometime between that date and April twentieth, when they were shipped to Corsica.'

'Pascal's report from Marseilles was posted on March twenty-second. That narrows it down closer. The date of enlistment will be important. Go on.'

'The Marseilles police have been busy. They have retrieved six dead bodies from the harbour in the past four weeks.'

'That is not unusual,' Poujet grunted. 'It is a way of life in Marseilles.'

'Five of the bodies have been identified. The sixth is taking a little longer. His face had been at the receiving end of a shotgun. One of those who has been identified was a man nicknamed Picasso. He used to provide passports and documents, and was an artist at changing people's appearance. He was well known. He operated from a bar called *Le Chien Noir.*'

'Marseilles must have hundreds of such men as this Picasso,' Poujet said.

'Picasso's speciality was providing papers for the Legion,' Dupois pointed out.

Poujet rubbed his chin.

'Perhaps the Fox used Picasso,' he suggested, 'to give him an acceptable cover, and somebody eliminated Picasso. But why?'

'Because Picasso could identify the Fox,' Raphael said.

'The Fox wouldn't give away anything about himself, but our friends could be making sure that there is no trail for anybody to link the Fox with the Legion. Which means that they have their own man right there with him.'

The arrival of the Inspector from the Marseilles Sûreté interrupted any further discussion on the subject. The Inspector also had an assistant with him. They were both sombre, grim-looking men and carried briefcases. Poujet briefly made the introductions, and offered them some refreshments. They politely refused. They appeared apprehensive of Poujet.

'And the Legion officer?' Poujet asked.

'In fifteen minutes, Monsieur,' the Inspector replied. 'I thought it would give us some time to talk together more freely before he arrives.'

Poujet nodded his head in silent agreement.

'Tell me about the Legion,' he said. 'Legionnaires — where they are recruited and what happens to them.'

The Inspector replied without hesitation. He had been expecting such a question.

'There are twenty recruiting stations throughout France. There is one in Marseilles. Many recruits, however, simply present themselves at the camp in Aubagne.'

'Some are also directed into the Legion by the police,' Poujet suggested, 'and your department.'

The Inspector looked uncomfortable.

'Come,' Poujet said. 'It is well known. Some are "encouraged" to join. It is a service to the Legion.'

'Perhaps some are,' the Inspector agreed reluctantly.

'In the last few weeks?'

'That is quite probable, Monsieur.'

'*Bien*,' Poujet said with apparent pleasure. '*Bien*. Do any foreigners from abroad apply?'

'Some do. Some are recruited in Paris.'

'What happens when they enrol?'

'They are all sent to the camp at Aubagne. There they are given a strict medical examination and a series of interviews with Legion officers.'

'Any fingerprints taken?'

'No. Nothing is recorded. The interviews are confidential. The Legion officers are only interested in whether the recruit will make a suitable legionnaire. The recruit is encouraged to talk about himself.'

'Are papers of identification necessary?'

'No, Monsieur.'

'Then why do some of them use people like Picasso?'

The Inspector shrugged his shoulders.

'Many who enlist in the Legion like to keep their past from the Legion. They are, perhaps, suspicious that the Legion will not protect them.'

'And are their fears justified?'

The Inspector shook his head.

'The Legion does not accept men wanted for a serious crime or felons. If the Legion thinks that they have such men amongst their recruits, they will quietly get rid of them. However, they do accept men who have,' he shrugged, 'shall we say, committed lesser crimes, and will protect them against all authority.' He looked pointedly at Poujet. 'Once the recruit has enlisted, he is given a new identity. His past is forgotten and it is protected by the Legion.'

'Very commendable,' Poujet muttered. 'But it still reserves the right to dismiss a man within ninety days of enlistment if he is not found suitable.'

Poujet cast his lazy eye on the Inspector. The Inspector grunted his agreement, and had a feeling that Poujet knew as much about the Legion as he did himself.

'How long do these interviews last?' Poujet asked.

'Two weeks, sometimes longer.'

'And the recruit is not enlisted until the Legion is satisfied?'

'That is so.'

Poujet frowned.

'So it will not be possible to find the exact date that a recruit presented himself at the camp. Some could take longer to enlist than others.'

'That is so, Monsieur. Many are enlisted on the same day, even though they might have been in the camp for some time.'

Poujet looked at his assistant, Raphael. Raphael knew what he was thinking. There was going to be no way of telling who had attracted Pascal into the Legion, if Pascal, or the Fox, had joined the Legion at the camp.

'What else happens at Aubagne, Inspector?'

'The recruits get the wrong impression of the Legion,' the Inspector replied. 'The camp is very comfortable. The recruits are well fed. They listen to tape recordings of the Legion's glorious past. They receive daily instruction in French. They do aptitude tests. And then they are shipped to Corsica. To the Citadel at Corte. The Citadel is very old and very spartan. There they will find out what the Legion is really like. They will have four months of initial training. It is very, very tough, Monsieur.'

Poujet grunted. He was momentarily thinking of Pascal.

There was a moment's silence.

'No fingerprints,' Poujet muttered. 'No dates that could help us. A new identity and a forgotten past.' He looked up at the Inspector. 'They do note where the recruit was supposed to have come from? His nationality?'

'They note their nationality, their original identity and certain other details.'

'They will also know whether they presented themselves at Paris, or one of the other cities, and when?'

The Inspector frowned.

'Perhaps the place, Monsieur, but the date…' He shrugged. 'You must appreciate, Monsieur, the Legion is only interested in the recruit once he is accepted and enlisted. Before that…' He shrugged again.

Poujet took another sandwich. He waved his arm, indicating that the rest of the men were free to help themselves. Raphael and Dupois did so; the Inspector and his assistant declined.

'I think I must advise you at this stage, Monsieur,' the Inspector said, 'that you are not the only official who has been enquiring about this last shipment to Corsica.'

'I think you should,' Poujet agreed.

'Three days ago, I had a visit from Inspector Rossini of the Italian Department of Interpol, and Inspector Paledo of the Criminal Investigation Department of the Naples Police Department. They were also very interested in the recent recruitment into the Legion. They also requested permission to examine the documents.'

'For what purpose?' Poujet asked.

The Inspector withdrew a sheet of paper from his briefcase. He read from his notes.

'On the night of March thirteenth of this year, a burglary occurred in the offices of a firm of importers and exporters owned by a Signor Bassito. During the course of the burglary, one of the watchmen shot dead one of the burglars. The man killed was an employee of the firm, called Garcini. On Garcini's body was found a piece of jewellery which has been confirmed as part of a large collection of jewellery that had been stolen a few months earlier from the home of a Contessa Vallego. The missing jewellery was valued at about one thousand million lire — about six million francs. Garcini's accomplices were not apprehended in Italy. It is believed that they escaped into France.'

'And into the Legion?' Poujet asked.

'That is so. Their trail ended in Marseilles.'

'Fingerprints? Descriptions? Anything to identify them?' Poujet asked.

'Nothing.'

There was a moment's silence.

'There was nothing that could warrant the arrest, or the removal from the Legion, of any of the men,' the Inspector added.

'They inspected the documents?'

'No, it was not permitted.'

Poujet grunted.

'Why should such men join the Legion?'

'The Italian Inspector strongly suspects that there is a link between the missing jewellery and a Mafia type of organisation, and a syndicate that operates in the States.'

'Mafia!' Poujet exclaimed. '*Sacré bleu*! The Legion does attract some strange men.'

'And dangerous ones, Monsieur.'

Poujet shrugged. 'I am not concerned about criminal matters, Monsieur,' he said. 'I am sure that your department can handle them. What I want is the cooperation of the Legion.'

'That might be difficult to get, Monsieur,' the Inspector warned.

'We shall see,' Poujet sighed.

They didn't have to wait long for the Legion representative to join them. He arrived punctually at the appointed time. He was a tall, dark haired *Chef de Bataillon* — a Major — responsible for the documentation of its recruits.

The Inspector made the introductions. The Major appeared crisp and formal. Poujet in contrast looked untidy, slow and casual.

They sat at a table. Poujet spread his body over a chair.

'Monsieur,' he said, 'we both serve France, although in somewhat different ways. Let us see if we can serve France together.'

'What is it that you require, Monsieur?' the Major asked.

Poujet gave the Major one of his rare smiles.

'You have amongst the men you recently sent to Corsica for training, a man who is of great importance to France. He is neither a criminal nor a felon. He is in fact a political refugee.'

'He has enlisted into the Legion for protection, Monsieur,' the Major said. 'The Legion honours their recruits' anonymity. I do not think such a man exists, Monsieur.'

'Come, Monsieur,' Poujet urged. 'Let us not play games with each other. This man exists. He is not going to be harmed. On the contrary, we want to protect him. I am not even asking that you hand him over to me.'

'What are you asking, Monsieur?' the Major asked.

Poujet put his bulky frame on the table.

'I want to inspect all the documents that you have in your possession belonging to the last group of men that you sent to Corsica. From that collection, I will select a group of men that I will want watching. That is all.'

He sat back.

'The documents are confidential, Monsieur.'

'So they are,' Poujet replied, 'and will be confidential with me.'

'They are particularly confidential to the Legion,' the Major insisted. 'If the man was wanted for some serious crime, or if you can prove that he is a hardened criminal…'

Poujet dismissed his words with a wave of his hand.

'Let us not get into disarray,' he said. 'Let me speak quite frankly, *mon Chef de*. My director is a powerful man. He is also a useful ally. He has the ear of *Monsieur le President*.' He cast his lazy eye on the Major pointedly. 'Let us fully comprehend,' he said. 'I want those documents.'

The Major frowned.

'I will have to speak to my Colonel, Monsieur.'

'By all means,' Poujet said. 'I will be spending some time here. I will await your return.'

The Major left the room to return to his headquarters and report to his Colonel.

'There will be no written record of any of their discussions, Monsieur,' the Inspector warned.

'That is a pity,' Poujet replied, 'if a recruit was encouraged to join the Legion through the advice given by members of the Marseilles Police Force.' He was being diplomatic in his terminology; there was no trace of sarcasm in his voice, but the Inspector found himself feeling uncomfortable again. 'Would the Police department also have any records of such interviews? Any dates, any details?'

The Inspector shook his head.

'No, Monsieur,' he said.

'So,' Poujet sighed. 'We will see what the Legion's records show.'

It took the Legion Major precisely two hours to get his Colonel's permission and return with the dossiers. Poujet and his two assistants took them into another room. The two Police Officers and the Legion Major waited elsewhere.

Poujet looked at the folders thoughtfully, and then at his two assistants.

'We know a lot about the Fox,' he said. 'We know that he has been trained from a very early age to operate in the West. He can speak several languages including French. He is intelligent, shrewd, careful, astute, observant and so on, but all these things he can change or camouflage. What can he not change, Messieurs? What will be the same as the man who left the Rostov Academy? Perhaps the face will have even been changed, but what do we know for sure?'

He fixed his eyes on his two assistants.

'He is Russian,' Raphael said.

'Not good enough,' Poujet replied. 'That he will quickly try to forget.'

They sat in silence.

'He cannot change his height,' Raphael said.

'Good,' Poujet agreed. 'He cannot change his height, and we are ninety-nine per cent sure that he is not a giant of a man, or a dwarf. He will not have any outstanding features.' Poujet paused and frowned. 'He might now, though. He might have added some. No, we know he will not be very tall or very small. What else do we know?'

'He will not be too young or too old.'

'Precisely. He will be a man — he will not be a boy. The K.G.B. does not entrust anybody to a mission abroad until they are thoroughly trained. That takes many years. He will be a man of about...' He raised his eyebrows, inviting his assistants to comment. He was like a college lecturer holding a tutorial.

'Twenty-five to forty-seven, but a man over his forties would not join the Legion.'

'He will be between twenty-five and thirty-five,' Poujet agreed. 'So let us look for that type of man. We can dismiss the young boys — the so-called adventurers. We can dismiss those who enlisted in Paris. We can dismiss those who made their enquiries from abroad before March thirteenth. We will look for legionnaires between twenty-five and thirty-five years of age. The Fox could have given a wrong age, so look carefully at the photographs. He will be a man of about one hundred and seventy centimetres to one hundred and eighty in height, and weigh about seventy kilograms, and he was recruited either in Aubagne or Marseilles.'

They opened the folders and started examining the documents. Each recruit had been photographed. The photographs had been taken after their heads had been cropped.

Their faces looked unreal.

Many of the recruits were quickly discarded. The Legion attracted a lot of young adventurers and many young Frenchmen. There were also many who had been recruited in Paris. The documents were studied meticulously, one by one. Each of the three men examined each document and they made their own selection. They took their time. Poujet wanted the Fox and he wanted him alive. There had to be no mistakes. Finally, they compared notes. From forty names, they had selected ten possible candidates.

Poujet looked at the ten sets of documents.

'I want a copy of all of them,' he said to Dupois.

'Including the discards?' Raphael asked.

'Including the discards,' Poujet agreed. 'Those we check on.'

'And the ten suspects?'

'We leave them well alone,' Poujet warned. 'We do not want our friends — or enemies — to know that we are concerned. We must also protect Pascal. If we eliminate the other thirty, we are getting very close to our man.' He looked at his assistant, Dupois, and said, 'I am sure that the Legion Major will remember something about our ten candidates. That is as far as our enquiries will go —'

'I understand, Monsieur.'

'Good.'

Poujet stood up and returned to the room where the Legion Major and the two policemen were waiting.

'We would appreciate a copy of the documents,' Poujet said to the Inspector.

'Certainly, Monsieur,' the Inspector replied.

'I am particularly interested in these ten.'

The Inspector accepted the ten sets of documents and glanced through them.

'I might be able to add some information about some of these men,' he said.

Poujet looked at him. 'They volunteered at the Police Station?'

'Two of them did, Monsieur.'

'That is encouraging,' Poujet said, and turned to the Major. 'Perhaps you might also give us the benefit of your knowledge of these men, Monsieur.'

'I have been instructed to cooperate, Monsieur,' the Major replied.

Poujet turned again to the Inspector and took him to one side. He spoke to him quietly.

'Monsieur, you know the Legion. If a man was going to try to kill one of his comrades, when do you think he would do it?'

'Certainly not while he was under training,' the Inspector replied. 'They are watched over day and night. They are drilled and disciplined to obey. They are not allowed to even talk to each other. A man would have to be desperate to try then, and there are no means of escape. Very few have ever made the break from Corte without outside help. No, Monsieur, I think such a man would wait until they have finished their basic training. If he could arrange a posting to the same unit as his intended victim, I think his chances would be greater.'

'Thank you, Monsieur, you have confirmed what I was thinking.'

'The training period does not last long,' the Inspector warned. 'Only four months.'

'Then we will have to have it prolonged,' Poujet said.

They rejoined the others. Poujet thanked the Legion Major.

'My assistant will return to Marseilles with the Inspector,' he said. 'When he has the necessary copies, the documents will be handed back to you. I appreciate your cooperation, Monsieur.'

The Major gave a formal nod of his head and muttered, 'Monsieur.'

Poujet formally shook hands with him and the two Police Officers.

'I will expect the copies on my desk in the morning,' he said to Dupois.

He left the Chateau with Raphael. In the car, Raphael said, 'We have selected the men who could be the Fox, Monsieur, but if the K.G.B. also have a man…'

'So?' Poujet interrupted.

'Well, Monsieur, we cannot apply the same rules of identification that we did for the Fox… They are very clever. They could use a young Frenchman.'

'Very good, Raphael,' Poujet said. 'Very good. You are learning quickly. What you say is true. We can produce a handful of possible Foxes, but not a single potential killer. If we knew when Pascal and the others had presented themselves for recruitment, we might have been able to produce a much shorter list of Foxes, and even a K.G.B. killer, but the Legion does not have such information. *Sacré bleu!* My heart bleeds for Pascal.'

'What do we do about the killer?'

'Nothing,' Poujet said. 'Their man will try to get close to the Fox, and don't forget, he is the only one who might be able to pick him out. My hunch is that he will be amongst those that we have selected. The others had generally enrolled elsewhere. Like Pascal, their man would not have enlisted in the Legion unless he knew that the Fox had also enlisted. He will have enrolled in Marseilles, like Pascal. He will be amongst those that we have selected. He will try and get close to the Fox. We might have to extend their training to give Pascal more time.'

'But if their man is not in that group we have selected?' Raphael persisted.

Poujet sighed and cast his lazy eye on his assistant. 'In that case,' he said, 'he will have to enjoy the life of a legionnaire and wait for an opportunity to desert.' He gave a chuckle. 'It will be good for him. He will not learn many military secrets, but he will learn how tough the Legion can be.'

Chapter Seven

Poujet returned to Paris. He spent the late hours studying the reports from the different sections of the department. When he reported to the Director the following morning, he had a clear picture of the activities of the department. So had the Director.

'The Russians are wary,' the Director said. 'The Americans are envious and the British anxious. They all know something — especially the Americans. Carson offered a deal. I am still suspicious of him. The British have been making suggestions of cooperation, and the Russians are watching every move, like a cat playing with a mouse. You have read all the reports?'

'Yes, Monsieur.'

'I am being courted on all sides — and *le Corps Diplomatique* have never enjoyed such popularity. They don't understand why.'

'The Russians also seem to have reduced their activities in France.'

The Director's dark eyes looked grave.

'*Mon Dieu.* I hope that nothing will prick the bubble before *Monsieur le President* visits Moscow, Marcel,' he said. 'If it does, there are many who will have their knives ready, and it will be our backs that they will stab.'

Poujet was well aware of the gravity of the situation. '*Le Renard* is in the Legion, Monsieur,' he said. 'He might as well be in a prison, or a monastery. For the next few months, he will be safe.'

'Unless the K.G.B. become desperate.'

'It is always a possibility.'

The Director sat back.

'So, the Fox is in the Legion,' he muttered. 'He has eluded the tentacles of the K.G.B. from Budapest to Marseilles. He has been well trained, but why the Legion?'

'He is a very frightened man, Monsieur. He has dynamite in his pocket. He knows that the K.G.B. are after him, and he knows how efficient they are. He probably thinks that every other spy network is also after him. He fears the C.I.A. as much as the K.G.B., otherwise he would have approached them in Budapest, and he knows that we cannot accept him. All that he wants, now, is to protect himself and to stay alive.'

The Director rubbed his chin.

'Frightened, scared,' he muttered. 'Not knowing who he can trust. So he takes protection in the Legion. I suppose it is understandable. And now what do we do?'

'Watch and wait until we are sure.'

'And when we are sure?'

Poujet shrugged. 'We will review the situation, Monsieur.'

The Director sat upright, and looked business-like.

'Agreed. What have you got?'

'Ten sets of documents. Nine of them suspects.'

'Tell me about them.'

'They all have several things in common. They are not young boys, or middle-aged men. Their ages range between twenty-seven and thirty-five. These have been supported by medical reports. They are not giants or dwarfs. They are all about average height, and none of them have any outstanding features about them that would make you look twice at them. They were all recruited into the Legion from the Marseilles area, either at the recruiting centre in Marseilles, or at the camp, and they can all speak some French. Some were directed into the Legion by the Police. I have their dossiers and photographs.'

He handed a photograph to the Director. The face was rough, and bruised. It was not a pleasant looking face, and beneath it was a thick neck that joined the face to a broad pair of shoulders.

'Beauchamp,' Poujet explained. 'That is the name that he gave the Legion. Now he is Baron. Claims to be a Belgian, but he speaks French as if he had lived all his life in the gutters of Marseilles. He was involved in a fight in a brothel in Marseilles. He had no papers. He said that he was waiting in Marseilles to meet another Belgian who had promised to get him a job in a mine in South Africa. He gave his former occupation as a miner. He offered his services to the Legion without being pressed. He was arrested along with this man.'

Poujet handed the Director another photograph. It showed the face of a man with eyes set wide apart and a large forehead. He had a pointed nose and thin lips, and bruise marks on his face, but it was the eyes that held the Director's attention. They were round, and had a fixed, vacant, looked about them.

'Calyspi now called Calowski,' Poujet said. 'Claims to be Polish. Said he was waiting to pick up a ship to go to the States. Said that he jumped a ship bound for Gdynia, but the police have had no reports from any Polish shipping company about missing persons, and there have been no ships bound for Gdynia in Marseilles in the past month. He also speaks remarkably good French for a Polish seaman. He was brought in with Baron. They had been living in the same brothel. He had no papers. Also volunteered to join the Legion.'

'Did the Police make enquiries about him and Baron?'

'No, but they will if we ask them. They believe that Baron is well known in the Marseilles area and probably an ex-convict, but if they pass one on to the Legion, they forget about them.'

'Clear their books.'

'That's about it. Neither the Police nor the Legion go looking for problems. The Legion wants men — the Marseilles Police want to rid themselves of any troublemakers, so they cooperate. Once the men enlist in the Legion, the Legion disciplines them into their ways. The past is irrelevant.'

'Next,' the Director said.

Poujet handed the Director another photograph. It showed an even-featured, handsome face that was more refined than the previous two. The hair was shaved short, but was dark, and so were the man's eyes.

'Name Karuz. Entered the camp at Aubagne with a Swiss passport. Renamed Klaus by the Legion. Seems intelligent. Age thirty years. Gave his former occupation as a clerk, but he speaks fluent French, German and English.'

The Director grunted and laid the photograph to one side.

'Another so-called Swiss,' Poujet said, and gave a photograph to the Director. 'Name now Luker.'

Luker's face was oval shaped with a full mouth and a straight nose. His eyes were dark. It was not a particularly handsome face, but it looked a sensitive one.

'With their haircuts, they all look like convicts,' the Director muttered, 'but this one has the look of a thinker.'

'Age thirty-two. Claimed that he worked in a hospital in Geneva. He also speaks French and German fluently. He had a Swiss passport and was recruited in Marseilles.'

The next photograph showed a Germanic, square-shaped face, with light coloured eyes. It was not a sensitive looking face like Luker's, or handsome like Klaus. It had nothing special about it.

'Malik,' Poujet said. 'That is his new name. An Austrian. Claims that he comes from Graz, near the border with Yugoslavia. Age thirty-one. He is fit and doesn't look too intelligent, but looks can be misleading. Gave his former occupation as a truck driver. Also speaks French. Was recruited at the camp in Aubagne.'

'Probably make a good legionnaire,' the Director said, and put the photograph to one side.

Poujet picked up another photograph.

'Ah, Thompson the Englishman,' he said. 'Another one supposed to have jumped ship. Age thirty-two, but looks much younger. Originally called Timson. Failed to pay a hotel bill. The police were called in. Claimed that he had jumped ship because he didn't want to return to the U.K. because there was a paternity charge waiting for him. He said that he wanted to join the Legion. He is a brash, cocky individual. Speaks French well enough to get by, and seems a bit of a troublemaker. He has already been involved in a fight during his short stay in Aubagne.'

'He will soon get that knocked out of him,' the Director said. He studied Thompson's photograph and details. Thompson had a slim pointed face that didn't impress the Director. His nose was more pronounced than his other features. His height was average, but he had a slim build. The Director laid the photograph aside.

'Another of the same build as Thompson, but not so brash.'

Poujet gave the Director another photograph. Despite the haircut, the face was quite handsome. It was lean and even featured. The eyes looked sharp and alert. The Director glanced at the man's physical characteristics. In build, he was smaller and slimmer than Thompson.

'Name Focelini, now called Ferelli,' Poujet said. 'Gave his age as twenty-eight, but is probably older. He admitted that he was on the run from the police for petty thieving. He claimed that he used to operate in the popular Italian tourist resorts during the summer, stealing from the tourists, but moved into the Riviera for the winter. Had an Italian passport and joined the Legion at the camp in Aubagne.'

'To escape arrest.'

'So he said.'

'Doesn't look Italian.'

'He speaks fluent Italian and French, Monsieur.'

There were three more photographs and details. The first was a Slav called Knojasky, renamed Trojasky by the Legion.

'He arrived at the recruiting centre in Marseilles with no papers,' Poujet explained. 'Age about thirty-five. He looks tough and not too intelligent. Speaks fluent Italian, and a little French, as well as his native Serbo-Croat. Gave his former occupation as a mortician. Lived for some years in Trieste.'

Trojasky looked like a Slav and a hard one. He had a prominent chin and a long face that looked as if it had seen a lot of life. There was a dark look in his eyes. The Director laid the photograph to one side.

'Svenson the Swede,' Poujet said. 'Arrived with all the necessary papers.'

The Director looked at the Swede. He saw a round, Nordic face. The shaven hair would have been blonde, he thought. The eyes looked intelligent, and the mouth cruel.

'Twenty-eight years of age,' Poujet explained. 'Physically fit and tough. Speaks a little French. Claims that he worked in a factory in Gothenburg, and before that in a mine. Joined the Legion for adventure.'

'Adventure,' the Director grunted.

'The last one is Verdi,' Poujet said. 'Originally named Verden, now Verdi. Claims to be Canadian — French Canadian.'

The Director looked at Verdi's photograph. It was a face that was also bruised like the Belgian, Baron. It was not a handsome face, nor was it ugly, but it was a defiant one. The defiance was in the man's eyes and the set expression on his lips. Beneath the face was a very broad pair of shoulders.

'The Legion is getting some useful recruits,' the Director said. 'This one looks as if he can take care of himself.'

'Verdi volunteered to join the Legion, at the camp,' Poujet explained. 'He had a Canadian passport that was out of date. He claims that he had been living in France for the past six years, doing any kind of job. Speaks fluent French with a rough Parisian accent. His English has a strong American accent. This one has been around. He is physically tough, and is probably more intelligent than he appears. Gave his former occupation as labourer.'

The Director sat back.

'That is ten, Marcel,' he said.

'Correct, Monsieur.'

'And Pascal?'

Poujet gave a smile. 'The shaven head, Monsieur, and the uniform can change a man. It can make him look ugly, distinguished, tough or even handsome!'

The Director gave a throaty chuckle.

'Good, Marcel, good. And which one is *le Renard?*'

'I have an open mind, Monsieur, and so far no suspicions.'

'Can we reduce the odds? We could start some discreet inquiries?'

'At the moment it is too great a risk. Once we make a move to show that we are in any way concerned about the Fox, we will lose all that we have gained. Russo and some of our other agents are still being watched by the Russians. If the Russians see us make a move, they will threaten us with Bichante. For the present we must wait. We must leave them all well alone. We must not underestimate the tentacles of the K.G.B. They have their informers everywhere, even in the Elysée Palace. They will also have them in the Legion. When we do bring in our man, it must be like catching a fly.' He made a swift, grabbing gesture with his hand. 'There will only be one opportunity. When we move we must be certain and quick, and it must be safe. Nobody must know but us.'

'It certainly is a game of patience and bluff,' the Director sighed. 'Marcel, you must be a good poker player.'

Poujet smiled. 'Unfortunately, I prefer bridge. It taxes the brain more.'

'Just as well. You would make too much money at poker, and I would lose a good deputy.' He shuffled his frame more comfortably into his seat.

'Is our man safe if we leave him alone?'

'So long as they are undergoing training, the Fox is safe. They have not time to think. They are too exhausted.'

'And after their training?'

'Some undergo special training, and many will join one of the Legion's regiments at home or abroad. That is when the Fox will be most vulnerable.'

'So?'

'We prolong their training as long as possible, if necessary.'

The Director looked at him questioningly.

'It is rather coincidental, Monsieur,' Poujet explained, in a matter-of-fact manner, 'but I have a cousin, who in turn has a cousin, who is in the Legion. I do believe that he has recently been posted to take command of an advanced infantry training centre in the North of Corsica, close to Calvi. I will see if I can arrange for our ten men to be sent there after they have completed their period of training at Corte.'

'You never cease to amaze me with the prolificacy of your ancestors. They must have spent more time in bed than at their work.'

'It has been an advantage, I agree.'

The Director sighed.

'So it is all up to Pascal?' he said. 'A lot rests on his shoulders.'

Yes, Poujet thought, a lot did rest on Pascal's shoulders. Perhaps it would be advisable to have somebody else on the side-lines. Somebody with intelligence who could be called upon to help if necessary. It wasn't a sudden thought. It was something that he had been thinking about ever since he had heard of Pascal's whereabouts. He had thought about it as he had returned from Marseilles, and the man he was thinking of was Simon Ducan. There had been something fresh and challenging about Ducan. Ducan could be of great service to France if he was given the right direction.

'I feel rather sorry for Pascal,' the Director said. 'I understand Madame Catherine Cantois sleeps alone in her bed with a heavy heart. She is under the impression that her Pascal has deserted her for some wealthy Hungarian widow. I met her a few nights ago at a party. She looked quite sad. Could you not arrange for her to have some company?'

'With Pascal serving his country in the Legion?'

Poujet shook his head in mock concern. 'Besides, just think how fit he will be when he returns. She will not know such virility and such passion.'

'If he survives,' the Director added.

Pascal would survive, Poujet thought. He would survive and he would be close to his man until Poujet or the Fox made a move. Pascal was like that, but he would suffer. They were all going to suffer.

Chapter Eight

The town of Corte is the old capital of the mountainous island of Corsica. It clings to a peak that rises sharply from a bare plateau. The island has great beauty, but Legion recruits only see this beauty as they are driven across the island from the seaport to the Citadel at Corte. In the Citadel, there is no beauty — only discipline. The Citadel is old, it is spartan, and it is very basic. It is the camp where men with close-cropped heads and ill-fitting uniforms, used to the soft life of a civilian, are forged into disciplined, obedient, and physically fit legionnaires. It is where they are drilled to obey immediately, without question, and without thought. It is a process that is physically and mentally exhausting. The past has to be quickly forgotten. All that matters is the present.

The ten men selected by Poujet for special attention were part of an assignment of forty men who all occupied one of the floors of the barracks. *Debout* — the order that started the day was at four a.m. The first parade was at five a.m. The men returned to their bunks at nine p.m. in the evening. In between, they were beaten, drilled, cursed and driven to their breaking point. There was no talking, no smoking and no relaxing of the pace. There were only two concessions. One was the liberal amount of 'vino' that the men were allowed to drink with their evening meal. The second was the opportunity to enjoy the local prostitutes who were brought into the camp at regular intervals. The 'vino' and the mess hall brawls allowed the men to let off steam. The girls prevented them from looking elsewhere for their sex. The Legion had thought of everything.

The ten men, like the others, were all individuals. Unlike most of the others, they did not particularly encourage company. The younger elements in the section and certain nationals gradually drifted together for comradeship and support. The ten men took what company came their way. They didn't remain aloof, but they neither sought each other's company nor that of any of the other men. There was no apparent link or interest between any of them. However, there was one particular feature they all did have in common during their four months of training at Corte. They all fell afoul of the system at some stage of their period of training. Each of them rebelled, and each of them suffered the consequences.

Verdi was the first, Ferelli the last. Verdi suffered at the beginning, Ferelli at the end. In between, each of the other eight also suffered. It was not surprising that Verdi should have been first. Verdi looked tough, he was tough and he suffered at the beginning because of his toughness. The men had to be shown what was expected of them, and how they would suffer if they stepped out of line. Verdi was to be the example. It was essential for the corporal in charge of the section to establish his authority and power over the men. It was a standard procedure — pick the toughest looking recruit, make him suffer and the rest would respond that much quicker. The corporal in charge of the section had no hesitation in picking Verdi. Verdi was tailor-made for the part.

On the first day of their training period, the corporal inspected the lines of men, but he had already selected Verdi for his display of authority. He finished his cursory inspection and returned to face Verdi, who was standing in the front line of men.

'Name?' the corporal demanded.

'Legionnaire, second class, Verdi,' Verdi replied.

'Corporal!' the Corporal snarled.

'Corporal,' Verdi said with obvious reluctance.

'Nationality?'

'Canadian, French-Canadian.'

'Corporal!'

'Corporal,' Verdi added after a pause, and with less enthusiasm than before.

'I don't like Canadians,' the Corporal snarled, 'particularly French-Canadians.' He hit Verdi full in the face with his fist. Verdi fell back into the arms of the man behind him. He saw red. He recovered his stance.

'Your nationality, Corporal?' he asked, tight-lipped.

The Corporal's eyes lit up. Verdi had committed the crime of asking a question. He was setting himself up for more punishment.

'Mongolian,' the Corporal mocked.

'I don't like Mongolians,' Verdi hissed, and crashed his fist into the Corporal's face. The Corporal fell to the ground, unconscious. Verdi was immediately set upon by two other Corporals and a Sergeant who had been watching the proceedings. He was bodily dragged away from the parade ground and taken to a cell where the three *sous-officiers* set about him. That was just the start of his punishment. He spent three nights in the cell and three days with a full pack of rocks on his back, running circles around a Sergeant who slowly walked around the citadel until Verdi would collapse, exhausted, and be dragged back to his cell.

Verdi was the first to suffer. He learned the hard way to control his temper. He was also an example for the others to heed, but in the charged atmosphere of the strict, iron discipline and physical hardships, the others had their breaking points. Malik, the Austrian, was the second to suffer. Malik spoke French fluently. He kept pace with the Corporals as they instructed them in the songs of the Legion, but for some reason — known only to the Corporal — his accent was not to the Corporal's liking. The Corporal intended to change it. He kept hitting Malik with his baton as Malik repeated the words of a song. Malik knew that he had to endure the constant smacks and the Corporal's sarcastic remarks, but he began to hate the Corporal and the hate built up inside him until he reached his breaking-point. He reacted one night in the barrack room. He was going through the regular performance of repeating the words of a song, and the Corporal was hitting him with rhythmic blows to his body. Malik snapped and lashed out with his fist. It connected with the Corporal's face, which was the only moment of satisfaction that he was allowed to enjoy. He got two days of the hell that Verdi had suffered. Verdi had been the example — Malik was the reminder.

Calowski, Baron and Svenson, the Swede suffered on the training range. Calowski watched people. He would stare at them as if trying to read their minds. He had stared at the Swede. The Swede had not liked it. As they were eating their rations on the range, the Swede's boot connected with Calowski's leg and a message of warning was hissed to him.

'Stop staring — or else!'

The Swede moved on. Calowski's foot tripped him up. The Swede went his length. There was a ripple of laughter from the men. The Swede got to his feet and turned on Calowski. He dragged Calowski to his feet. Baron also got to his feet. He had attached himself to Calowski and had intended to part the Swede from him, but another Swede decided that national pride demanded his support. There was a free for all. The Sergeants and Corporals watched for a while, and then broke it up.

'So much energy,' the Sergeant said, and shook his head. 'We shall see.'

The four men ran all that afternoon over the rough, gorse covered ground with their packs filled with rocks. Svenson's compatriot collapsed with fatigue. The others managed to keep going until they were route marched back to the camp.

Klaus, Thompson and the Slav, Trojasky, who had been nicknamed Tojak, were involved in a brawl in the mess hall, but Thompson was always in trouble. It seemed to follow him around. He had been in a fight in Aubagne. He was frequently involved in fights in the training camp, and spent many nights chained to an iron ring on the staircase in the barrack block.

Klaus had tried hard not to get involved. He was more concerned about keeping his good looks than proving his ability to throw a punch.

In the crowded mess hall, Thompson and Tojak crossed swords. They had both gone for the same seat. Thompson told Tojak to 'piss off.' He added that the Slav was just a 'big bag of shit!' His comments were delivered in English. The Slav hadn't understood their meaning, but he insisted on occupying the vacant seat at that particular table. He got his way through his sheer weight and size. Thompson joined another table and sat opposite Klaus.

'He's a big guy,' Klaus said in English.

'He's like all big guys,' Thompson replied. 'He falls heavier. They don't worry me. Nobody does.'

'That why you spend the nights chained to the staircase?'

'I prefer my own company.'

Klaus saw the Slav from the corner of his eye moving towards them. Somebody had obviously translated Thompson's remarks into French. The Slav didn't look pleased. He couldn't afford to. He couldn't lose face, or he would be ridiculed. He stood over Thompson and glowered at Klaus.

'You speak English?' he snarled at Klaus.

'No,' Klaus lied, and continued to eat his meal.

The Slav knew Klaus was lying. He knocked Klaus' plate away. Klaus had to make a stand. The room went quiet.

'You tell me what he said about me,' the Slav shouted.

Klaus slowly stood up.

'I don't know what he said about you,' he said loudly, 'but I know what I think about you. I think you are a big bag of shit.' His description had been delivered in English, but he added in French, 'You are *merde*, and a *cochon*.'

Before the Slav's brain had time to react, Thompson hit him in the pit of his stomach with the full force of his two fists clenched together. The Slav groaned and crumpled to the floor, but he had an ally who enjoyed a good fight. There was an uproar, and another mess brawl. Several others joined in.

As a result, Thompson spent more nights chained to an iron ring on the staircase. Klaus, Tojak and the others involved in the fight spent the night in the cell block. The following day, they all suffered on the circuit.

Luker, the other Swiss, suffered because he was not a robot. He had been educated. He was a thinker. Whatever the Corporals ordered of him, he seemed to think about it, as if looking for a reason for the order or a shortcut. But often there was no logical reason or shortcut, and Luker didn't react quickly enough. On the rifle range, his shooting was not up to standard. The Sergeant had had enough of him.

'Legionnaire Luker,' he snapped. 'Not only must your shooting improve, but also,' he paused, 'but also, so must you.' Again he paused. 'I am going to give you some time to think over my warning. You are going to spend the afternoon on field discipline.'

Luker did think about it as he started his field punishment, but he soon stopped thinking about it. He concentrated on satisfying the Corporals who were supervising his punishment. The physical pain soon became an all-consuming torture. The heavy pack of rocks on his back tore at his shoulders, his legs became like lead weights, and his inside was like a burning furnace. Finally, when he had collapsed twice, he was relieved from his torture. He didn't think about the Sergeant's remarks, but he intended to make sure that he didn't suffer again. He would react more quickly in future — he would obey, and not think.

Ferelli, the slim, ferret-faced Italian, became known as 'Fingers' when some of his past came to light. The men watched him closely. He was not popular and he was the last to suffer.

In build, Fingers was very similar to Thompson. He was also as tough as Thompson, but he was much shrewder. He had tried to gain Klaus's friendship, but without success. He had also tried to get close to Verdi, but Verdi had ignored him. Fingers was on his own. Nevertheless, he had made up his mind that he would survive the training period without any additional punishment. He was even prepared to eat humble pie, or crawl, rather than cause a mess brawl. Towards the end of the training period, somebody else decided that Fingers must suffer. A well placed boot sent him crashing down the staircase as the section was assembling for a ceremonial parade. The men had moved quickly when the order had come to assemble. So had Fingers, but somebody had helped him on his way. Somebody else helped him to his feet, and somebody ripped his shirt in the process. Fingers went on parade, he had to. He stood to attention, knowing that he had been set up for punishment. He knew that he had enemies. Whoever they were, they were not disappointed. Fingers suffered one day of hell on the circuit and four days of extra duty. Nobody felt sorry for him.

At the end of their training period in the Citadel, the men were route marched across the mountainous island. Again, they didn't appreciate its beauty. They only appreciated that it signified the end of their initial training. They were tested and interviewed. They made their requests for the units of their choice, and they waited for their postings.

The ten men selected by Poujet had been together for over four months, including their stay at Aubagne. They had been part of a larger section of forty men. They had been aware of each other. They had not become close; they had not become comrades. Klaus had become friendly with a young Frenchman. Luker had kept to himself; so had Verdi. Thompson had occasionally spoken to Klaus, but after their brawl, Klaus had kept away from the Englishman. Trouble was Thompson's only close companion. Malik, the Austrian, was another loner. There were many Germans in the section — men younger than Malik. Occasionally they had spoken to him, but Malik had not sought out any of them for special company. Only Calowski and Baron kept a close relationship. Baron seemed to have become Calowski's protector, although Calowski was quite capable of looking after himself, and the others were well aware of it. Tojak, the Slav, had become friendly with another Slav. Occasionally he was seen looking suspiciously at Malik, but it was only Malik, and the few observant men of the barrack room who noticed it. He had also been seen talking to Fingers.

Svenson, the Swede, had been close to another of his countrymen. They had both seemed to enjoy their physical fitness, and had been prepared to take on anybody in the mess hall.

None of Poujet's ten made any request for further specialist training. They all requested a posting to a regular infantry unit, but all ten were officially posted to the Advanced Infantry Training Centre, for further training. For the first time they were made aware of each other — or so it appeared.

A full report on their behaviour and attitudes during their training period at Corte was sent to Poujet. He had earlier received a report on the men that he had discarded. Nothing had come to light to indicate that any of them should have been included on his list of suspects. The Fox was one of his selected group. He received another piece of information. One of the prostitutes who had been in the camp during the last week of the men's training had agreed to despatch a bunch of flowers to an address in Paris for one of the legionnaires. Poujet received a message that three pink and three red carnations had been delivered. Poujet was impressed.

'Pascal is getting closer,' he remarked to the Director, with confidence.

'Pascal must be a man of unusual talent,' the Director muttered.

Poujet studied the reports in detail in his office. He knew that the sands were running out for the Fox. The posting to the Advanced Training Centre was only a temporary stopgap. Poujet couldn't keep the group together for further training without arousing suspicion. After their training, they would be posted for service in East Africa. Poujet had thought long and hard about that. The training period was nine weeks, but the President's visit to Moscow was still several months away. A posting to East Africa would take the Fox out of Metropolitan France. It would take him into a wild, desolate country where the Legion's posts were often small and isolated. It would open up an opportunity for a different ball game. It would make the Fox more vulnerable, but it could also give Poujet more freedom of action. He might be able to use it to his advantage. There was a seed of an idea in his brain. He would let it germinate and take root. In the meantime, he would also reinforce his hand. It was time to have a reserve for Pascal. Somebody who was in a position to help if necessary. He decided it was time for Lieutenant Ducan to serve his country.

Chapter Nine

Ducan again presented himself at Poujet's office. It was a hot sunny day, but Poujet didn't seem to notice the heat. His small window looked as if it couldn't open and he sat at his desk, still wearing a thick, woollen suit. Ducan, in contrast, was smartly dressed in a lightweight suit.

Poujet waved him to a seat. He watched him out of the corner of his eye. Ducan still had that youthful freshness about him that Poujet had noticed before. There was a feeling of gaiety about his appearance and manner. He was still amused by it all, Poujet thought.

'It is some time since we last met,' Poujet said.

'Yes, Monsieur.'

'And are you still being used as a clerk?'

Ducan's eyes danced. He smiled.

'I regret to say, Monsieur, that there has been little change.'

Poujet's face didn't show any sign of amusement. He held Ducan firmly in his gaze. The smile left Ducan's face.

'Colonel Gourbet recommended you to me, Monsieur, because he thought that I might be able to make use of your services. Also he wanted my opinion as to your usefulness for his staff.'

'Yes, Monsieur.'

'I have studied the matter carefully, Monsieur, and I have made my recommendation for Colonel Gourbet.'

'I understand, Monsieur.'

Ducan smiled again. It was a confident smile.

Poujet placed a piece of paper in front of him.

'That is my recommendation,' he said.

Ducan glanced at it and saw the words quite clearly — 'Not recommended for Military Intelligence. Recommended for service with a regular unit'. Poujet watched Ducan's face closely. He saw no change as Ducan read the words, not even in his eyes.

'I regret that you have made such a decision, Monsieur,' Ducan said.

Poujet recognised a trace of sadness in Ducan's voice.

'What will you do?'

'I will serve where I am posted, Monsieur,' Ducan said.

His disappointment was obvious by his tone, but his face had remained impassive. 'I will see if it is in the best interests of France.'

Poujet was curious. He decided to explore Ducan's reactions before informing him what was proposed.

'And if you think that it is not?'

'I will seek a re-assignment to Military Intelligence.'

'But this obstacle.' Poujet waved his hand at his brief report.

'Obstacles can be overcome, Monsieur,' Ducan said. 'Obstacles can be like sand dunes that erode in time.'

'And if they don't erode?'

'They can be bypassed.'

'And how will you do that?'

'There is *Monsieur le Ministre de la Defense*, and *Monsieur le President*.'

'You would go to such lengths?'

'If I thought it in the best interests of my country.'

'And yourself?'

'Perhaps they are both the same, Monsieur.'

Poujet slowly nodded his head in approval.

Ducan stood up.

'Is that all, Monsieur?' he asked.

'No, it is not,' Poujet said. 'Sit down, Monsieur.'

Ducan sat down. Poujet looked at him. Ducan returned the look politely, but defiantly. Poujet had blunted his ego and his confidence, but Ducan wasn't going to show it. Poujet admired him for it. Ducan had backbone. Poujet was pleased.

'This is the recommendation that will go to Colonel Gourbet,' Poujet said, 'because *Monsieur le Ministre de la Defense* has agreed to assign you to my department.'

He looked at Ducan.

Ducan said, 'Monsieur?' with a questioning look on his face.

'Before we go any further,' Poujet added. 'You are at liberty to refuse. If you do so, I will tear up the recommendation and you will continue to serve on Colonel Gourbet's staff.'

'I do not know what you propose, Monsieur.'

'No you don't,' Poujet agreed, and sat back.

The two men looked at each other. A faint smile appeared on Ducan's lips and his eyes lit up.

'It is a challenge, Monsieur,' he said. 'I like a challenge.'

'Good.'

Poujet sat forward again, and put his arms on the desk.

'As you are aware, our territory in East Africa is very soon to be given its independence.'

'Yes, Monsieur.'

'I am sure that you will also be aware that both Somalia and Ethiopia are watching our movements very closely.'

'I am, Monsieur. The two countries are also on the verge of open conflict with each other.'

Poujet nodded his head in agreement.

'*Bien.* You will also be aware of the Russian influence in the area.'

'Yes, Monsieur.'

'Then you will understand why it is possible that I will need the services of a man of your talents.'

Ducan smiled, but there was a look of suspicion in his eyes.

'There is a unit being formed in Corsica that is to be posted to East Africa on the completion of its training. I want you to join this unit.'

Ducan looked thoughtful.

'Corsica, Monsieur? Is it *la Légion Étrangère*?'

Poujet cast his lazy eye in Ducan's direction.

'Yes, Monsieur. It is *la Légion*.'

The two men looked at each other. Ducan frowned.

'It is a challenge,' Poujet said.

'*La Légion* is always a challenge, Monsieur.'

Poujet sat back and watched Ducan. Ducan was puzzled by the selection of the unit. He was also curious.

'I have not posted you to the unit lightly, or without reason,' Poujet said. 'It is very possible that you will be of great service to me, and to your country. At the moment, I can say no more.'

Ducan gave a wry smile.

'Am I permitted to ask a question, Monsieur?'

Poujet shook his head decisively. 'No,' he said. 'You are not.'

But Poujet wanted to know more about Ducan. He wanted to know how shrewd and intelligent he could be. He wanted to know what potential the man had.

'However,' he said. 'I would be interested to know of any observations that you have in mind.'

Ducan dropped his head thoughtfully, and then looked up.

'The Legion is unique both in the men that it recruits and in the role that it performs. You could not have selected a more challenging unit for me to join. I will be interested to study its methods. However, it did cross my mind that I am not in need of any infantry training myself, and that the Legion already has units in East Africa. Also, Monsieur, you would not have called me to your office if you did not have any need for my services.'

'So you conclude, Monsieur?'

'Perhaps it is the role that this unit will be called upon to perform in East Africa, or it is the men.'

Poujet raised his hand. He had heard enough. Ducan had given a remarkably shrewd analysis of the situation that was very close to the mark. Poujet was impressed and encouraged.

'You are very shrewd, Monsieur. I wonder how perceptive you can be also. Study the ways of the Legion. Get to know your men. I will be watching your progress closely. We will meet again soon.'

'Yes, Monsieur.'

Poujet relaxed.

'*Bien.* The necessary arrangements will be made. Colonel Gourbet will be informed.'

He dropped his eyes and looked at some papers on his desk. Ducan was being dismissed. Ducan understood. He excused himself and left the room.

Later, Poujet informed the Director. The Director knew of Ducan. He had read the reports on the man. He also knew of Poujet's interest in Ducan for the department, but Ducan was untried.

'Why did you pick Ducan?' he asked. 'There are others far more experienced.'

'Precisely,' Poujet said. 'Ducan is a young, inexperienced Lieutenant who is still wet behind the ears, but he has certain qualities. He speaks fluent Russian and also Somali. He is intelligent and observant, and he could prove to be a most promising prospect.'

'Could, Marcel?'

Poujet frowned.

'There is a flaw in his character. He lacks the dedication that is needed to get to the top. He has the ability, but not the drive. Life is still something for him to watch and be amused by. He needs some challenge, some cause. He needs to struggle to survive.'

'Perhaps he needs a woman,' the Director remarked lightly. 'Good or bad.'

Poujet smiled.

'You have a sense of humour, Monsieur.'

'Has Ducan?'

'Yes, he certainly has that.'

'Good. He is going to need it in the Legion.'

Again Poujet smiled. Perhaps the Legion would be the stimulant that Ducan needed to spur him on, he thought. It would certainly do something for him.

Chapter Ten

The Legion's Advanced Infantry Training Centre was a small camp set in a rocky valley in the Northern part of Corsica, close to the Legion's base at Calvi. It was a collection of single storey buildings and dusty, unmade tracks surrounded by the rugged mountains that dwarfed everything around them.

The purpose of the Centre was to retrain and produce elite sections of infantrymen for the regular units. Men who would be above the normal standards of fitness and expertise, and who could be used by their units for special duties. With the situation that was developing in East Africa, most of the sections at the Centre were earmarked for special duties in that theatre of operations. The centre was also used by the regular units as a means of reminding some of their more troublesome legionnaires of the standards of fitness and obedience that were demanded by the Legion.

The training period was nine weeks, and the instructing staff were as hard and unyielding as the rugged mountains that were the training ground.

The Captain of the camp was Maurice Moutoner, and he ran it with a small nucleus of officers and permanent staff.

To this camp were posted Poujet's ten men from Corte and Lieutenant Simon Ducan. A posting to the centre for a newly commissioned officer was normal procedure. It was a method of giving them an insight into the Legion's ways.

The ten men from Corte travelled to the Centre in the rear of a truck. There was a cautious atmosphere amongst them as they journeyed, as if they were unsure of one another. Immediately, as they arrived at the camp, two corporals pounced on them. They both carried short canes which the men sensed were significant. The corporals introduced themselves and warned the men what to expect.

'The Sergeant-Chief is called Schiller. He is a bastard. If one man falls out of line, the whole section suffers.'

The corporal who spoke was a big man. The other corporal was smaller, but meaner looking.

'The men of your section are from regular units. They know the Legion. They know the Sergeant-Chief, and they don't like to suffer unnecessarily.'

The two corporals walked the line of the ten men.

'You are here for nine weeks only.' It was the smaller of the two corporal's turn to speak. 'You all know the routine. It is going to be harder than you think.'

The following morning, the men met the Sergeant-Chief. So did Lieutenant Ducan. Ducan had arrived the previous evening and reported to Captain Moutoner. He had been detailed to Number One section. That was Schiller's section. He hadn't met Schiller and he proposed to watch him, and the men, before being formally introduced.

In the early hours of the morning, as the mist lifted from the valley, Ducan stood aside and waited for the men to assemble. The mountains looked majestic and beautiful. The air was still and there was a sweet scent of the *maquis* plant. There was peace in the valley.

All that abruptly changed.

A series of raucous voices ordered, *Rassemblement!* The camp came alive. The legionnaires rushed out of their blocks and stood to attention. The ten men from Corte, and Lieutenant Ducan, saw Schiller for the first time. He walked in front of his section smacking his cane, impatiently, against the palm of his large hands. He was taller and broader than the other Sergeants and wore a traditional dress hat that looked as if it was perched on the top of a lump of stone hewn from the mountainside. He looked hard, tough and physically fit. There was nothing about him to suggest that he was anything other than a bastard. He stood to one side as another sergeant inspected the men. The section was brought to attention. The drill of the morning parade was performed. The *Tricolore* was hoisted. The section sergeants took over again.

Schiller spoke gruffly to the other sergeant. The ten new arrivals were told to stand fast. The rest of the section was taken out of the camp at the double. One of the corporals remained with the Sergeant-Chief.

The Sergeant-Chief faced the ten men.

Verdi braced himself. He knew that he would be made to suffer. Klaus saw a bird hovering in the sky. It was free, he thought, free — and he gritted his teeth. Calowski stared and waited. He had disciplined himself not to think. Thompson also stared. He had decided that he would keep out of trouble. There was a feeling about the Centre that it was for real, and he had had enough punishment. Malik wondered why they had been selected for the posting. He wondered if they had been specially selected, or if it had been accidental. His eyes caught the Sergeant-Chief and he quickly concentrated his thoughts on the white-washed walls of the building facing him. Luker saw the Lieutenant standing alongside the administration block, and wondered what was going through his mind. Svenson thought that Schiller's bark would be worse than his bite. Baron thought otherwise and knew that it was going to be hell. Tojak confidently thought that he could take whatever Schiller was going to dish out. Fingers stood as rigidly to attention as was humanly possible. His fingers were pressed to the side of his leg. He gripped his rifle butt. His chin was upturned. He didn't want any trouble.

A stillness hung over the camp. The other sections had disappeared behind a cloud of dust. The dust had settled. The sun had poked its head over the peaks of the mountain.

Schiller gave a smirk.

'You have been sent here for toughening up,' he called out. His voice was coarse, his tone aggressive. There was no finesse about him.

'We are also going to prepare you to fight and serve the Legion wherever you are needed. That might be in the sewers of Paris or in the desert of East Africa.' He smacked his cane against the palm of his hand. 'Wherever you are sent, you will be ready. I will see to it.'

He looked along the line. His eyes settled on Verdi. He snarled and went up to him. He flicked his cane into Verdi's side. Verdi didn't react, although he had felt the whiplash of the cane.

'Don't you ever upset me, Legionnaire,' he snarled. 'Don't you dare.'

He walked along the line. He stopped in front of Klaus. He looked into Klaus's dark, handsome face.

'A gentleman,' he snorted.

Klaus didn't reply.

'Nationality?'

'Swiss, Sergeant-Chief.'

'Liar!' Schiller hissed, and whiplashed the side of his large hand into Klaus's body with a short, sharp, karate type blow. Klaus winced — the pain burned through his ribs. He gave a mental prayer of thanks as Schiller moved along the line. Schiller stopped in front of the Englishman, Thompson. The Englishman looked directly to his front. Suddenly, Schiller's fist hit the Englishman's stomach. Thompson grunted and his body crumpled. Schiller held him upright. The Englishman gasped for breath.

'Next time,' Schiller hissed, 'you will be prepared.' He held the slim Thompson by the scruff of the neck. 'You had better be.'

He moved along the line dishing out sharp, short blows to the men's bodies. He used his hand, his elbow, or his fist. Nobody was missed out — nobody escaped. That was Sergeant-Chief Schiller's way of introducing himself. He returned to face Fingers.

He tapped his cane on Finger's shoulders with regular strokes. He knew that the man was called Fingers and he knew why. He knew about them all. He knew the names that they called each other. They were the names by which Schiller would also think of them, but he wondered why some of them were in the camp. He wondered why the Englishman was there and why Fingers had been sent. Fingers was physically different to the rest of the men. He had a slim, fragile looking figure. He was smaller and slimmer than Thompson. He looked more suited for a desk post, or even the cookhouse. He didn't look the type to be trained as a killer. Schiller stopped tapping Finger's shoulders and put his cane, ominously, under Finger's chin. He pushed Finger's chin upwards so that Finger's eyes were directed to the Sergeant-Chiefs. Schiller shook his head slowly and hissed.

'Don't ever use your fingers,' he warned, referring to Finger's nickname. Fingers got the message. He mentally swallowed and prepared himself. A sudden movement by the Sergeant-Chief and his cane had connected with Finger's testicles. Fingers gave a sharp cry of pain, but he stood his ground.

'If they are going to trouble you,' Schiller snarled, 'we will have to remove them. Understand?'

'Yes, Sergeant-Chief,' Fingers replied.

The Sergeant-Chief stood in the centre of the line.

'If any one of you steps out of line, if any one of you fails me — the whole section will suffer.' He looked along the line. 'They don't like to suffer.'

He turned to the corporal.

'Take them away,' he snapped.

The corporal saluted. The men doubled out of the camp. The Sergeant-Chief followed behind. Lieutenant Ducan watched them. They left a trail of grey, sandy dust behind them. They were the last group to leave the camp. The camp had come to life like an army of insects coming out of the ground. Now it was quiet again, but Ducan didn't find the morning pleasant any longer. The mountains didn't look so attractive, and there was no scent of the *maquis* plant. There was the first hint of the hot Corsican sun, and the thought of Schiller making his men suffer. The Legion had started its training.

'That was your Sergeant-Chief,' a voice said.

Ducan turned to see Captain Moutoner approaching.

Ducan saluted. Moutoner returned the salute.

'Yes, Sir,' Ducan said.

'You have met him formally?'

'No, Sir.'

'Then I will introduce you to him when he returns. Come and have some coffee with me. You look sad, Monsieur.'

Ducan gave a half smile.

'I had been thinking, earlier, what a beautiful morning it was,' he said.

'And now that you have met the Sergeant-Chief?' Moutoner asked.

Ducan shrugged.

'We shall see, Sir.'

They returned to Moutoner's office and drank their coffee. Moutoner introduced Ducan to some of the permanent staff and explained the training. Ducan was interested. He asked questions, and Moutoner decided that he was going to be a useful officer to have around.

They watched the sections returning to the camp. They had been away for an hour of recreation. Schiller's latest recruits had been given an insight into Schiller's version of the term 'recreation'. They were all in agreement that he was a bastard.

Schiller was ordered to report to the Captain's office. Schiller presented himself. Moutoner introduced Lieutenant Ducan.

'*Monsieur le Lieutenant* will be in command of Number One section.'

'*Oui, mon Capitaine*,' Schiller replied.

The Lieutenant and the Sergeant-Chief faced each other, and dutifully acknowledged each other's presence. Schiller saluted. Ducan acknowledged the salute. Neither man spoke. Moutoner watched them silently weighing each other up. It was like putting two opposite ends of a magnet together, he thought ruefully. They were opposite in almost every way.

The Sergeant-Chief turned to the Captain.

'Will that be all, Sir?' he asked.

It was Schiller's way of showing his disapproval of Ducan. Schiller had little time for newly commissioned officers. They came and they went.

Moutoner saw a smile appear on Ducan's lips and knew that Ducan had appreciated the slight. It also appeared to amuse him.

'*Monsieur le Lieutenant* will be spending some time with you on the range, Sergeant-Chief. He wants to get to know the men.'

The Sergeant-Chief's features didn't change, but both Moutoner and Ducan sensed his resentment of the proposal.

'Yes, Sir,' Schiller said. He saluted and withdrew.

'I gather he doesn't approve,' Ducan said, when he was alone with the Captain again.

'He doesn't approve of any newly commissioned officers,' Moutoner said. 'It is nothing personal. I also got the impression that you did not take to him.'

'First impressions can often be misleading,' Ducan pointed out, but he knew that the Captain was correct. Ducan hadn't taken to Schiller. Schiller had reminded him of part of his past. Of his days at school where he had met some younger versions of Schiller.

'You are quite right,' Moutoner said. 'You will come to respect Schiller. Schiller has his faults, but he is the Legion. He is also of the opinion that officers should direct and give orders, and not expose themselves unnecessarily to the men. In battle, the officer is important. In training, it is the *sous-officier*.'

'And do you agree, Sir?'

'You will find that it can be more difficult to give an order, or make a decision, than it is to train a section of men.'

'And the Legion has its own brand of *sous-officiers* for training its men?' Ducan asked.

Moutoner smiled patiently.

'The Legion's ways have worked well in the past. Schiller is no exception.'

A bugle sounded. The training had begun again.

Ducan left the Captain and joined the Sergeant-Chief and the section on the range.

The Sergeant-Chief was assisted by another Sergeant, Sergeant Hultz, and two corporals, but it was the Sergeant-Chief who was in charge. He bellowed and cursed the men and mocked them when they didn't come up to his standards. He also whiplashed them with his cane or with the side of his large hands.

Ducan watched. The Sergeant-Chief suffered his presence.

The day wore on. Ducan remained with the section. The Sergeant-Chief acknowledged him only when it was absolutely necessary to keep the respect of the officer in front of the men, but there was no hiding his resentment of Ducan's invasion of his territory, nor his attempt to intimidate Ducan into returning to camp.

It was a long, gruelling day. Schiller drove the men hard, but they knew what was expected of them as legionnaires and from Schiller, Ducan found out, and he was not surprised. It was as he had expected, but he was soon aware of a growing feeling of antagonism towards both the system and Schiller's sadistic methods.

The following days were the same. From early morning until evening, the men were drilled and disciplined. The dusty surface, kicked up from their boots, choked in their throats. The sun shone; the sky was an idyllic blue. The sergeants and corporals kept on top of their men. They did everything at the double. They sang and they sweated and some fell out of line, and they all suffered for it.

Poujet's ten men kept together. The other men in the section were from serving units. They had already formed their own survival groups. Poujet's ten had to stick together or go it alone, and they soon felt the need for support in case trouble flared up. The Legion was a jungle, and Poujet's ten had been thrown into the lion's den.

In the mess hall, they ate together.

'That Sergeant-Chief is a *cochon*,' Verdi growled. He had felt the lash of Schiller's wrath that particular day. 'One of these days, somebody will fix him.'

'He's been in the Legion a long time,' Klaus said with a patronising smile.

'There's always a first,' Verdi retorted.

'But it won't be you, Verdi,' Klaus said, 'or any of us.'

'And why not?' Fingers chipped in.

'Why not?' Klaus asked. 'Because from this Godforsaken camp there is no means of escape. If anybody does any fixing, it has to be from where there is means of escape.'

Calowski looked at him from across the table and dropped his eyes.

'It could be an accident,' Verdi growled.

Klaus shrugged. 'It's not only the Sergeant-Chief. It's the others as well. They watch all the time. What do you say, Luker?'

Luker continued to eat his meal.

'We are here for nine weeks. After that, life will be easier. Why make trouble?'

'Sure,' Thompson added. 'I go along with that, but why the hell were we sent here in the first place?'

'Yeah, why were we sent?' Tojak grunted in his stilted French accent.

'You hadn't sweated enough, Tojak,' Malik said. 'You needed more discipline.'

Tojak glowered at him.

'What do you mean, Austrian?'

'Nothing personal, Tojak,' Malik said. 'We all suffered at Corte, one way and another. Perhaps they thought we needed more discipline.'

Tojak gave a grunt and looked away. He was suspicious of Malik, but it didn't seem to bother Malik.

'We are only here for nine weeks,' Svenson said. 'That's not long.'

'Eight more weeks of bloody hell,' Thompson grunted.

'It's better than the pen,' Baron said. He didn't speak very often, but when he did, his remarks always had a lot of feeling about them.

'You been inside?' Thompson asked.

'Schiller is like a Fairy Godmother compared to some pigs you come across.'

'I spent a spell inside in Naples,' Fingers said. 'They were bastards as well.'

'The world's made up of bastards,' Thompson said.

'So we just take it and don't look for trouble,' Klaus said.

Verdi looked at him.

'Just why did you join the Legion, Klaus? You seem to know all the answers.'

'I got fed up of working as a clerk. It wasn't doing my health any good,' Klaus said, his face beaming. 'I needed a change and a rest, but I don't intend to stay five years. Perhaps a few more months and then I will be off.' He gave a long sigh. 'It is the thought of what I'll do then that makes me prepared to put up with the Sergeant-Chief.'

'What about you Verdi?' Fingers asked.

'Some whore in Marseilles fixed me,' Verdi snarled. 'We had a difference of opinion. She went to the pigs and told them my papers were out of date. I joined the Legion before the pigs could pick me up.'

'They would have sent me back to Italy,' Fingers grumbled.

'What was wrong with that?' Klaus asked. There was a touch of sarcasm in his voice. 'Wouldn't you be welcome there?'

Fingers scowled and looked away. 'That's my bloody business.'

The others at the table didn't volunteer to confess to their pasts, or their reasons for joining the Legion, but Klaus had drunk a lot of wine. He was in a talkative mood.

'What about the rest of you guys?' he said. 'We eat, drink, sleep and sweat together. I like to know my company.'

'Don't push it,' Baron snarled.

Tojak added his weight. 'If you don't like what you see, Klaus,' he said, 'go and find some other company. Nobody asks a legionnaire about his past.'

He stood up to reinforce his point. There was suddenly tension at the table.

'Sit down!' Malik called out.

Tojak turned on him. 'What's it to you?' he snarled.

Malik didn't stand up.

'We stick together,' Malik snapped. 'Don't be a bloody fool.'

'You don't tell me what to do, Austrian,' Tojak retorted.

'Sit down!' a voice called out.

It was from an adjoining table.

'Sit down you mug,' the voice said again. 'If they find you fighting, they'll think they aren't working us hard enough.'

The man who had spoken stood up. He was as big as Tojak and looked as if he had seen a lot of service.

'Use your brains, not your arse,' he said, and walked away.

'He's right,' Thompson said. 'They'll make us suffer, and *Mon Dieu*, we are suffering enough.'

Tojak sat down. The atmosphere relaxed again.

'I worked in a steel factory,' Svenson said abruptly. 'In Gothenburg. I wanted a change of scenery.'

'I worked in a hospital,' Luker said. 'As a porter. There was some trouble — I decided to get away.'

'Sure,' Malik added. 'Me too. It was time for a change of scenery. I got fed up with being a bloody truck driver.'

Nobody believed any of their stories, but they were satisfying Klaus and not offending Tojak.

'It was a woman,' Thompson said in his bright, chirpy manner. 'She claimed I was the father of her twins.'

'And were you?' Verdi asked.

'How the hell should I know? I only poofed her one night.'

Tojak, Baron and Calowski didn't volunteer anything. Tojak still looked sullen and glum. Baron also had a dark look on his face. Calowski just stared at his food.

'Tojak,' Klaus called out.

Tojak looked up. He eyed Klaus suspiciously.

'You were right, Tojak,' Klaus said. 'I ask too many questions. Your past is your own affair.'

Tojak dropped his eyes.

'Where I come from — and where Calowski comes from — it is better that way.'

'Sure,' Thompson said. 'That's right. What the hell?'

But it was impossible not to learn more about each other. During the day, they sweated and suffered. It was like being driven by a pneumatic drill. Their only breath of freedom was in their sleep or at the mess hall where the wine made them talk. They learned that Tojak was on the run from the police. He claimed he had run a black market operation across the

Yugoslav border into Trieste. One of his operations had gone sour. The police began investigations. Tojak didn't wait for the outcome.

Calowski and Baron said very little other than that they had met in a bar in Marseilles and had teamed up together. Like Klaus, they didn't intend to see their term out. The others also talked about deserting, but with Calowski and Baron there was a feeling that they had it already planned.

Chapter Eleven

Ducan had no wish to openly clash with the Sergeant-Chief. He had formed a deep dislike of Schiller's methods of discipline, but he was also resentful of a system that demanded such methods and denied the men initiative and imagination. He suffered Schiller as he suffered the system, with an attitude of cynical amusement. The system didn't react, but Schiller did. He showed his reaction by the look on his face. The glint of amusement in Ducan's eyes and his casual remarks only kept the flame burning. Schiller resented Ducan's invasion of his territory and his invasion of the Legion. Ducan was using the Legion. He was critical of it, and he was inexperienced. That was what Schiller felt, and Ducan was intelligent enough to realise it, but Ducan was not concerned enough to do anything about it.

Twice he came into open conflict with the Sergeant-Chief, and twice he added to the Sergeant-Chiefs resentment by overruling him.

The first incident occurred on a battle course. It was a steep, rocky incline. Schiller and his men were making the course realistic, and they were driving the men hard. Ducan was following in the rear. One of the men of the section missed his foothold and fell badly, crashing down a slope onto some rocks. Ducan saw the fall. He also saw Luker immediately go to the aid of the man and bend over him. Luker had acted instinctively, without thought of the Sergeant-Chief and his battle training.

'Luker!' Schiller yelled. 'Move it!'

Ducan was following behind. He saw Luker examining the fallen legionnaire's leg. He seemed to know what he was doing. Ducan was curious.

'Sergeant-Chief!' he shouted.

Schiller turned.

'Let Luker examine the man,' Ducan ordered.

Schiller's lips curled and the veins of his forehead became more prominent.

'We have medical orderlies, *mon Lieutenant*, with the vehicles.'

'Let Luker examine him,' Ducan said again.

He left the Sergeant-Chief and went to where Luker was bending over the groaning legionnaire. Schiller fumed his way up the mountain, yelling and shouting at the men.

'Is it broken?' Ducan asked.

Luker looked up. 'I don't think so, *mon Lieutenant*,' he said. 'It will be badly bruised. An x-ray will tell.'

'Help him down the mountain.'

'Yes, *mon Lieutenant*.'

The rest of the men fought their way up the mountain. Luker helped the man to his feet and struggled with him down the incline. Ducan watched him thoughtfully. He was curious about the men and their backgrounds. He wondered if Luker had had medical training.

The second incident was with the self-defence training. The Legion called it *savant*. It was their form of karate. It was a regular part of their training, but Schiller decided to make it more realistic. The instructors were to use open knives. The men were going to have to be extra careful. An open cut or scratch would be troublesome in the heat and sweat of their daily routine. There was an air of uneasiness. They were split into three groups with the instructors. The first group was paired off. Verdi, who was with the group, stood alone.

'No partner, Verdi?' Schiller snarled. 'Nobody you would like to use the knife on?'

'Yes, Chief,' Verdi retorted. He didn't say who, but the men knew that Verdi's resentment of Ducan was as great as his resentment of Schiller. Either man would have pleased Verdi.

Ducan heard all that had been said. He called the Sergeant-Chief to him.

'I will take on Verdi,' he said.

Schiller's face immediately showed his contempt for the suggestion.

'*Mon Lieutenant,*' he hissed. 'This is for real. This is not pretend. You are an officer.'

'And I am not a fool, Sergeant-Chief.'

There was a glint of amusement in Ducan's eye, and a smile on his lips. They only added to Schiller's irritation.

Schiller clenched his fist in annoyance.

'I also believe,' Ducan added, 'that an officer should be as good as the men he commands. Would you not agree?'

Schiller was not in the mood for an academic discussion. He snarled his disgust and turned away and called Verdi. A smile appeared on Verdi's face when he was given his order. The other legionnaires watched with interest. Verdi had the knife.

Verdi faced Ducan. There was a look of glee in his eyes. They sparred with each other. Verdi made his lunge, Ducan side-stepped and threw him expertly. Verdi got to his feet and came for Ducan again. The Lieutenant moved swiftly and the two men became locked in a grip. Verdi was broader and heavier than Ducan, but Ducan had strength that neither the Sergeant-Chief or Verdi realised. He suddenly gave a grunt and jerked himself free of Verdi. At the same instant, he sank his knee into Verdi's crotch. Verdi grunted.

Ducan threw him again. Verdi went sprawling. For a moment there was silence. Ducan had shown an expertise that had even surprised Schiller, but the Sergeant-Chief quickly recovered. He ordered Verdi back to the section and turned on the men. He gave them a verbal dressing down as if Verdi's failure had been their failure. Ducan turned away and adjusted his uniform.

'I don't know who I hate most,' Verdi growled, in the mess hall that evening. 'The Lieutenant or the Sergeant-Chief. Why doesn't he keep his nose out of it?'

'He's a watcher,' Malik said.

'A watcher?' Verdi asked sharply. He looked at Calowski, who was sitting opposite him. 'What about it, Calowski?'

Calowski was also a watcher, but he had been accepted, he was one of them. Nobody ever asked what he was looking for, or what he was afraid of.

'He's a watcher,' Calowski agreed.

'Well let him watch,' Thompson added. 'He might recommend me for promotion. He even talked to me in English when I was on *sentinelle*.'

'You have to be a bastard to get promotion in the Legion,' Malik said.

'Make me a corporal and I'll be a proper bastard,' Thompson retorted.

'*Merde* to the Lieutenant,' Verdi snarled. 'He's a *cochon* like the rest of them, and he's making us suffer.'

'But why is he watching?' Klaus pondered.

'Yeah,' Tojak added. 'Why does he watch? What do you think Malik?'

Malik looked up to see Tojak's dark eyes watching him closely, as if challenging him to speak out.

Malik returned the look and shook his head.

'Your guess is as good as mine,' he said.

'Perhaps he's a reformer,' Luker suggested.

They looked at him. Luker expanded on his remark.

'I think he's watching and waiting. He is a thinker. He is also different from the other officers. I think he would like to change the system.'

'Change the system!' the Swede scoffed.

'He is young and newly commissioned,' Luker said. 'He has new ideas. Why else would he be so interested in what goes on?'

'Will he succeed?' Klaus asked seriously. 'In making changes?'

'No,' Luker said equally seriously. 'He will not succeed.'

'Then he's wasting his time,' Klaus sighed.

'If nobody ever tries,' Luker said. 'Then there is no hope.'

Verdi looked up at Luker, but said nothing. Malik momentarily hesitated in eating his meal. Calowski watched. Thompson looked thoughtful. Tojak scowled.

Klaus said, 'Forget the Lieutenant. Let Schiller worry about him. If anybody hates the Lieutenant more than you, Verdi, it is Schiller. He also thinks the Lieutenant is a reformer.'

There was a grunt of agreement. They knew how Schiller felt about the Lieutenant. That was why they were all suffering. But Luker's suggestion about the Lieutenant had put a different thought about him in their minds. Some of them felt easier.

Ducan was not the reformer that Luker had suggested, but he did want to make changes. He had accepted his posting with an open mind. He had followed Poujet's instructions and got to know the men and the system, but it was not in his nature to accept the established ways of any institution without questioning them, and he certainly questioned the ways of the Legion, which brainwashed its men into blind obedience. He wanted to make changes in the men's training schedule. He wanted to give them the opportunity to use their initiative and their intelligence. He had already made his ideas known to the Captain, and he was waiting for the opportunity to put forward his proposals.

Chapter Twelve

Pascal allowed himself one reminder of times gone by and that was the night the girls came into the camp. There were three of them — all experienced prostitutes. Paula was small, dumpy, insensitive, satisfying, but quick. Claudette was big, with a well-shaped body and an attractive face. She could have worked in a high-class brothel, but she had been born and bred locally, and she was content with the steady income from the Legion. Suzette was the youngest of the trio, and had a shapely, youthful figure with firm breasts. She also had plenty of vigour and fire about her. She was not so attractive to look at as Claudette, but she had a quick smile and a quick wit. She could hold her own with the men and the other girls.

Pascal always hoped that he was detailed to Suzette. Her shape and size reminded him of his Catherine, and the last time he had slept with her. He was not always fortunate in getting Suzette, but on this particular night, he got his wish.

He joined Suzette in the small bedroom. It was supposed to be a quick drill, but as he lay on the mattress alongside her, he again thought of Catherine in Paris. His hand gently caressed the girl's firm breasts. He moved closer to her and had a strong desire to make love to her. He kissed her gently on the cheek. She turned her face and he kissed her long and passionately on the mouth. She gently eased herself away from him.

'No, *mon chéri*,' she said. '*Non.*'

Pascal withdrew his hand from her breasts. He looked at her. There was regret in her dark eyes. She gave a faint smile.

'*Non,*' she said again. 'There isn't time.'

Pascal gripped the iron rail of the bed with his hand. The girl was not going to let him make love to her. She did not have time. There were others waiting. It was another Legion drill.

'Sorry,' she said. 'Come.'

He relaxed his body and smiled at her. She smiled back.

'There is something else you can do for me,' he whispered.

'What, *mon chéri*?'

'It is my ageing Mother. I have to get a letter to her.'

'Certainly, *mon chéri*.'

Pascal performed his drill, but his thoughts were elsewhere.

Chapter Thirteen

Poujet sat in his office deep in thought. He had just returned from a talk with the Director. The Diplomatic Corps had got wind of veiled references to matters of internal security. They were asking questions about Bichante and the President's forthcoming visit to Moscow. The Director could not hold them off much longer.

Poujet glanced at the files on his desk that contained all the information and reports of the Fox. He knew a great deal about his suspects, but he was making little progress. Only one of Pascal's cryptic messages had given him any vital information. Pascal had not been the last of the group to join the Legion — Svenson had. That was the only step forward that Poujet had made, and he knew that it was not enough to act on. Nevertheless, he had to make a move.

He called his assistant, Raphael, into his room.

'The Russians are still watching our contacts?' he asked.

'Yes, Monsieur.'

Poujet frowned. The Russians were playing a very patient waiting game. They were making no noises and there was no action. They were waiting and watching. To Poujet, that meant only one thing. They had their hound close to the Fox, ready to pounce, and they were starting to consolidate their position with a web of diplomatic intrigue.

'The Russians are being very clever,' he sighed. 'They are waiting at the front door and knocking on the back door.'

'*Le Corps Diplomatique*, Monsieur!'

'Yes, *le Corps Diplomatique*. If they learn of our agreement with the Russians, our hands will be tied, very tightly.' Poujet spread his bulky frame over his desk to get closer to his assistant.

'We make some discreet moves,' he said, barely above a whisper, as if the walls of his own room had ears. 'Tell Russo to lose the Russians and go to Geneva. We have been patient with him long enough. I want you to stand by to fly to Geneva and talk to Monsieur Russo. Also contact the Marseilles Police. There was an unidentified body fished out of the harbour at the time the Fox joined the Legion. I want to know if it has been identified yet.'

'Yes, Monsieur,' Raphael said. He waited for further orders.

'Get onto Stockholm. I want a check put on Svenson. He was the last to join the little party. It is most unlikely that he will be the Fox.'

Poujet looked thoughtful.

'There was that Italian Inspector making enquiries in Marseilles,' he said. 'Get onto Interpol, see what they know about his enquiries. We might be able to cooperate.'

'Yes, Monsieur. Anything else?'

'Yes. Make absolutely sure that Russo arrives in Geneva alone. We cannot afford to make a false move.'

'Yes, Monsieur. I understand.'

Poujet waved his arm, dismissing his assistant. When he was alone, he remained sitting at his desk pondering over the situation. His ten suspects would soon be posted to a unit in Africa. Several ideas had taken root in his fertile brain on how to deal with the situation, but he was beginning to suspect that time would run out on him before he could put them into operation. If something didn't break for him very soon, they were going to be trapped in the Russian web, and he wouldn't be able to help the Fox.

Chapter Fourteen

Something did break for Poujet, but not in the manner that he had expected. It broke soon after his discussion with the Director. Poujet was in his bed, but he was not asleep. He often lay awake during the night thinking of Pascal, the Fox, and the Legion. His thoughts of Pascal were always tinged with a certain feeling of sympathy, especially when he was in his comfortable bed, enjoying the scented atmosphere and warmth of his wife's body. He had no illusions about the Legion. He knew what Pascal was suffering, and he knew that Pascal would get no medals for it. He would just get another assignment. Poujet didn't have the same feeling for Ducan. Ducan needed the Legion. It would do him good, he thought.

Poujet was thinking of Pascal when his bedside telephone rang. He picked up the receiver before the ringing noise could disturb his wife.

'Monsieur Poujet?' a voice asked.

Poujet affirmed his identity.

'This is Carson — Frank Carson.'

Poujet simply said, 'Hello Frank,' as if such a call at such a time was an everyday occurrence, but Poujet had never received a telephone call from Carson before at his home number. Carson was the head of the C.I.A. in France. The two men knew each other. They occasionally did deals. Sometimes they opposed each other. They rarely contacted each other personally — unless it was very urgent.

'Can I see you immediately?' Carson asked.

Poujet saw the dial on his illuminated bedside lamp. It was two a.m.

'Have the Russians dropped an atom bomb?' he asked.

'It's important,' Carson replied. His voice was stern and concerned.

Carson always took life too seriously, Poujet thought, but so did all the American C.I.A. agents.

'Where are you?' he asked.

'Five minutes away from your apartment. I could come around. It is safe.'

'Do so, but you won't mind if I don't dress?'

The telephone went dead. Poujet got out of bed. His wife stirred, but did not wake up.

Carson arrived on the fifth minute. Poujet expected no other; Carson was always prompt and exact. He stood at Poujet's entrance door, hatless, bespectacled, grim faced and smartly dressed. He was older than Poujet, and always looked to Poujet as if he had the cares of the U.S. Government firmly planted on his shoulders. In turn, Poujet always looked to Carson like a character from his old French textbook. On this occasion, Carson was not thinking about Poujet's image. If he had, he might have thought that Poujet's long, thick, floral dressing gown only needed a night cap to put him in an even older French textbook.

Poujet beckoned Carson into his home. He did not glance along the boulevard at Carson's aides in the shadows. He knew that they would be there, all grim faced and trigger happy, and all wearing dark suits like Carson. Poujet took him into his study. It was thickly carpeted and it was comfortable. The walls were lined with books, and there was a drinks cabinet and two comfortable leather chairs. There was a feeling of security in the room.

Poujet poured Carson a whisky on the rocks. He knew his habits and his likes, just as Carson knew that Poujet preferred a Benedictine at that hour of the morning.

They took their drinks and settled into the chairs facing each other.

'Here's to you Marcel,' Carson said.

They were on first name terms, but that meant little. They would both stab each other in the back if it was for the good of their respective countries.

'We have one helluva problem,' Carson sighed.

Poujet wondered if Carson's collective 'we' was meant to be particular to the Americans, or if he intended it to include Poujet. He decided to find out.

'We?' he asked.

Carson did not take the point.

'We have a kidnapping on our hands,' Carson growled.

Poujet pushed his point further.

'A French national?'

'Yes,' Carson said, 'a French girl, but she's not the real problem. There is also an American girl.'

'So it is we after all,' Poujet remarked.

'The American girl is the daughter of Jackson-Lang, the President of American Electrics. He is big and influential in the States. He is also very close to the President. In fact, he's one of the President's biggest supporters.'

'And he is also big on the Continent,' Poujet added. He was beginning to get the gist of Carson's concern.

'He has a lot of interests over here, that is true. He is also looking for expansion.'

The bait was not lost on Poujet.

'Suppose you tell me about this kidnapping. The French girl interests me. Where is this kidnapping?'

'Ethiopia,' Carson grunted.

Poujet raised his bushy eyebrows.

'A long way from home,' he said.

'The American girl was Governess to the two children of Princess Towaja, a distant relative of the former Emperor. The French girl was a nurse in the same household. When the military took over, the family fled from Addis Ababa to their estate in the mountains near a town called Jimna. The Prince was later arrested and has not been heard of since. The Princess and her relatives were allowed to remain at their estate under house arrest. A friend of the American girl secretly arranged to fly the Princess and her family, and also the American and French girls, to Eritrea in the North. That was where the Princess came from before she married the Prince. She still has family friends in that area who could protect her. As you know, there is trouble in Ethiopia with the Eritreans.'

Poujet knew. Carson did not wait for a comment.

'Very briefly, this friend got the party aboard a light aircraft, and set off for the Northern territory. On the way, they were forced to land. Probably shot at by the group of bandits who now hold the party hostage.'

'And the pilot?'

'They disposed of him in their usual barbaric way. The rest of the party are still alive. They are being held at a camp on the fringe of a small range of mountains that borders your territory in East Africa, towards the North of the territory. The group of bandits are led by a Mohammed Azir. They claim to be a group seeking independence for Eritrea. That is a cover. We know that Azir is in fact a Somali from the south. He is an educated Somali who has a group of Somalis with him. He is stirring up trouble and trying to make the local Danakil tribes unite against the Ethiopian Government and against your

Government. The Eritreans and Danakils in Azir's group are being paid, and I don't have to tell you who by.'

'The Somali republic has a lot of Russian advisers,' Poujet said. 'It is well known.'

'It is also well known that they want a united Somali Republic, which would include the Somalis in the French territory as well as in Ethiopia.'

Carson was telling Poujet nothing that he didn't already know.

'Has this Azir a large force?'

Carson shrugged. 'A hundred or so.'

'And how have you been informed about his hostages?'

'Through the Sultan of Aussa. He is the traditional head of the Danakil tribespeople. He is acting as intermediary along with a Catholic missionary. They live in Tandaho. The Catholic missionary is Father Emmanuel Gargone, a Belgian who is now more native than Belgian. He is the link between the Sultan and Mohammed Azir.'

'I see, and what are their terms for handing over the hostages?'

'We either pay one million dollars in ransom money and give formal recognition to the cause for an independent Eritrea, or the girls will be shot.'

'And the Ethiopian Government — the Dirg?'

'They are sympathetic to the American girl, and of course the French girl, but they have no concern for the Princess. They are sitting on the fence.'

'But they would be very concerned if the U.S. Government gave any sign of recognition to an independent Eritrea.'

Carson looked glum.

'They know we damned well would never do that.'

'So why don't they act?'

'They claim that if they make one move to attack Mohammed Azir's base, the girls would be immediately shot.'

'You accept their case?'

'Partly,' Carson growled, 'but there are ways and means which they haven't explored. They are playing cat and mouse with us. They are putting us to the test. They want to see how clever we are — or how stupid. The Russians are also courting them. So we are in one helluva spot.'

'And how can I help?'

'The President is onto this one, Marcel. It is in his court. Two of his big fish are on their way to Paris. McNew and Senator Fielding.'

Poujet knew the two names. McNew was the U.S. President's adviser on French affairs and Senator Fielding was Chairman of the U.S. Foreign Aid Committee. They were two powerful men in the U.S. Senator Fielding was also influential in Europe. There was a hint of pressure being brought to bear.

'They will be arriving in about six hours' time. I would like you to arrange a secret meeting with whoever you think could help us. We would like somebody close to the President.'

'There is your Ambassador,' Poujet suggested. 'There is the protocol.'

'Let's forget them, Marcel. We don't want the diplomatic boys involved. They can play the game according to their rules and negotiate with Azir. This has to be behind the scenes.'

'How do you think my Government can help yours?' Poujet asked.

'The camp where Mohammed Azir is holding the captives is only thirty kilometres from your border, Marcel. Azir is with his main force about a hundred kilometres away, directing the negotiations.'

'What you have in mind is, perhaps, a small commando raid of French troops?' Poujet made a sweeping gesture with his hand. 'In and out and everybody back safely.'

'Something like that.'

Poujet gave a non-committal shrug. It was a gamble that could go wrong, and France's relations with Ethiopia were delicate to begin with. He couldn't see his Government agreeing to such a proposal, even though they might be sympathetic.

He didn't tell Carson his thoughts. Instead he said, 'Thirty kilometres of rocky canyons, dust and tremendous heat can be an awful long way.'

'I'm sure your men could do it,' Carson said.

They had it already worked out, Poujet thought. The whole of their intelligence and military chiefs would have been pumping advice and proposals into their computer in the Pentagon. He had a mental picture of their top brass all studying the maps and reports. They were taking it very seriously. There had to be a good reason.

'In the words of your own people, Frank,' he said, 'lay it on the line for me. No diplomatic jargon. That can be played at the meeting. But you and I are going to be the ones to spell it out.'

'OK, Marcel, here goes. The President is having a rough time and a bad press. He needs all he can get going for him. If we have to eat humble pie over this affair, his critics will jump on him. If the girl gets shot, he's a bad guy. He can't win either way. Number two. The girl's Father was the President's biggest financial backer at the last election. It will soon be election time again. Without Jackson-Lang's support, the President is going to need a charity box. Do you get the gist?'

Poujet did. 'So, a bomb has been dropped in your President's lap,' he sighed, and calmly asked, 'but what about my Government? Lay that on the line.'

'American Electrics are looking for European expansion. It has been half promised to the British, but they are having certain labour troubles. A major part of their expansion could be channelled into France.'

Carson handed Poujet his empty glass and shook his head in refusal of a re-charge.

'That's the official line,' he said quietly, as if the room was bugged. 'Off the record, Marcel, let me just say that my President would be very grateful and so would I. We would owe you a favour. I would owe you one, Marcel.'

Carson really had the bit, Poujet thought. The U.S. President must have been onto him personally. He had never seen Carson so keyed up and tense. It was an opportunity not to be missed. He decided to exploit the situation.

'The Americans are well known for their generosity,' he said. 'I will help you as much as I can. There is no question of favours. Besides!' He gave a shrug that was intended to emphasize his following remarks. 'There have been no defections for how long? Six months? The market is very quiet. There is nothing new.'

'There is always something happening, Marcel. You know that.'

Poujet shrugged. 'Not for France, Frank. Not at the moment.'

'You French certainly play it close,' Carson said, taking the bait. 'You've been sitting with your aces, waiting for the right moment to take the pot.'

So the C.I.A. did know about the Fox, Poujet thought. The Director was right. The C.I.A. had got hold of something.

'There is always a joker in every pack,' Poujet said, and watched Carson carefully.

Carson gave a knowing smile.

'There are undercurrents,' he said. 'They say that a joker is lost in a pack, and there are three sharks after him.'

Poujet smiled. It was a genuine smile of pleasure. Carson had just given him some very valuable information. He had shown his hand and made a grave mistake. There were only two sources from which Carson could have got his information, and Poujet knew both. He had Carson on the hook now, and he was going to make him wriggle before he let him go. He stood up. Carson did likewise.

'I will arrange the meeting, Frank,' Poujet said. He gave Carson an encouraging pat on the shoulder. 'Don't worry, Frank. We will see what can be done.'

Carson looked fractionally relieved. At least he was getting to first base.

'There is a small cafe called *Le Cardinal*,' Poujet explained. 'It is close to the Boulevard Saint Germaine. Upstairs is a room. It is ideal for such a meeting. Say twelve noon, sharp?'

'Noon it is.'

'And Frank, please leave your boys behind. I will make sure that we are not interrupted. OK?'

'OK, Marcel.'

Carson left the room, still with the cares of the U.S. President on his shoulders. Poujet watched him safely escorted to his car by his assistants and then returned to his study. For a moment he stood in thought. Then he poured himself another drink in celebration. He could see his way into the future more clearly. He finished his drink and returned the bottles to the

117

drinks cabinet. He opened a drawer in the cocktail cabinet and lifted out a telephone. There were three buttons on the telephone. Each one was a direct line. One was to his Director, another to his office, and the third to Raphael, his assistant. He pressed the Director's button first and gave him all the facts. The negotiations with the American delegation were then the Director's concern. Poujet put them to one side. He pressed his assistant's button. Raphael had probably been asleep, but it was not unusual for Poujet to use the line. Raphael was wide awake when he answered the call.

'Have you made arrangements with Russo?' Poujet asked.

'Yes, Monsieur. He arranged a business trip to Geneva. He arrived there last night.'

'Good. I want you to go there immediately. Take all necessary precautions, but I want action and answers quickly. Get him out of Geneva into France. Take him into the mountains. Take him to Flaine. That is innocent enough. He will enjoy the scenery and Marcel Breuer's architecture. On the way, make sure that he talks, and make sure he leaves nothing out.'

'Any special line?'

'Yes. Try the Judas angle, but instead of silver, find out how many dollars he was paid. And Raphael…'

'Yes, Monsieur?'

'I want the answer before midday tomorrow.'

'You will have it, Monsieur, and after he talks?'

'He is no use to France anymore,' Poujet said thoughtfully. 'It will depend on what our American friends feel about him. I will let you know.'

'I understand.'

Poujet rang off and pressed the button that connected him with his office. The duty assistant answered anxiously.

'Get onto Special Branch in Marseilles,' Poujet ordered. 'The Marseilles Police had an unidentified body in their morgue last March to April period. Get Special Branch to check it with their list of American shipping agents. I want an answer as soon as possible.'

'Yes, Monsieur.'

Poujet replaced the receiver on its stand, and the telephone in its secret drawer. He returned to his bed well pleased with the turn of events.

Chapter Fifteen

Le Cardinal was a small, intimate, and expensive restaurant that attracted the discerning gourmet. It was situated close to the offices of State in the area of the Boulevard Saint Germaine and was often used as a meeting place by members of the various departments. Their meetings were held in a private room on the first floor which was reached by a staircase, hidden from the main part of the restaurant. It was a room where matters of State could be discussed openly and without fear of publicity. The room was long and narrow, and panelled in dark mahogany. It was simply furnished with a long, mahogany table and matching chairs. There was also a smaller table on which refreshments were usually placed.

It was to this room that Poujet had invited Carson and his delegation. The French party arrived first. It consisted of three members and Poujet. It was led by Monsieur Hugan, a close adviser to the President and a man to match Senator Fielding as a prominent political figure. Hugan was small, slim and astute. With him was Colonel Gourbet of the Intelligence Section of the French Military Command, and Monsieur Marchand, Poujet's superior. Gourbet was grey haired and sharp featured, with a military bearing and an expert knowledge of *le Territoire des Afars et des Issas*.

Poujet was not expected to participate in any of the discussions, unless asked to do so by his Director. Poujet was in charge of the security arrangements, and he had made sure that there were no foreign, or French observers.

The three French delegates had met earlier in the President's chambers. They had also cross-examined Poujet. They were aware of what was going to be put to them.

The American party arrived at the appointed time. They were also four in number. Three delegates and Carson.

McNew was the leader of their delegation. He was a man in his mid-forties, who had the reputation of being a shrewd negotiator. Senator Fielding was a big, bluff looking man, with thick, grey hair and an acute business brain. Both men were known to the French party. The third member of the American party was from the U.S. State Department. His name was Ellis. He was from the Yale School of U.S. diplomats. He was tall, slim, bespectacled, with short hair and a high intelligence rating. He carried a thick briefcase.

Carson made the introductions. There was no language difficulty. All the French party spoke English and all the Americans spoke French. Only Senator Fielding was not a fluent speaker of French, but Ellis was there to help with translations. As a matter of courtesy, and diplomacy, the Americans spoke in French. The U.S. Government was playing its hand tactfully.

The exchange of Presidential greetings and pleasantries that protocol demanded were kept as short as possible, and it was to be a working lunch.

Monsieur Hugan soon started the meeting by a casual, 'Gentlemen, shall we sit at the table?' remark.

The two parties took their seats and sat facing each other. Carson was still nervous. The President was putting pressure on him, Poujet thought. He gave him an encouraging smile, but he intended to make him sweat even more. He had heard from Raphael. Russo had been very cooperative. Poujet had his hooks well and truly into Carson.

Ellis unzipped his briefcase in readiness to produce whatever documents were required.

Hugan started the proceedings officially.

'I suggest, Monsieur McNew, that you begin,' he said in his grave but quiet voice. 'We have, of course, been briefed on the problem.'

'We know where the rebel bandits have the hostages,' McNew said crisply. 'We have a very good pictorial picture of the region from our satellite.'

Ellis quickly produced a number of aerial photographs and a map of the area. The map was spread out on the table facing the French party. It was an enlarged map of the area and showed the French territory of Afars and Issas and Ethiopia. A cross had been placed on the map at a location in Ethiopian territory, a short distance from the border with the French territory.

Colonel Gourbet examined the aerial photographs. They had been enlarged to show a native encampment around a group of buildings, close to the rocky hills that formed the barrier between the French territory and Ethiopia. There were several photographs of the area.

McNew briefly recapped the situation.

'You appreciate that it is not a question of the money,' he said finally. 'A million is neither here nor there. Azir is being prompted by the Russians. To recognise his cause would be really playing into their hands.'

'We understand the position fully,' Hugan replied.

Senator Fielding decided to get to the meat of the problem.

'We have a large force in the Mediterranean,' he said. He kept his words to the French that he knew. 'We have planes, ships, marines. We have men who would give their right arm to go in and take Azir apart. But we have not got the expertise of the area, and politically it would be dynamite. It would open the door for the Russians to make a countermove.'

There was a delicate pause. The Senator had put the ball in the French court. The French leader gave it back to the Americans.

'Monsieur McNew,' Hugan said. 'Do not think that we do not appreciate all that has been said, but I must point out that we are also in a very delicate position. The British and the Italians gave the Somalis their independence. Very soon, the territory of Afars and Issas is also to be granted its independence. The date has been agreed. The territory is small, but it is strategically important to France and the Free World. When the territory becomes independent, it is essential that we maintain peace in that part of Africa. Both Somalia and Ethiopia have designs on the territory. Along our borders are many tribes whose allegiance is divided between Somalia and Ethiopia. At the moment they are at peace with us, but they watch us very closely. They watch our every move. If we were to commit our troops — even a very small force — to an act of aggression across our borders, it would not only be an invasion of Ethiopian territory, but also of the territory of these border tribes. It could be the spark to unite them together in rebellion. We could find ourselves in open conflict with both Ethiopia and the border tribes. I regret, Monsieur, it is not possible.'

McNew's face was hard set and grim. He looked at his watch, and played his final trump card.

'We are flying to London in four hours,' he said. 'If the French Government will not help us, I am sure we can rely on the British.'

'The British are experts in the Middle East,' Hugan said, 'I agree. They have had their Lawrences and their Gordons, but could the British Government honestly commit itself to such an act?'

'Perhaps not,' McNew agreed, 'but the British are a strange people. They like these sorts of problems. They have a great imagination. They will have somebody who will make such an attempt, I am sure.'

Ellis quickly retrieved his map and photographs, and replaced them in his briefcase.

'We leave the Embassy at three thirty,' McNew said. 'If we do not hear from you before then, we will assume that, regrettably, you are not in a position to help us.'

The French leader looked genuinely concerned at his inability to offer help.

The two delegations formally shook hands. Poujet stood by the door.

The American delegation left the room. Carson looked at Poujet.

'The John is over there,' Poujet said, indicating a door.

Carson got the message. He excused himself from his party and went to the toilet. Poujet joined him. The two men stood in the washroom and set about washing their hands as if they had dirt all over them.

'How is it going?' Carson asked.

'Slowly,' Poujet replied, 'and cautiously. These negotiations always remind me of the mating habits of the animal species. There is the courtship, the rejection, then re-consideration, and sometimes the mating.'

'Will they mate this time?'

'That depends on many things.'

'Such as?'

Poujet shrugged.

'Such as *Monsieur le Président*,' he said. 'Monsieur Hugan, the state of the border tribes.' He looked at Carson. 'On many things,' he said. 'Including Russo.'

Carson turned sharply.

'Russo?' he asked. 'Who is he?'

'Nobody you know, Frank,' Poujet said diplomatically, 'but let me tell you about him.'

'Go on,' Carson said, tight-lipped. He started to wash his hands again.

'Karl Russo is a Doctor in Zurich,' Poujet said. 'Not a particularly good one, but he has other uses. Russo is now taking a vacation. Like your American girl, Mademoiselle Jackson-Lang, he is being looked after. Whether Russo returns to his medical practice, or remains in the mountains, can have a bearing on whether Mademoiselle Jackson-Lang also returns to her home.'

'Go on. What's the pitch?'

Poujet soaped his hands.

'There are three sharks in the pool,' he said. 'I want to know their identity. It is as simple as that.'

'That was only hearsay,' Carson said. 'The waters are calm. There has been no activity.'

'That was not hearsay, Frank. That was an undercurrent.'

'But how can we get hold of such information?'

'By four-thirty,' Poujet added.

'My God, Marcel, I've told you the market is dead. Where are we supposed to get the information?'

Poujet lifted his soapy hand. He drew a wet line on the tiled wall. He placed two soap marks on one side of the line to indicate himself and Garson. He looked at Carson and placed his finger on the other side of the line. He said no more. Carson got the message.

'It is still impossible,' Carson grumbled.

'You Americans are always running yourselves down, Frank. You get men to the moon. You have a computer library that can produce a picture of almost every individual in the world. You can get aerial photographs of Azir's camp.' He grabbed two towels and gave one to Carson. 'Come Frank,' he said, like a benevolent uncle encouraging a hesitant nephew. 'I know you can do it.'

He put his hand on the door handle.

'The American girl?' Carson asked.

'That is up to *Monsieur le President*,' Poujet said, and opened the door.

Carson joined his party. Poujet returned to the room where the French delegates were still seated at the table. As he entered the room, Marchand, the Director, caught his eye. A slight movement of his head by Poujet told the Director that he had come to an understanding with Carson.

'The British!' Hugan exclaimed, and made a gesture with his hands. 'Why do the Americans always think that if they mention the British to us, we will rush to outsmart them? On one hand, they say that they want us all to be friendly and united, and on the other they try to divide us. The British are no fools. They would not dare risk such an adventure.'

'No,' Marchand agreed. 'They would not, but they would make an attempt.'

Hugan looked at him. 'I don't believe you.'

'The British Government will make the gesture. They will make every possible move to help the Americans, and they will end up doing nothing.'

Hugan moved and sat at the table facing Marchand.

'How will they do that?' he asked.

'Like McNew said. They will get someone who is an expert in the territory of Eastern Ethiopia. They will probably get a group of mercenaries together. They might also make sure that their group of mercenaries never gets to its destination, but they will have made the gesture. They will not let the Americans go back empty-handed.'

'Their group of mercenaries might even pull it off,' Colonel Gourbet added. 'But even if they don't succeed, they will have got the prize.'

'Prize,' Hugan grunted. 'There is more at stake than American Electrics. We must safeguard our position in the Middle East.'

Hugan started to pace the floor. 'American Electrics, and what else we could squeeze out of them,' he muttered, 'against a possible weakening of our position, and a confrontation with the Ethiopian Government.' He shook his head sadly. 'No,' he muttered, and paced the distance of the room. He returned and stopped abruptly, in front of Marchand.

'I know what you are thinking,' he said. He turned to Colonel Gourbet. 'Tell him,' he said. 'Tell him that it is not possible.'

'We have the greatest army of adventurers in the world,' Colonel Gourbet said sadly. '*La Légion Étrangère.* The operation is tailor-made for them, but what Hugan says is true. If we make one move and send in any unit of the French Command, it could cause the border to erupt. The territory of Afars and Issas is containing its subversive elements, but such an operation could have very serious repercussions.' The Colonel looked glum. 'Besides,' he added, 'the natives either have a natural instinct for sensing such a move, or a very good intelligence service. They would be informed the moment we made any preparation to send out a patrol.'

'There,' Hugan said to Marchand. 'Now do you agree?'

Marchand slowly shook his head in disagreement.

'No, I do not,' he said. He slowly lit a cigarette and smoked it.

'Well?' Hugan demanded.

'We could produce a small army of mercenaries,' Marchand said, 'just like the British. We could give them to the Americans.'

Hugan and Colonel Gourbet digested the suggestion.

'And where would you get such a group?' Hugan asked. His tone had softened. He was interested.

Marchand turned to Poujet, who had been studying the various furnishings in the room during the discussions.

'Where would you get such a group?' the Director asked. The question gave the impression that it had been Poujet's suggestion in the first instance, but Marchand wanted support for his proposal.

'*La Légion Étrangère*,' Poujet said.

'The Legion?' Hugan said. 'But Colonel Gourbet has just told us…'

'Please, Monsieur,' Marchand hastily interrupted. 'Please hear me out. I agree with Poujet.'

Hugan remained silent.

'Such a unit would have to be disciplined and well trained to succeed,' Marchand explained. 'It would have to have a leader who knows the area. It would have to have a chance of success or it would be murder.'

'If one man left the Legion in the territory, it would be known,' Hugan persisted. 'It is not possible.'

Marchand insisted. 'It is, Monsieur. We take a group of men — legionnaires. Not from the territory of Afars and Issas. Not highly trained parachutists or specialists. That would be too suspicious. We take a group of ordinary trained infantry men and discharge them, temporarily, from the Legion. We offer them to the Americans for a sum of money. The money is paid to the French Government, but legally the men will have become paid mercenaries. We can destroy all records of their past service with the Legion. They will be international, and they will have become the Americans' responsibility.'

There was a pregnant silence as Hugan and Colonel Gourbet thought over Marchand's remarks. Colonel Gourbet looked enthusiastic, but diplomatically, he waited for Hugan to make his decision.

Finally, Hugan looked across the table at Marchand and said solemnly, 'I like it,' and said it again with more enthusiasm, 'I like it.'

There was a feeling of relief in the room. They had a possible way out of their dilemma. Poujet felt the immediate change of atmosphere.

'There must be somebody available to lead such a force,' Hugan remarked. 'Somebody who knows the area.'

'There is,' Colonel Gourbet said eagerly. 'I had a Lieutenant on my staff until a month or so ago. He is now serving with the Legion in Corsica. He has lived most of his life in Djibouti. He speaks the native language. He knows the area well.'

'His name?'

'Simon Ducan.'

Immediately, as Ducan's name was mentioned, Marchand turned to his assistant. Poujet was calmly studying the ceiling at the time, but he felt obliged to look in his Director's direction. He saw the Director's questioning look and returned it with a look that said — 'let it be so'. He also gave a faint smile. The Director's features softened.

'So we have a possible leader,' Hugan said. 'That is good. And how many men would you suggest, Marchand?'

'I would leave that to the leader, but I rather think he will take ten.' He turned to Poujet again. 'Any comments, Poujet? About security?'

Poujet sat more formally in his seat.

'No, Monsieur. It can all be taken care of.'

Marchand was satisfied. He turned to Hugan. Hugan looked from Marchand to Colonel Gourbet and said, 'We report now to *Monsieur le President.*'

Chapter Sixteen

The French delegation reported to the President. Poujet remained in the vicinity of the restaurant. When the delegation returned, Poujet was informed that the President had given his agreement to the proposal.

The Americans were summoned. They arrived within minutes. They had been sitting by their telephone. The formalities were brief. The two parties faced each other, again, at the table. The Americans looked at Monsieur Hugan.

'We have consulted with *Monsieur le President*,' Hugan said. 'He has the interest of your President very much at heart, and also the concern that would be felt by your people, and the French nation, if any harm should come to an American and French national at the hands of any terrorists. He is also aware of the delicacy of the situation. The French Government has commitments in the area. They have agreements with the Government of Ethiopia which must be honoured...'

The Americans listened patiently. Hugan was obliged to make the French position quite clear and discharge themselves of any involvement that could embarrass their Government. The American party knew that they had not been recalled for a lecture on France's foreign policy, or French diplomacy. They were prepared to let Hugan deliver the *hors d'oeuvres* and the first course. They were interested only in the meat dish. Finally it was served.

'*Monsieur le President* cannot commit any unit of the French Forces, no matter how small, to an act of aggression. However, he is prepared to second a volunteer section of men to...'

Hugan gave a diplomatic pause, 'to an intermediate mercenary that perhaps you can arrange.'

'A volunteer section from the Foreign Legion?' McNew asked.

'A volunteer section of men who are disciplined and trained in the art of warfare, Monsieur, and led by an officer who is knowledgeable about the area in question. Such a unit could well come from the Foreign Legion.'

The Americans relaxed. There were smiles on their faces.

'We are grateful to your President, Monsieur,' Senator Fielding said for the party.

'Let us make it quite clear, Monsieur,' Hugan added. 'These men will be hired mercenaries. Hired by an intermediary that you will arrange.' He smiled. 'I am sure that Monsieur Carson already has somebody in mind. These mercenaries will be issued with foreign weapons and uniforms, and will not bear any insignia to indicate that they are ex-French soldiers. They will be led by a French officer who will, today, resign his commission for personal reasons. He will make all the necessary arrangements for the operation with your intermediary or representatives. *Monsieur le President*, the French Government, and the French people, are in no way involved.'

Having wiped the slate clean for his country, Hugan then felt it wise to add, 'The Foreign Legion has some very fine men. They also have some very fine officers and *sous-officiers*. They will act and fight in the tradition of the Legion. I do not think you will find them lacking.'

'I am sure we will not,' McNew said with feeling.

For the second time that day, Poujet felt the atmosphere in the room suddenly relax. It was almost as if the room had been in darkness and someone had switched on an electric light. The change was so sudden and so noticeable.

Colonel Gourbet produced a bottle of brandy and a tray of glasses. All the men in the room toasted the success of the mission. Then they got down to details.

Carson took over for the Americans. He explained their intentions.

'Mr McNew, Senator Fielding and Mr Ellis will fly to London as arranged. In London, they will discuss the situation with the British Government and get their backing. It could also give the impression to any interested parties that you have declined to become involved. I don't know where your volunteers are stationed, but I have two aircraft at Geneva Airport available to pick them up and fly them to a small Greek island. The island is owned by a friendly Greek who assists the U.S. Government from time to time. I will arrange for the issue of weapons and clothing. We will also arrange for them to be flown to a location close to the rebel camp. After that, it will be up to your men. As for the return…' He shook his head and looked hopefully at the French party.

Poujet hoped that he got some positive response. It was apparent that the American party had been prepared to back anybody that was prepared to help them. Carson had laid everything on, including getting the small force close to the terrorist camp. He was now looking for some means of support in getting them back safely.

There was no immediate response from the French party.

'We can land an aircraft close to the camp,' Carson said, 'but to leave the aircraft in the open for two or three days would be too dangerous. Besides, the Ethiopian Government's Air Force patrols the area. To bring the aircraft into the territory at an agreed time is a possibility, but there could be problems.'

Again he looked hopefully at Monsieur Hugan. Hugan made the gesture.

'The French Government cannot be involved,' he said, 'but probably the men who are transferred to you will be from the Legion. The Legion patrols the border, and the Legion protects its own.'

It was what the Americans had wanted to hear.

'I am sure we can look for a satisfactory conclusion to the mission,' McNew said, in a manner that suggested that he wanted to be on his way.

'Colonel Gourbet will be flying to Corsica this evening,' Hugan explained, 'to find suitable volunteers. If you arrange for your aircraft to fly at once to Calvi airport, we will see that they are looked after. The officer who will lead the party will be at your disposal from midnight tonight. He will be taken to the airport.'

'In that case, he can go in advance,' Carson said. 'I will arrange for him to be fully briefed.'

'Then it is agreed.'

Hugan stood up. The meeting was over. The two parties formally shook hands.

Carson took Poujet to one side.

'One hour?' Carson asked.

'I will be here,' Poujet replied.

The Americans departed. The Frenchmen sat down again.

'Lieutenant Ducan will resign his commission immediately,' Hugan instructed. 'The records of the volunteers will be temporarily removed from the files of the Legion.' He turned to Marchand. 'You will arrange the necessary cover in case anything should go wrong.'

'And if everything goes well?'

Hugan opened the palms of his hands.

'There will be no public glory for France,' he said with regret, 'but we will have a large share of American Electrics and a grateful American State Department. They are generous people and they don't forget, but let us be cautious in our thinking. The outcome of this gamble has yet to be determined.'

Chapter Seventeen

Poujet was still seated in the chair that he had occupied during the meeting when Carson later rejoined him. Carson got the immediate impression that Poujet had been catching up on his disturbed night of sleep but was shrewd enough to dismiss the suggestion. In fact, Poujet had been thinking and planning ahead. He had been thinking about Ducan and the proposed mission, and planning how he could protect their particular interest in the Legion. He had also been planning how to squeeze the full investment out of American Electrics for the benefit of France. Carson's arrival had not disturbed his thoughts. It had only put the wheels of his plans into motion.

Carson had been escorted into the room by one of Poujet's assistants. Poujet dismissed the assistant with a wave of his hand and stood up to greet Carson. He offered him a seat.

Carson took a seat facing Poujet. Poujet sat down again.

'A satisfactory outcome,' Poujet remarked.

'Satisfactory,' Carson agreed. He unzipped a leather briefcase, not unlike the one Ellis had had with him. Poujet wondered if they were a standard issue.

'You will appreciate, Marcel, that we have no special sources of information.'

It was a reversal of the previous situation. It was the American's turn to be on the defensive and safeguard their interests. To Poujet, the remark meant that Carson had not deemed it necessary to contact their agent in the opposite camp. The information was on their files.

Carson placed three photographs, face down, on the table. On each was typed, in the style of a computer printout, the details of each man. Besides their original identity and their alias names, there was a full description of their physical appearances, and a history of their previous roles and operations. Poujet read the details of each man only once. The facts were then stored in his brain, and would later be reproduced for his department's files. He slowly turned the photographs over one by one, as if displaying a winning hand at poker. He looked at the three faces. One of them he recognised. One of them was the face he had wanted to see. He was content now that his plans were going to materialise. He passed the three photographs across the table to Carson.

Carson picked them up and replaced them in his briefcase.

'You will also appreciate, Marcel,' he said, 'that we have no knowledge, or interest, in a Karl Russo.'

So the C.I.A. was also finished with Russo, Poujet thought. He had outlived his usefulness to them.

'It is just that the world is short of good doctors,' Carson added.

'Quite,' Poujet agreed. 'He can still serve society.'

Russo would be returned safely to Zurich.

Carson stood up. So did Poujet. For a moment, Carson studied the room.

'There is history in this room,' he said. 'I can feel it.'

'It is an old building,' Poujet remarked.

'I feel as if I am in the past,' Carson went on. 'The restaurant is aptly named.'

'*Le Cardinal?* Are you thinking of a Cardinal in particular?'

Carson gave the first smile that Poujet had seen from him, since their meeting in his home the previous evening.

'Perhaps,' he said, 'but you also remind me of someone from the past, Marcel.'

Poujet gave a surprised look of concern. He frowned.

'You remind me of Richelieu's right hand man. He must have had one.'

Poujet's features relaxed. He looked relieved.

'I am pleased you didn't give me the crown,' he said. '*Monsieur le Director* would not have approved.'

'Not a king, but a king-maker,' Carson said.

They shook hands.

'I will be in touch,' Carson remarked.

'Certainly,' Poujet replied. He would see to it.

They left the restaurant together. There was a lot for both of them to attend to. Carson went about his negotiations. Poujet returned to his office and joined the Director.

'Gourbet is flying to Calvi,' the Director said. 'I have arranged for you to go with him, to look after our interests.'

'Yes, Monsieur.'

'Did Carson deliver the goods?'

'He did, Monsieur. They have a most impressive library.'

The Director gave a snort of disgust.

'So Russo sold us out to the Americans,' he said. 'The traitor. What do we do with him?'

'I have agreed to his safe return.'

The Director gave a disapproving grunt and changed the subject.

'That explains why the Fox joined the Legion.'

'When the Fox found out that he was being shipped to the States, Monsieur, he came to the only conclusion possible — that we had washed our hands of him and passed him over to the C.I.A. The Fox has personal reasons for wanting to defect to us. What they are, unfortunately, we do not know, but he certainly didn't want to be shipped to the States.'

'At least we know what went wrong.'

'We also know that Russo had no knowledge of what he was handling. It was the C.I.A. who knew otherwise. They gave Russo his orders.'

'They were quick off the mark.'

'They got inside information. They have a well informed source working for them. As soon as the Fox took flight, the C.I.A. were informed.'

'In which case, Marcel, they might have the Fox's identity.'

'They might, Monsieur, but I think otherwise. They have made no move. They will know more about him than we do, but my hunch is that they lost his trail in Marseilles along with their shipping agent, when the K.G.B. caught up with them.'

The Director agreed.

'And now we have Ducan going on this adventure,' he said.

'With ten men, Monsieur.'

'Our ten men?'

'Yes, Monsieur. Our ten men.'

'Is that wise, Marcel?'

'It is essential, Monsieur, if we are to make any move to net the Fox. The opportunity is ideal. It is not of our doing. It is a Legion affair. We do not know the identity of the Fox, so…' He gave a resigned shrug.

'But in the wilds of East Africa, our Fox could be killed.'

'He could, Monsieur. It is a gamble we must take. Certainly it would be to our advantage if some of them did not return…'

Poujet looked up at the Director. He gave him a knowing look. The Director understood.

'What about Ducan?' the Director asked. 'Do we confide in him?'

Poujet shook his head solemnly.

'No, Monsieur, I think not. I think that Lieutenant Ducan will have his hands full. I do not wish to overburden him.'

The Director sighed.

'So it is all up to Pascal again.'

'Yes, Monsieur, Pascal, but now that Carson has cooperated, we can give Pascal some ammunition.'

'Ah! Carson. It has been quite a day for Monsieur Carson.'

'It has, Monsieur,' Poujet agreed. A faint smile came to his lips. 'Carson was even reminded of the intrigues of the past. He likened me to Richelieu's right hand man.'

'So I am Richelieu,' the Director said, and gave a deep chuckle of delight.

'For one moment, I thought he was going to liken me to some other infamous man of our past.'

'Who, Marcel? Who?'

'Robespierre.'

'Robespierre! That devil and his reign of terror! You? Never.'

The thought amused the Director even more than the reference to Cardinal Richelieu.

'I'm relieved that you find the thought unlikely, Monsieur.'

The Director shook his head.

'You a Robespierre? No, Marcel, never, but don't underestimate the C.I.A. They will also know that you could not be a Robespierre.'

'How, Monsieur?'

'Because they will know you almost as well as I do. For instance, they will know that beneath that floppy, casual exterior of yours is a steel hearted machine that has one unmechanical-like quality.'

Poujet raised his bushy eyebrows questioningly.

'You are a romantic, Poujet,' the Director said with a smile.

'A romantic, Monsieur?'

'Yes, a romantic, and they will also know that your favourite poet is an Englishman called Byron.'

Poujet looked chastened. The Director's smile broadened. He had told Poujet something about himself that Poujet had not thought the Director knew.

'Ah! *Mon* Lord Byron,' Poujet muttered and looked uneasy.

'Fortunately the romantic in you, Marcel, is tempered by the logic of your thinking.'

Poujet looked more uncomfortable. 'This is most interesting, Monsieur,' he said.

'In fact, it is the romantic in you that is allowing Ducan to go on this wild adventure into Africa,' the Director said.

'It was too late to stop, Monsieur,' Poujet replied. He was on the defensive, but he had recovered from his embarrassment at being called a romantic. 'Once his name was mentioned, there would have been a question asked if we had opposed him. Also, Monsieur, it gives us the opportunity to solve our problem, once and for all.'

'Perhaps, but even without our ten men, I think you would have recommended Ducan. You want him to lead this mission, Marcel. You see it as his challenge.'

'I see it as a means of bringing a number of things to a head, Monsieur, that is true. It is said that Africa brings out the best in people — or the worst. If it brings out the best in Ducan, it will have produced a man who can be of great service to France. If it brings out the worst, then it is well to know that now and dispense with his services.'

The Director sat back in his chair. Poujet had conceded the point.

'Ducan needs this challenge,' Poujet went on. 'It is time that he was put to the test.'

There was a moment's silence.

'I will make arrangements for the flight, Monsieur,' Poujet said.

He stood up to take his leave.

The Director looked at him.

'I would hate to have a Robespierre as my deputy, Marcel,' he said.

'Thank you, Monsieur.'

'I am also a bit of a romantic,' the Director added.

Chapter Eighteen

It had been another hot day. Schiller had been at his blistering best. Ducan had felt for the men, but there was to be no change in the training programme. He had tried to persuade Captain Moutoner to introduce some changes, but he had had no success. He had found the Captain as inflexible as he would have found Schiller. The only difference was that the Captain had a more charming and diplomatic way of refusing him. Schiller was aware of Ducan's discussions with the Captain and of their outcome, but he still made the men suffer.

At the end of the day, the section returned to the camp. Schiller reported to Ducan.

'Permission to dismiss the men, *mon Lieutenant.*'

Ducan gave a faint smile.

'Are they finished for today?' he asked.

Schiller's eyes narrowed fractionally.

'Unless you want them for special training, *mon Lieutenant.*'

'I think they have done enough, Sergeant-Chief. You have excelled yourself today. We will continue with the good work tomorrow.'

His eyes had a glint of mischief in them. He wasn't going to give the Sergeant-Chief any indication of the disappointment that he felt that his ideas for changes in the routine had been turned down.

'Dismiss the men,' he added.

'Yes, *mon Lieutenant.*'

The men were formally dismissed. Ducan returned to his quarters. Schiller was a sadist, he thought — a sadistic bastard. He wondered if all the Sergeant-Chiefs were like him, or if

Schiller was special. He sat on his bed. He was grimy, sweaty, and his limbs ached. He felt a seething resentment of the Sergeant-Chief.

There was a knock on his door. It was an orderly. Ducan was to report to the Captain immediately. Ducan sighed and went to Moutoner's office.

'A hard day?' Moutoner asked.

'It was no different from the rest, Sir.'

Moutoner smiled encouragingly.

'Well perhaps tomorrow will be different, Simon.'

'Sir?' Ducan asked.

'We leave immediately for Calvi. You are to wear civilian clothes. You are to hand all your belongings over to the Quartermaster for safekeeping. You are being sent on a special assignment.'

'Special assignment, Sir?'

'I can help you no further,' Moutoner said. 'I too am in the dark, and you must tell no one where you are going.'

Ducan frowned. The Captain saw the frown.

'In the Legion, anything is possible,' he remarked. 'We are here to obey.'

'It is just that I was getting used to my assignment.'

'Were you, Simon?' Moutoner asked. He thought otherwise. He thought Ducan was showing signs of frustration. He didn't wait for an answer. 'You had better start packing. Colonel Gourbet does not like to be kept waiting.'

'Colonel Gourbet?'

'Yes, you know him, I believe.'

'Yes, Sir.'

Ducan was puzzled as well as surprised. He thought that he had been posted out of the Colonel's department.

The Captain was also puzzled. The telephone call from his Colonel in Calvi had been brief, but to the point. It was a matter of extreme urgency and secrecy. The Captain was to bring Lieutenant Ducan with him immediately to Calvi. The Lieutenant was to wear civilian clothes, and would not be returning to the camp for some time.

The two officers travelled by car. They did not refer to the special assignment as they journeyed. There was no point in conjecture.

It was dark when they arrived at the Legion camp at Calvi. The duty officer was at the entrance gate waiting for them. He took them immediately to the Commandant's office. In the office were three senior officers and a civilian. One of the senior officers was Colonel Gourbet. The civilian was Marcel Poujet. He sat slouched over a chair at the end of a long table. He looked out of place in the room. His suit was crumpled, whereas the three senior officers were all smartly dressed, and he sat in an un-military like pose, with his knees crossed and his back bent.

Captain Moutoner saluted. Ducan stood stiffly to attention in his civilian attire. He knew Colonel Gourbet and Poujet, but not the other two officers. They were both Colonels, and both wore rows of campaign ribbons on their chests.

Colonel Gourbet shook hands with Moutoner and Ducan. He gave Ducan a warm smile. He briefly introduced him to the two Colonels and Poujet. The two Colonels were introduced by name and rank. They were both Colonels in the Legion. Poujet was simply introduced as a Monsieur Poujet from Paris without giving him any official, civilian position. Poujet didn't look at Ducan as he was introduced. He simply nodded his head as his name was mentioned. Ducan made no sign of recognition. The two Legion Colonels watched him. Their names were not known to Ducan and in turn he was not known to them. So they studied him critically.

'Sit down, Captain Moutoner,' Colonel Gourbet said, 'and you Lieutenant Ducan.' He indicated the chairs on which they were to sit. Moutoner was given a seat in the wings. Ducan was given one in the centre of the stage facing the three Colonels.

'You look fit, Simon,' Colonel Gourbet said informally. 'The Legion suits you.'

'I am fit, *mon Colonel*,' Ducan replied, and purposely refrained from praising the Legion. He could feel the eyes of the two Legion Colonels on him, and wondered if they had got the point. He was beginning to resent the feeling of being the subject of interrogation. He wondered why Poujet was in the room, but was pleased that he was present.

Colonel Gourbet cleared his throat.

'Lieutenant Ducan,' he said, being formal again. 'You know the French territory of Afars and Issas very well. That is so?'

'Yes, *mon Colonel*,' Ducan agreed. 'I lived in Djibouti for many years. I was brought up in the territory.'

'Let us assume that none of these gentlemen know the territory. Tell them about it. Give them the facts.'

As Ducan marshalled his thoughts together, he wondered what it was all leading up to. He was aware that Colonel Gourbet knew the territory as well as himself, and probably the two Legion Colonels also. They were playing for time, he thought. They wanted to watch him perform.

'*Le Territoire Francois des Afars et des Issas*,' he said crisply, 'was formerly known as French Somaliland. It was renamed after a referendum held in 1967 produced a majority vote in favour of continued French rule. The name of the territory represents the names of the two indigenous peoples who make up the population. The Issas, who are a Somali people, are in the

146

majority. The Afars are the same as the neighbouring Danakils who live in Ethiopia. The population is about one hundred and forty thousand people. The country itself is a comparatively small enclave surrounding the Gulf of Tadjonra, near the mouth of the Red Sea. It covers about twenty-three thousand square kilometres. It is bordered to the South by the Somali Republic, and to the West and North by Ethiopia, with the Ethiopian territory of Eritrea to the North. The territory has, perhaps, the hottest climate in Africa, and ninety per cent of the country is classified as desert. It has barren hills, deep, dry wadis and a plateau of desolate scrub. It has a coastal plain with sparse scrub vegetation, and an important sea port at Djibouti. The sea port has strategic importance for France. There is also a railway link from Djibouti to the Ethiopian capital of Addis Ababa. The majority of the natives are settled in the coastal plain. The remainder are nomads who move from water hole to water hole with their cattle and camels.'

He paused to collect his thoughts. The Legion Colonels continued to watch him. Poujet sat with an air of apparent nonchalance, but he had been most impressed by Ducan's description of the territory.

'The border territory?' Colonel Gourbet suggested.

'To the North it is mountainous, but generally it is either barren hills of volcanic origin or desert scrub. It is a barren, harsh region and the tribes that roam the area have a miserable existence.'

'You have a sympathy for the natives?' one of the Legion Colonels asked.

Poujet moved slowly in his seat and cast his lazy eye on Ducan. Ducan was looking at the questioner.

'One has only to see the way they survive, *mon Colonel*,' he said, with a hint of defiance in his voice, 'and one cannot help but have sympathy for them.'

Poujet returned to his study of the table top.

'What is the political climate?' Colonel Gourbet asked.

'The whole area is a smouldering cauldron,' Ducan replied. 'In the territory there has been a desire for home rule for many years, which has been perhaps symptomatic of the times. They have been encouraged in this cause by the Somalis who have stirred up trouble along our borders. Now that the date for independence has been agreed, there is an uneasy peace. The Somalis are seeking a larger united Somali Republic. The Ethiopians need our support. Both countries are seeking the support of the border tribes. The situation is very tense, and fraught with dangers.'

'You speak the native language?' one of the Colonels asked.

'I do, *mon Colonel*. However, there are many dialects, but I can make myself understood.'

'You have travelled into Ethiopia?' Colonel Gourbet asked.

'I have,' Ducan agreed.

Colonel Gourbet turned to the Colonel sitting on his left, who had been introduced as Colonel Dennier. Colonel Dennier stood up from his chair and left the table. He went to the wall behind where Ducan was sitting, and pulled a cord hanging from the ceiling. A large map of the French territory in East Africa and its borders was displayed. The Colonel picked up a wooden pointer and pointed to an area in Ethiopia, known as the Danakil Depression. It was to the North of the French territory.

'You have been here?' he asked.

'Yes, *mon Colonel*,' Ducan replied. 'It is a blazing desert, where the Danakils mine salt. It is probably the hottest desert in the world.'

The Colonel moved his pointer to the South of the desert and pointed to two marks on the map. They were two villages. One was only about thirty kilometres from the French border.

'Two dusty, oppressive villages, *mon Colonel*,' Ducan said. 'One is called Sarda and the other Tandaho.'

The Colonel pointed to the area North of Sarda, which was the village that was closest to the French border.

'The area to the West and North is a desert of scrub and large boulders,' Ducan explained. 'It is only marginally more bearable than the Danakil Depression.'

'And the border?'

'It fringes the mountains to the North. It is a very rugged area of small, stark hills, of volcanic origin, and massive boulders.'

'There are passes through the hills into the French territory?' the Colonel asked.

'Yes, *mon Colonel*,' Ducan agreed. 'There are narrow canyons, but there are also passes.'

'And the people in the area?'

'They are Danakils *mon Colonel*. Nomadic tribes who roam the area. They are fierce warriors. Some of them are engaged in the guerrilla war against the Dirg.'

'And the others?' the Colonel asked. 'What is their allegiance?'

'To their water holes, *mon Colonel*,' Ducan replied. 'Water means survival. They have tribal loyalties and they do not welcome strangers. They believe that one extra stranger means less water for one of them. They also have an unswerving faith in the will of Allah. Whatever happens, it is Allah's will.'

The Colonel, at the wall map, nodded his head in silent agreement. He looked pleased, as if Ducan had impressed him with his knowledge of the area.

He turned away from the wall map and resumed his position at the table, on the left of Colonel Gourbet.

Colonel Gourbet took up the questioning. He turned to Ducan and asked, 'Do you think it would be possible for a very small, well equipped group of men to land near to the border, carry out an offensive action, and return into French territory?'

'Anything is possible, *mon Colonel*,' Ducan replied. 'It depends upon the preparation, the planning and the men. They would not only be fighting their offensive action, they would also be fighting to survive. The terrain, the climate and the natives are all hostile.'

The next question was obvious. Poujet moved himself in his seat so that he could observe Ducan's reactions. How Ducan reacted was important. It could give him an indication of the outcome of the mission.

'Would you be prepared to carry out such a mission?' Colonel Gourbet asked.

Poujet was disappointed. Ducan's features didn't alter and his eyes didn't flicker.

'If the Colonel is convinced that such a mission is essential for France,' he said, without any trace of feeling.

Poujet looked away. Ducan had prepared himself for the question, he thought. The build-up had warned him, and Poujet's own presence had given the question his official seal. Ducan had been prepared, and he had been given no choice with his answer.

Colonel Gourbet seemed satisfied with their progress.

'The Government considers that such an action is necessary,' he said, and explained about the captives and the ransom. 'The

French Government,' he added, 'has agreed to send a small force to an independent mercenary, who will arrange and finance a raid into Azir's territory to try and rescue the captives. You will lead this small commando raid, Lieutenant. However, as you will appreciate, the situation is very delicate. The French Government cannot be involved in any way. Consequently, you will be required to resign your commission. When you leave this room, you will no longer be an officer in the service of your country. Your records will be temporarily removed from our files. You will become an independent mercenary working for a foreign power, and so will the men who go with you. We will, in fact, arrange an assumed identity for you, if anything should misfire. Do you fully understand, Lieutenant?'

'I do, *mon Colonel.*'

'Good. We have many photographs for you to study, and many details to discuss, but are there any initial questions?'

The Colonel sat back in his chair, as if giving Ducan the right to question all the men at the table.

'How small is the force that was mentioned?' Ducan asked.

'About ten men.'

Ducan moved his head in agreement.

'The French girl, *mon Colonel?* Tell me about her.'

Poujet cast his eyes in Colonel Gourbet's direction, as if trying to penetrate his mind. What Gourbet said now was important, he thought. Very important.

'Mademoiselle Michelle Casanou,' the Colonel replied. 'She is part Algerian and part French. Her father was a doctor. Her mother came from an Algerian family.'

It was the Colonel's way of putting it that the girl was half Arabic and half French. At least he had been tactful, Poujet thought, and looked at Ducan. Ducan's attitude had changed.

There was an eager, youthful look on his face, as if he had got the bit.

'Is she part of the ransom?' he asked.

'The French Government has not been approached, but we are very concerned. She must be saved.'

'Yes, *mon Colonel*,' Ducan said promptly.

Poujet frowned. The way Ducan had previously conducted himself and spoken had impressed him. It had been a serious, controlled, Ducan. Just the type of man who would undertake the mission with all the seriousness that it demanded. Now he saw another Ducan. It was the Ducan he had seen when he had first interviewed him. It was a Ducan who didn't take anything particularly seriously. A Ducan who wanted some adventure. Poujet frowned and studied the table in thought.

'What is the attitude of the Dirg, *mon Colonel*?' Ducan asked.

'Sympathetic, but hindered. The Princess does not interest them. She is Eritrean by birth. The American girl does interest them.'

But the French girl does not, Poujet thought. Gourbet was adding more fuel to Ducan's fire of adventure.

'The strength of Azir's band, *mon Colonel*?' Ducan asked.

'His estimated strength is between eighty and one hundred in number, but he has made one bad, tactical mistake. The Americans strongly believe that the captives are being held at a small camp about thirty kilometres from our border. Azir himself is encamped with his main force close to Sarda. That is also close to our border, but about one hundred and thirty kilometres from where the captives are being held.'

'He has split his camp in two,' Ducan remarked. Colonel Gourbet gave a shrug.

'It is very possible that Azir is tempting us to make a move from our territory,' he said. 'He knows that such a move would be a diplomatic blunder on our part, and just the flame that he needs to start a bush war along our border. Or, perhaps, he does not realise how advanced the Americans are with their satellites. Even I have been most impressed.'

'They have photographs of the camp, *mon Colonel?*'

'They have very detailed photographs which will be most valuable to you, and there is no evidence that Azir has any mechanical transport.'

The Colonel looked at the two Colonels by his side.

'Perhaps we can get down to some detailed planning,' he suggested.

Poujet decided it was time for him to make some plans also.

'*Monsieur, le Colonel,*' he said.

Colonel Gourbet looked at him. 'Monsieur?' he asked.

Poujet stood up.

'If you gentlemen are to discuss details with *Monsieur le Lieutenant,*' he said in his slow drawl, 'perhaps Captain Moutoner and I could be excused. There are matters which I would like to discuss with *Monsieur le Capitaine.*'

Colonel Gourbet seemed pleased with the suggestion. It was as if he had been waiting for an excuse to free himself of Poujet.

'Certainly,' he agreed. 'The detailed planning will not interest you.'

Poujet slowly moved away from the table and shuffled towards the door. When he came close to Ducan, he stopped and turned to face him. Ducan was watching him.

'This is an unexpected assignment, Monsieur,' Poujet said, 'but it is an ideal opportunity for you to serve France. Take care, Monsieur, and *bon chance.*'

'Thank you, Monsieur.'

Poujet left the room followed by Captain Moutoner.

Chapter Nineteen

'*Debout! Debout!*'

The order came for the men to waken. Malik woke immediately. He looked around the row of beds as if in a daze. He realised where he was and a moment of panic passed through his body. He had slept fitfully. He had dreamed of the past. Had he also spoken out in his sleep? he wondered anxiously. He looked at Thompson, who occupied the nearest bunk. Thompson was on the move. He turned to Klaus. Klaus gave him a weak smile and started to move. He felt easier. He looked across the room at the Slav, Tojak. Tojak was out of his bunk. He saw his profile. It was an unusual shape, like a pear, and Tojak had particularly long ears. Suddenly something clicked inside Malik's brain. He had seen the profile before. It was the profile in a record file.

As if his thoughts had been telepathically transmitted to Tojak, the Slav shook himself and turned in Malik's direction. Malik saw a dark look appear on Tojak's face. He looked away. He was going to have to watch the Slav, he thought. The Slav was dangerous.

'A bad night?' Thompson asked.

Malik looked at him sharply, but Thompson looked as if he was only making conversation.

'Yeah! A bad night,' Malik agreed.

'I get them as well,' Thompson said.

There was a faraway look in his eyes. Malik saw it.

Thompson had lost a lot of his aggression, he thought. He was being drilled into submission like the rest.

'Sometimes I have a good one,' Klaus said cheerfully. He had overheard their conversation. 'Sometimes I dream I am in a luxury hotel with a beautiful blonde.'

'You'll be on extra drill if you don't move it!' a voice called out. It was the room Corporal. 'You won't have time for dreaming. Move it! Pronto! Pronto!'

The men moved it. Malik forgot about his bad night, but not about Tojak.

'*Rassemblement! Rassemblement!*'

The order came to assemble. The men fell quickly into line outside the hut and prepared themselves for another day of toil.

'*Guarde à vous!*'

They came to attention and faced their front. The parade went through its daily routine. The *Tricolore* was hoisted as the sun poked its head over the mountains. The only thing different from the previous days was the absence of Lieutenant Ducan. Some of the men noticed his absence. Klaus did, so did Verdi, Malik and Luker.

The other section sergeants shouted out their orders to their sections. Schiller marched ominously amongst his men. His cane came to rest on ten men. At each one, he paused and gave them a look of intimidation. The ten men selected were Poujet's ten men. They wondered what delight Schiller had in store for them.

Schiller called his assistant to him. The sergeant ordered the ten selected men to stand fast. The remainder of the section started their day of toil.

The ten men were paraded in single file. The camp was still and silent again. Schiller walked along the line.

'Stand still,' he snarled at Thompson.

Thompson's eyes had been attracted to Captain Moutoner, who had appeared on the scene. He thought that he had not moved, but Schiller had been watching him.

Schiller reported to the Captain. He returned to the men and gave the order to stand at ease. The men obeyed. Captain Moutoner came in front of them. He spoke to them in guarded tones, but his message was brief and simple. Lieutenant Ducan had been assigned to an act of combat. He needed ten volunteers to undertake a small commando raid into territory close to the border of the French territory in Eastern Africa. There would be no rewards, but it would be an act of combat for the service of France. It was a mission in keeping with the traditional role of the Legion. It would be arduous and dangerous. The Captain delivered his message. He left the rest to the Sergeant-Chief.

Schiller waited until they were alone.

'*Monsieur le Lieutenant* wants ten volunteers,' he said aggressively. 'When I give the order to fall out, any man who volunteers will collect his belongings together and take them to the Quartermaster's store. Any man who does not wish to volunteer…' He paused and said as an aside, 'And I don't know why you scum have been selected — any man who does not wish to volunteer will join the section for special training.'

His reference to special training was the sting in the tail, but he did not give the men time to even consider it. He dismissed them.

'*Rompez!*' he barked.

The men came to attention, saluted, and fell out. For a moment, they stood looking uncertainly at each other.

'You're not a pack of cowboys,' Schiller snarled. 'Move it!'

'I could do with a change of scenery,' Klaus said.

'So could I,' Malik agreed.

Calowski looked at Baron. 'Yeah!' Baron agreed.

They turned and walked to the hut. Thompson followed. So did Verdi and the others. They had all volunteered. Luker had been the last, but he had made his mind up earlier. So had some of the others.

Chapter Twenty

Klaus got his change of scenery. So did the other volunteers, and the pace of events took them by surprise. No sooner had they handed in their equipment than they were driven to the airport at Calvi, where a civilian aircraft with Greek markings was waiting for them. Two hours later, they were landing on a small island deep in the heart of the Aegean Sea.

The aircraft taxied to the end of the runway where a truck was standing. Silently, the men disembarked. They saw a row of three Nissen huts and an aircraft hangar, but no other signs of life. They were on a flat, barren island that was pockmarked with a handful of thick gorse bushes and nothing else. The sun shone from a clear, blue sky, and the island was surrounded by the deep blue of the sea.

'Bloody hot,' someone grumbled.

'Wait until you get to Africa,' Baron grunted.

As they boarded the open truck, the aircraft taxied to the far end of the runway. The men watched it. It did a quick turn and roared down the runway and into the sky. The men turned their attention to the row of Nissen huts. A solitary figure in a khaki uniform stood waiting to greet them. As they drew closer, they recognised the figure as Lieutenant Ducan, but they did not recognise his uniform. He wore a khaki bush jacket and trousers. They were a shade of khaki, and style, that were not French. He also wore calf high, brown leather boots and a leather belt from which hung a large knife. On his head was a bush hat not unlike those issued to the legionnaires. He wore no badges of rank, but had a blue silk cravat around his neck.

He stood erect, still and expressionless. The truck stopped in front of him and the order came to de-bus. The men jumped out and started to form rank. They were dressed in khaki fatigue, and each man carried a small duffel bag.

Ducan looked at them. They were ten men from his section. Another figure emerged from the passenger seat alongside the driver. It was the granite-faced Schiller.

Ducan's features did not change, but his heart sank and he felt as if some of the wind had suddenly been taken out of his sails. Schiller was the last man he had wanted with him on the mission.

Schiller sharply brought the men to attention. The truck drove away. Schiller marched up to Ducan and saluted. Ducan looked Schiller straight in the eyes. The Sergeant-Chief saw his red rimmed eyes, and knew that the Lieutenant had spent a sleepless night.

'Welcome,' Ducan said. He gave a faint smile. 'This is indeed a surprise.' Schiller knew what was in the Lieutenant's mind. His face hardened.

'*Mon Lieutenant*,' he growled respectfully.

'We do it my way, Sergeant-Chief,' Ducan said. Schiller didn't reply.

'Stand them at ease.'

Schiller gave the order. The men responded. He faced Ducan again.

'The men will go immediately through the small door behind me, Sergeant-Chief,' Ducan said. 'They will all strip off. Their uniforms will be placed in their duffel bags along with their personal belongings — their rings, their money, and anything else they might have with them. They will give their bags to one of the Greeks inside the hangar. There are three Greeks. None of them speak French. The men will then go into the adjoining room where they will be given a uniform like mine, and underclothing and socks. They may take their time. Their uniforms must fit, Sergeant-Chief, and it is essential that their boots are comfortable. We are going to do a lot of walking in the sun. There will be no means of exchanging their boots. The men will be given everything they will need, including a framed rucksack and a sleeping bag. They will not receive any weapons. They will get them later. When they have received their clothing, you will take them to the first hut. The second one is for you and me. You will then collect your own equipment. I will then explain our mission to the men. After that, they will return to the hangar and receive their weapons. The weapons are Czech. You might be familiar with them. I am. The men will go to the rifle range behind the hangar, and there they will familiarise themselves with their weapons until dusk. They will then return to their hut where they will find food and wine waiting for them. They will be left to their own devices. At dawn, you will assemble them again, and they will return to the range. Some of them will receive special instruction in the use of explosives and booby-traps. At midday, we fly out of here, and tomorrow evening we start our mission.' He looked the Sergeant-Chief squarely in the eyes. 'Do you fully understand, Sergeant-Chief?'

'Yes, *mon Lieutenant.*'

'The men will not question any of the Greeks, Sergeant-Chief. They will not help themselves to anything that is not being issued to them. Also, Sergeant-Chief, they must not leave anything on their persons that could link them with *la Légion*. There will be no badges of rank.'

The Lieutenant saw a fleeting look of concern appear in the Sergeant-Chief's eyes. He gave a faint smile. Schiller saw it and a cheek muscle on his rugged face twitched, but he remained silent.

'Now I will leave it all to you, Sergeant-Chief,' Ducan said.

Schiller saluted. Ducan returned the salute.

'That will be the last salute,' he said, and walked away towards the Nissen huts.

The Sergeant-Chief took a deep breath and turned to face the men. He waited until the Lieutenant was out of earshot and then hissed menacingly, 'Remember — all of you. No matter what you are told. You are still the Legion, as far as I am concerned, and I am going to be with you all the time. When you are through with this little jaunt, we will all go back to Corsica. Don't ever forget that.' He walked along the line and glared at each man in turn.

'Now listen to me very carefully.' He gave them their orders as he interpreted them and added a few of his own. 'Now we begin our little charade,' he hissed, when he had finished.

The men were marched into the hangar. They entered a partitioned room where three smiling Greeks in white shirts and slacks waited to attend to them. The men stripped off. Schiller stood watching them. They entered the adjoining room. It was large and cool, and looked like a huge quartermaster's store.

'Aladdin's cave,' Fingers muttered.

'Keep your thieving hands to yourself, Ferelli,' Schiller snarled.

Again the Greeks attended to them. The men were given their clothing and equipment with great care.

'The boots,' Schiller called out. 'Make sure they fit. There is no exchange — except from the dead.'

'*Cochon*,' Verdi hissed.

'Miserable bastard,' Thompson added.

The men got dressed in their new uniforms and assembled at the end of the hangar. Schiller inspected them; they still looked like legionnaires, despite their change of garb. They had the suntanned faces and the lean look of physical fitness that were the hallmarks of a legionnaire. Schiller was satisfied. He marched them to their hut. It was not unlike the one they had left in Corsica, only the temperature was higher. There were two rows of beds, and a large centre table with two foam seats. On the table stood four jugs of iced lemon and ten mugs.

'Don't leave this building,' Schiller warned. 'I'll be back.'

He left them. The men helped themselves to the drink.

'Where do you think this uniform was made?' Thompson called out.

'Not by a Paris fashion designer,' Klaus said.

'It's not Greek, neither,' Malik said.

'What do you think?' Verdi asked.

'Hungarian,' Malik replied.

'How do you know that, Malik?' Tojak asked. 'You been there?'

'Sure, I've been there,' Tojak,' Malik retorted, and turned his back on him.

'You've been around — for a truck driver,' Tojak sneered.

'The boots are good leather,' Thompson chipped in cheerfully.

'You're going to need them,' Klaus said. 'I think we are going to do a lot of walking.'

'Some private store those Greeks have,' Svenson sighed.

'Yeah!' Klaus agreed.

'It would be easy to get in and help ourselves,' Fingers said.

His eyes seemed to light up at the thought.

'Easy?' Klaus asked.

'Sure, Klaus. It wouldn't be difficult.'

'You wouldn't get off the island,' Calowski pointed out.

'What makes you so sure?'

Calowski had a way of making remarks that had a deeper significance. The room went silent.

The Swede went up to him.

'What about it, Calowski?'

'Did you see the bushes?'

'Yeah! I saw them.'

The others all looked at Calowski.

'They are evenly spaced about the island,' Calowski said. 'Not in any pattern, but spaced about. They are camouflage.'

'Air shafts?' Thompson asked.

'It's all underneath,' Klaus said, with a whistle of surprise. 'A secret arsenal.'

'It doesn't pay to be too inquisitive,' Luker suggested, 'otherwise they will make sure we never get back to tell about it.'

'Yeah!' Verdi agreed. 'Let's forget about it. Luker is right. We saw nothing.'

He selected a bunk and started to unpack his equipment.

The others followed suit.

'Bloody hot,' Thompson sighed. 'Don't like the bloody heat.'

'You think that this is hot,' Baron snorted. 'Just you wait.'

'Have you been there before?' Thompson asked.

'Sure, I have been in Djibouti. Djibouti is OK. It has everything you would want, but inland it is as hot as hell. You just wait.'

'Do you think the Greeks might lay on a couple of girls tonight?' the Swede asked.

'Sure, why not,' Verdi said. 'Any particular fancy?'

'Yeah!' the Swede replied. 'A nice, big, Swedish girl.'

Luker turned to him.

'I've never poofed a Swedish girl. Are they good?'

He didn't get an answer. Schiller joined them instead.

'*Guarde à vous!*' came the order.

The men responded immediately. They stood stiffly to attention. Schiller walked amongst them, letting them see him in his new uniform.

'Take a good look,' he snarled. He walked up and down the room.

The men watched him, but kept their silence.

'*Rassemblement!*' he shouted. 'Assemble outside! Pronto!'

The men moved at the double and formed rank outside the hut. Schiller walked along the line. The men felt the heat of the overhead sun on their bodies, and braced themselves for Schiller's cane. He tapped them temptingly, but he did not lash out. He marched them to a shaded area between two huts where Ducan was waiting for them. Schiller brought the men to attention and went to report to the Lieutenant. He did not salute. Ducan took the Sergeant-Chief to one side, out of earshot.

'You need a corporal, Sergeant-Chief,' he said. 'Somebody to lead the men if necessary.'

'Who do you have in mind, *mon Lieutenant?*'

Ducan smiled. 'I think you know the men better than me,' he said.

Again Schiller's face muscles flinched. The Lieutenant's smile got under his skin. It irritated him.

'Verdi,' he grunted. 'He can handle them.'

Ducan raised an eyebrow, but nodded his head in approval.

'Get the men to sit in the shade.'

Schiller returned to the men. They formed a small semicircle. Ducan sat facing them. Schiller was at his side.

'Welcome to Signor Spiro's private army,' Ducan said, with a glint in his eyes. 'From this moment on, there will be no formal saluting. You are now officially mercenaries, and not legionnaires.' Schiller's presence seemed to contradict that statement. The men felt his eyes reinforcing their feelings.

'This is a temporary arrangement,' Ducan went on. 'You will nevertheless act, obey, and fight like legionnaires. Is that understood?'

He got no response.

'Verdi,' he called out. Verdi looked up at him.

'Yes, *mon Lieutenant?*'

'You will now act as Corporal,' Ducan said.

Schiller glanced at the men. They showed no reaction.

Verdi's face registered surprise, but he was not going to be allowed to question his promotion.

'That is an order,' Ducan said. 'The chain of command is myself, then Sergeant-Chief, and then Corporal Verdi. If the three of us are killed, it will then be every man for himself. Is that understood?'

This time the tone of his voice demanded a response. He got it.

'Yes, *mon Lieutenant*,' came the response.

'Good.'

Ducan gave them a smile of encouragement. Schiller looked surly. Ducan was enjoying himself. The Sergeant-Chief was not.

'I am going to tell you about your equipment, and then what our mission is,' Ducan said. 'It is possible some of you might die on this mission, so I am inviting you to ask questions. I want soldiers who are thinkers as well as fighters. Is that also understood?'

Again he got his response. He did not look at the Sergeant-Chief.

'There are only two questions that I will not answer,' Ducan went on. 'Why we are undertaking this mission, and who is providing all the equipment and transport. All you need to know is that we are working for a Signor Spiro.' He looked at the men. They were watching him closely. 'You will be issued with either an automatic rifle or a sub-machine gun. We will take four machine guns and eight automatic rifles. The weapons are Czech. You will find them similar to the weapons that you have used. You have already been issued with a framed rucksack. That is Norwegian. So is the sleeping bag. It is specially designed for tropical conditions. You also have a small medical pack in case of burns or bites, and an emergency bandage for anything more serious. You have four full water canteens and two boxes, each one containing five packages. Each package is a specially prepared meal — not very appetising, but nevertheless a meal. You also have a small box of anti-dehydration tablets. You will take a tablet when you take a drink of water. Your water is very precious. You will only drink when ordered. If you want to survive, you will not disobey that order.'

He paused to emphasise the importance of his remark.

'The water canteens are heavy,' he said, 'but they are vital to survival. The ration is half a canteen per day. You can survive on that. If you use more than that you might end up with no water, and you will certainly die. There will be no water holes and no spare water. What extra we take we will need for the people we are going to help. You must make your water last.'

Again he paused. He saw that the men had got his message. He continued.

'Tonight you will use your sleeping bags. Tomorrow morning, the Sergeant-Chief will inspect your equipment and your water canteens. Everything must be in order. After you have been issued with your weapons, you will go to a rifle range at the rear of the hangar. There you will familiarise yourself with your weapons until you are all experts. That is essential. Tomorrow morning, we will again use the range. We leave at midday tomorrow.' He studied the men's faces. His eyes fell on the Swiss — Luker.

'One man,' he said, 'will be issued with a special medical kit. That man will also be given special instructions by one of the Greeks on the use of various drugs in the kit. The Greek can speak English and German.' He hesitated momentarily. 'I need a volunteer.'

He got no response.

Schiller grunted, 'Luker!' He had been watching Ducan's eyes and knew that Luker was the man for the detail.

Luker looked up. 'Yes, Sergeant-Chief,' he said.

'You will volunteer?' Schiller asked in a manner that made his question seem like an order.

Luker lowered his eyes. 'Yes, Sergeant-Chief,' he said.

'Good,' Ducan said. 'I also want two volunteers to familiarise themselves with some rather special explosives and booby-traps.'

No one was forthcoming.

Schiller scowled. He did not like Ducan's way of asking for volunteers; Schiller's way was different. Men were detailed for a duty. He grunted, and was about to make his views heard when Klaus volunteered.

'I will volunteer, *mon Lieutenant*,' he said, with a flash of a smile. 'I have always had a fancy to blow things up.'

'I will also volunteer, *mon Lieutenant*,' Malik added.

Ducan was satisfied.

'You will both report to the hangar after you have been issued with your rifles. You also, Luker,' he said.

He opened a large, leather briefcase that he had brought with him and withdrew a map and a number of enlarged photographs that assembled into a panoramic picture of the area in which they were to operate. He spread out the map and the photographs. The map was simply drawn, not unlike a child's drawing, but it showed all the essential features.

'Now to our mission,' he said. 'I want you to listen carefully and fully understand.'

A tense silence fell over the group. The men's faces were serious. They hung on to every word the Lieutenant said as he told them about Mohammed Azir and his guerrilla band, and of the captives that he was holding to ransom. Ducan omitted nothing. He showed them the location of Azir's camp and he told them about the hostility of the country and the people. He left them in no doubt about what they were up against.

'If you are captured,' he warned, 'they will kill you, but they will kill you by staking you to the ground and emasculating you.' In case they didn't understand the full meaning of the word, he explained, 'That means they will cut off your penis and your testicles, and leave you to the insects and vultures. That is their way of dealing with enemies, and all strangers are enemies.' One or two of the men, like Fingers and Luker, shuffled uncomfortably at the thought of their manly parts being cut off. The others looked as if it did not bother them.

Ducan spread out the photographs in the middle of the group. They showed a rugged area of gorges and canyons between the volcanic rock hills.

'To the West and the East is the flat desert scrub of the plain,' he explained. 'The rock hills form the boundary between

168

Ethiopia and the French territory of Afars and Issas. They are only about two to three hundred metres in height and their tops are flat plateaus, but they form an ideal barrier and an ideal area for ambushes and guerrilla warfare. To the North are the foothills of a much higher mountain range that borders the French territory with Eritrea. Now I will show you our escape route. Study it carefully.' He pointed to a semi-circular shaped area that fringed the flat plain. 'That is where Azir has his camp and, we believe, his prisoners. Behind the camp the route into the French territory is through this narrow gorge.' The men followed the route carefully. From the narrow gorge, they saw a large, open area, then another gorge, not so long as the first. Again, a wider flat area, after which were two passes. The one to the North was cut short by a cover strip to indicate that it was not important, but the one to the South was shown winding its way through the rocky hills.

'The pass to the North,' Ducan explained, 'is the old pass into Eritrea. You must bear South.' He touched the point on the photograph where the South pass started, and another along its course. 'At this location, you should meet some patrols from *la Légion*,' he said.

He brought out another set of photographs from his briefcase. They showed a crude, square shaped, two-storied building with a flat roof, and a row of single storied outbuildings on either side of it. Surrounding the buildings were palm trees and bushes that indicated the presence of water, and a cluster of mud huts. There was also a small wall encircling the area. The buildings looked crude and primitive in their construction, but they gave the impression of being the small estate of a local chieftain.

'This group of buildings is Azir's camp, and we believe that the party of captives is being held in the outbuildings. The area around this encampment is flat, but it has good cover, and compared with the rest of the region it is reasonably fertile, because of the presence of water.' He passed the photographs to the men to study. 'It is close to the hills and to our escape route.'

He returned to his map. 'The main body of Azir's force is close to this village, Sarda. That is where he is carrying out his negotiations. It is about one hundred and thirty kilometres from their base camp. It is in that region that they will be expecting any reprisals from the Ethiopian armed forces. They do not expect any attack from their rear. In the mountains and hills, there are many warring tribes that keep the French forces occupied. Azir also knows that the French Government would not risk an invasion into Ethiopian territory.' He looked at the men, one by one. 'That is why we are now mercenaries,' he said.

The men remained silent.

'Our plan is to land at this point.' He indicated a position North of Azir's camp. 'We land at night and we march as quickly as possible. We take cover during the day. We should reach Azir's camp on the second night. We attack immediately and return with Azir's hostages, via the escape route into French territory.'

He gave a sigh.

'That is our mission, gentlemen. I am now inviting you to think — to ask any questions.'

The men did not respond. They had been drilled to obey, and not to question.

'Come,' Ducan said. 'Malik, Klaus, Corporal Verdi.'

He turned to Schiller and raised his eyebrows questioningly. Schiller turned to the men.

'If you have any questions,' he snarled, 'ask *Monsieur le Lieutenant* now. There will not be another opportunity.'

'How do we get to the starting point, *mon Lieutenant*?' Thompson asked.

'Aircraft.'

Schiller did not like it. He did not like it at all. Neither did Thompson.

'The natives will hear it, *mon Lieutenant*,' Thompson said. 'The word will get around.'

'The alternative is to parachute, but we are mercenaries, not trained parachutists. Besides, if one of you was injured in the fall, it could jeopardise the whole mission.'

Schiller settled the matter. 'We march, *mon Lieutenant*,' he said.

'More questions,' Ducan demanded.

'We could use helicopters, *mon Lieutenant*,' Malik suggested. 'They would get us nearer to Azir's camp.'

'From French territory, perhaps, but not from here. We cannot use our own bases. We fly from here. Speed is of the essence when we make our move.'

'What happens to any wounded, *mon Lieutenant*?' Fingers asked hesitantly.

'The wounded we help. It will make it harder for us, but we will not leave any wounded behind, if we can help them.'

'What are our chances of success, *mon Lieutenant*?' Verdi asked, 'and our chances of getting back alive?'

The men looked at Ducan. Verdi had asked the question they all wanted to know. Would they get back alive?

Ducan did not answer straight away. He hesitated as if picking his words carefully.

'You are all trained and disciplined,' he said slowly. 'If you maintain your standards, our chances are very good. Obey all orders. We are all physically fit, although the heat could affect us all differently. We should be able to move quickly. The advantage of surprise should be in our favour.' He looked thoughtful. 'To answer your question honestly, I would bet on getting back alive, but,' he shrugged, 'that is different from a successful mission. Whether we save the captives is not so certain. Or even if they are alive at all. We are up against barbaric people. They are fanatics. However, they have made the mistake of splitting their force into two. That is to our advantage.' He shrugged again. The men knew that success lay on a razor's edge. It could go either way.

There were no more questions. Verdi's question and Ducan's reply had wrapped it all up.

The Sergeant-Chief took over. The men collected their weapons and went to the range. They soon became experts with them. They were highly trained infantrymen, and one weapon was very much like any other. Luker, Klaus and Malik returned to the hangar and were given their special instructions by the Greeks. They learned quickly. Luker even asked some very technical questions.

As dusk approached, the men were marched back to their quarters. They were all quiet, as if the pace of events had suddenly caught up with them and made them realise what was in store for them.

Inside the hut, they found the table covered with food and wine. It looked like a banquet, yet none of them made any comment about it. They placed their weapons in a rack and kept their firing bolts. Some of them sat at the table, whilst others sat on their bunks. Luker examined his medical kit again.

'Like the last supper, Thomo',' Klaus said in English. Thompson looked up at him, a question on his face.

'What?' he asked.

'The last supper,' Klaus said again.

'What last supper?' Thompson asked in English, and frowned.

'From the Bible,' Klaus said.

'Oh, yes, of course.'

'There were thirteen of them,' Luker said, also in English. 'That's right isn't it, Thomo'?'

'Sure, if you say so. Not my strong point.'

'Talk in French,' Verdi ordered. He came over to the table and sat at the head. He grabbed a bottle of wine. 'We all speak French. Understand?'

'Sure,' Thompson replied, and moved away.

'OK,' Klaus added.

Verdi looked at Luker.

'Yes, Corporal,' Luker said.

'Good. Now let's all eat and enjoy the meal.'

The men sat down. None of them questioned Verdi's authority or promotion. They had either accepted it or ignored it. He had yet to find out which it was to be.

'Who do you think the American girl is?' Thompson asked.

'Jackie Onassis,' Klaus said, smiling. 'And it is the Onassis family who is paying for this trip.'

'He's dead,' Fingers said.

'So? There is still his money around.'

'I think it is a film actress,' Tojak beamed. 'The Americans like their film stars. Especially their women. Who do you think it will be?'

Tojak looked thoughtful. 'Shirley Temple?' he asked.

'*Sacré bleu!*' Luker said. 'Shirley Temple!'

'Could it be the President's daughter?' Klaus asked. 'What do you think, Calowski?'

Calowski looked at Klaus from across the table. 'It is somebody important, that is for sure,' he said.

'Perhaps she will be rich and reward us all,' Fingers said.

'What with, Fingers?' Klaus asked. 'What would you want?'

'What do you mean, Klaus?' Fingers asked.

'Pieces of silver, Fingers?' Klaus suggested.

'Now you are back to the Bible again,' Luker sighed.

'What's this all about?' Tojak asked. 'I'll take anything as reward, even silver.' He looked at Malik. 'How about that, Malik?'

'I only hope you get back to enjoy it, Tojak,' Malik said.

Tojak stood up.

'You going to see I don't, Malik?'

'Sit down!' Verdi snarled. 'Sit down Tojak, or I'll make sure you don't get up again.'

Tojak looked at Verdi.

'Sit down!' Verdi ordered.

Tojak sat down and looked glum.

'I just want to get back safely,' Luker said.

'That goes for me too,' Klaus added. 'I have too promising a future to miss it.'

'In the Legion?' Thompson asked.

Klaus gave a bland smile. 'Don't ask such bloody silly questions.'

'What do you think, Verdi?' the Swede boomed across the table. 'About our chances?'

Verdi looked up at him.

'Corporal,' he said.

The Swede didn't answer.

'Corporal,' Verdi said again, with more feeling.

The men looked at the Swede. There was no love lost on him. It was the testing time. He had always been so sure of himself and of his strength.

Baron picked up a bottle of wine very slowly and said, 'Some wine, Corporal?' He had made his position clear, and nobody ever thought of crossing Baron.

Verdi looked at Svenson. The Swede capitulated.

'Corporal,' he said.

The room relaxed. Verdi was their Corporal.

'The Lieutenant seems to know his side of the business,' Verdi said to them all, 'and the Sergeant-Chief has fought in the territory before. We should be OK, if the natives don't hear us landing.'

'They'll hear us,' Baron growled. 'I have dealt with their kind before. They have a sixth sense. They will know we have arrived. They will even know we are coming.'

The room went silent again.

'Good wine, this,' Klaus said, and helped himself. 'Don't let's spoil the night. Tell us about some of your happier memories, Baron. What about the poofing?'

A smile came to Thompson's face, and the others as well. Baron had poofed in every corner of the globe, or so he boasted. He had a wealth of experience to call upon.

'Yeah!' Luker sighed. 'Tell us about it, Baron.'

The men charged their glasses. Luker looked at Klaus. Klaus was also a leader, he thought, and he had brains. Klaus saw Luker watching him, and he looked away.

Chapter Twenty-one

Lieutenant Ducan's quarters were marginally more comfortable than the men's. The hut was partitioned off into a number of rooms, and there was a small dining room, but Ducan was not interested in his quarters. He had spent the whole of the previous night at a briefing session with a unit of the U.S. Air Force. He was tired and weary. All he wanted was to retire early to his room. The Sergeant-Chief reported that the men were in their quarters.

'There is plenty of wine and food, Sergeant-Chief. Don't stand on ceremony. Help yourself. I am going to take a shower and retire early.'

'Yes, *mon Lieutenant*.'

Ducan took his shower. So did the Sergeant-Chief, but he waited until the Lieutenant had finished. Ducan went to the dining room. He would have preferred to have been alone. He had no stomach for the Sergeant-Chief's company, but he resisted his desire to retire to his room.

Schiller joined him. There was a moment's uncertainty. It was the first time that the two men had ever confronted each other off duty. It was the first time that Ducan had seen the Sergeant-Chief without his *kepi*, or any other headgear. Similarly, Schiller had always seen Ducan in full uniform. Suddenly, it was as if the two men were seeing each other in a different context.

Ducan looked tired but relaxed. His appearance was refined and genteel. His hair was dark, fine and neatly cut. He did not give any impression of the toughness, hardness and steel core that Schiller looked for in his Legion Officers. He looked the

Parisian — the academic — the gentleman soldier. He was the things that Schiller did not like in Lieutenants. And Ducan felt it.

Ducan also saw Schiller differently. Schiller did not look so formidable without his headgear. He was like Samson without his beard. His hair was fair, but cropped short in traditional Legion fashion, and he had a scar at the back of his scalp. It was another reminder of his long history of service in the Legion. Schiller was the Legion, Ducan thought, but he was the old Legion. Ducan sighed. He wished like hell that Schiller had not been forced upon him. Any other *sous-officier* would have been preferable. He knew that there was no love lost either way. The feeling of antagonism even hung heavily in the room, as if the men's personalities were in open conflict.

Ducan decided to bring their differences out into the open.

'I didn't ask for you to join me, Sergeant-Chief,' he said.

'No, *mon Lieutenant?*'

'Then why did you come?'

'It is a Legion matter, *mon Lieutenant*. I have served in the territory. The men need a *sous-officier*.'

'Bah!' Ducan snapped. 'There are plenty of other good *sous-officiers*. Why you?'

'They are my men as well as yours, *mon Lieutenant*,' Schiller grunted, and stood his ground defiantly. 'It is natural that I should want to be with them.'

'To protect them?'

'Perhaps, *mon Lieutenant*.'

'What are you really concerned about, Sergeant-Chief?' Ducan asked. 'That the men will let the Legion down?'

'The men will not let the Legion down, *mon Lieutenant*. They are trained legionnaires, and I am here to remind them.'

Ducan hesitated in drinking his wine. Schiller had replied with feeling. He had left Ducan in no doubt of his concern. It was not the men that Schiller feared would fail the Legion, it was Ducan! Ducan smiled at the thought, and his eyes twinkled, as if the Sergeant-Chief's frankness had amused him.

He stood up, and still with a smile, said, 'We will see if your fears are justified, Sergeant-Chief.'

He walked away. Schiller watched him. He was not smiling, but neither was Ducan. Ducan's eyes had lost some of their sparkle.

Chapter Twenty-two

The men braced themselves. There was a *thud* and the aircraft wheels hit the ground. The aircraft shuddered, and every joint in its construction took the strain. It ran over the ground. The men clung to the straps. Gradually it reduced speed, and the shaking became less violent. The men relaxed. They had arrived at their destination. They were in Africa. The aircraft came to a halt. There was a feeling of relief in the dimly lit cabin. The men had been cooped up in the cabin for six hours. There had been one long stop on the journey, but the men had not been allowed to leave the aircraft. They had suffered the journey. Now they were ready to get under way.

One of the Greek crewman opened the hatch door, and the warm, roasted air of Africa drifted into the cabin. The men saw a dark, starry sky and collected their equipment. A ladder was lowered. One by one, they disembarked. They gathered together and stood adjusting their eyes to the darkness. They saw dark shapes all around them and felt the warm, airless, breeze that would turn cold during the night, and they felt the vastness of their surroundings.

Schiller went amongst them, quietly checking that they had all their equipment and were ready to move off. When he was satisfied, he reported to Ducan. Ducan was studying his compass.

'Ready to move off, *mon Lieutenant.*'

'Good.'

Ducan made a last check of his compass bearing and started their march. They walked in single file with Ducan in the lead and Schiller bringing up the rear.

They had only gone a short distance when they heard the aircraft taking off. Ducan did not stop. He kept the men going. The aircraft roared into the sky.

Thompson whispered, 'Why not send a bloody telegram?'

'Silence,' Schiller hissed from the rear of the line, but the men had all been thinking the same. The aircraft had been very noisy, and its sound would travel far.

Ducan kept a steady pace. The sky was clear and starry, and a deep, navy blue. There was a quarter, crescent shaped moon, which gave just sufficient light for them to pick their way. The ground was firm underfoot with a loose, dusty surface, but there were cracks and small crevices in the baked surface that would catch them unawares, and in the dark shadows all around them were prickly thorn bushes that seemed to grab at their packs and clothing as they walked past them.

The night was neither silent nor still. There was an incessant clicking noise from the nocturnal insects, and the warm breeze carried its own insects with it. The men were constantly brushing them from their faces.

After an hour, Ducan halted the column. The men rested. Nobody spoke. Schiller was there to see that they kept silent. After five minutes' rest, Ducan started the march again. It was the Legion's pace — one hour's march, five minutes' rest. Occasionally, one of the men would catch his foot and stumble, and Schiller would be quick to get him on his feet again.

They passed through several broad depressions that looked like dried up wadis, in which the ground was much softer and free of the bushes.

The night passed slowly. Ducan kept to the steady pace. The men kept silent. The terrain did not vary. Only the warm breeze gradually lowered its temperature, which the men felt when they rested. Towards midnight, they came to another wadi. Ducan halted the column and told Schiller that the men could have a thirty minute rest and eat some of their rations. Schiller gave the orders in a hushed voice. The men took off their packs and lay on the ground.

'Easy on the water,' Schiller warned. 'You're going to need it.'

The men got out a ration pack.

'Don't leave any wrappings,' Verdi hissed.

'Sure, Corporal,' Klaus sighed. 'Not as good as Signor Spiro's other dishes, but I suppose we will get used to them.'

'There are some packets of coffee and milk,' Malik said. 'They must think that we are on a safari.'

'Some safari,' Thompson muttered.

Schiller came amongst them.

'Luker, Svenson,' he said. 'Take *sentinelle*, one North and one South.'

The men collected their gear.

'How much further are we marching, Sergeant-Chief?' Klaus asked. 'I'm getting bored with the scenery.'

'Till you drop,' Schiller growled, 'and then you crawl.' He moved away.

'Bastard,' Klaus hissed.

A sudden swirl of breeze brought up the dust. '*Merde!*' Tojak swore. 'It is dry enough without the dust.'

The men cursed the breeze, and the grit that got into their food.

'Is it always cold at night?' Malik asked Baron. 'Always,' Baron grunted. 'It is like a furnace in the day, even the rocks crack with the heat, but at night it can be as cold as inside a refrigerator.'

'And the bloody breeze,' Thompson grunted.

'It is the summer monsoons,' Klaus said. 'It brings the rains, but not to these parts.'

'You know a lot about it,' Verdi said. 'You been to Africa before?'

'Sure, I've been to Africa. I always take my winter holiday in Africa — Tunisia preferably.'

'Not this year you won't,' Fingers chipped in.

Klaus looked at him.

'We shall see,' he muttered.

He stood up and walked away. Calowski watched him.

The Sergeant-Chief came amongst them.

'Five minutes,' he growled. 'Leave nothing behind. See to it, Corporal.'

'Yes, Sergeant-Chief.'

The men collected their gear. Schiller re-distributed the loads that they were carrying. Some had extra water rations and some had explosives. The machine guns were exchanged for automatic rifles. The men accepted their new loads without comment. Schiller reported to Lieutenant Ducan.

'We still have a long way to go,' Ducan warned.

They resumed their march. The men marched stoically as they had been trained. The scenery did not change, the temperature dropped and the men had to wear extra clothing. The only relief was that they were not plagued with insects when the breeze became cooler. As dawn approached, and the dark navy of the sky became a lighter shade, the men could see the distant mass of rocks that they had studied on the photographs. They were a dark line on the horizon, as if the earth had suddenly been uplifted by several hundred metres. The top of the hills looked flat like a plateau.

Ducan halted the column. The men took off their packs. Schiller, as always, reported to the Lieutenant.

'The men?' Ducan asked.

'One or two scratches from the bushes, *mon Lieutenant.*'

'They have marched well.'

'They are legionnaires, *mon Lieutenant.*'

Ducan sighed. Schiller never gave up, he thought.

'We must find some cover, before the sun attacks us.'

He studied the foreground with his binoculars. It looked unyielding.

'If necessary, we will have to use the sleeping bags as tents,' he grunted.

Again they marched, but now they could see a large, flaming ball poking its head over the horizon to the East. It cast a red and orange glow all along the horizon. It looked hot, and it looked angry. There was beauty in its shades of colour, but there was also a warning, and the temperature of the breeze had started to rise sharply. The men began to perspire.

Suddenly, Ducan halted the column. The men saw him study the foreground with his binoculars. They waited, glad of the unexpected rest.

'There is a small native kraal, Sergeant-Chief,' Ducan explained to Schiller. 'About four kilometres away.'

He handed Schiller the binoculars. Schiller saw the tops of a cluster of mud huts. He returned the binoculars to the Lieutenant.

'They haven't got our scent, *mon Lieutenant,*' he grunted.

'No, that is strange. They all have dogs. They usually pick up the scent.'

'A trap, *mon Lieutenant?*'

'I think they have gone to the hills.'

'The aircraft?'

'Or the lack of water.'

'They usually take their huts with them, *mon Lieutenant*,' Schiller growled.

'Yes, they do.'

Ducan frowned. It was unusual for the natives to leave their village deserted.

'Send one man to investigate, Sergeant-Chief.'

'Yes, *mon Lieutenant*.'

Schiller went back along the line. Verdi was sent forward. The rest waited and watched the dawn explode. The dark ridge on the horizon had now taken shape. They could see the irregular face of the rock hills that made a natural frontier. They also saw each other's grubby appearance. They were covered with a layer of dirty, yellow dust. They sat silently, and began to perspire.

Presently, Verdi returned and reported to Ducan.

'It is deserted, *mon Lieutenant*.'

'Recently?'

'The fire embers are cold. The animal droppings are dried up.'

'In this country, everything dries up in minutes,' Ducan said. 'Thank you, Corporal.'

Verdi returned to his position in the line. Schiller was beside Ducan, waiting for Ducan to make his decision. Ducan looked at the ball of fire that was approaching, and made his decision.

'We use the village for cover, Sergeant-Chief. The men can get some rest. We can't march in the heat of the day.'

'And if it was the aircraft that sent them away, *mon Lieutenant*?'

'Then we might get some visitors. Post *sentinelles* and make sure they keep awake.'

'They will keep awake, *mon Lieutenant*.'

They moved forward again, through the bushes that came up to their knees and thighs. Some over-towered them. The area had a thick growth of vegetation. There were even tufted lumps of strong, yellow grass. Close to the kraal was a deep, dry wadi. Its bottom was soft and not baked hard like the plain. Ducan halted the column in the wadi and the men took cover. Ducan approached the kraal alone. There were six mud and wattle beehive huts, set in no particular pattern. They were sited on a flat, open area close to the wadi. The ground in the village was stripped bare of any vegetation, but the surrounding area had bushes and tufted, sandy grass. Ducan inspected the huts. They stank of human and animal excreta, but they would offer protection from the sun, he thought. He studied the hills with his binoculars and the surrounding plain. It was a barren, desolate wilderness. There was no sign of life — but there was life, he thought, and the natives would be watching them. What the Sergeant-Chief had said was true. The nomads did not leave their huts behind. They always took them with them.

He returned to the men. Two were on *sentinelle*. He went up to the Sergeant-Chief and spoke in a voice that the men would also hear.

'Soon the sun will be like a laser beam,' he said. 'We must have cover. The huts are filthy and foul, but they will protect us. We will use only three. There are three close together. We can then warn each other, if necessary. We must have a constant lookout. The men can eat one of their rations, and use half a canteen of water.'

'The natives, *mon Lieutenant*? Have they been gone long?'

'There is no way of telling. The ground in this wadi is soft. There has been water here. They could have decided to move closer to the mountains.'

'And their huts?'

'If they intended to return in a few days, or weeks, they would leave them,' Ducan said. He saw no point in alarming the men. 'They don't usually get visitors.'

He turned away. He did not want to discuss the situation further. The party moved into the village. It had been a long night; the men were weary. Schiller detailed them to their huts and gave them their tour of *sentinelle* duty.

'Don't exceed your water ration,' he warned, 'and no smoking. Keep your eyes open when you are on duty, or God help us. We'll all have our balls cut off.'

The men went to the huts. Ducan, Schiller, Baron and Calowski took one. Corporal Verdi, Klaus, Thompson and Fingers another. In the third one was Tojak, Svenson, Malik and Luker.

'*Mon Dieu*,' Klaus hissed. 'The stench.'

'No smoking, Corporal?' Thompson asked hopefully.

'No smoking,' Verdi grunted.

'*Merde*,' Klaus went on. 'It is all bloody *merde*.'

'And animal droppings, Klaus,' Fingers said.

'It is all *merde* to me,' Klaus snapped.

'Put your sleeping bags on it,' Verdi ordered, 'and get some sleep. You won't notice it when you are asleep.'

'Then I'll dream about it.'

The men were all repulsed by the stench and the droppings that covered the ground. The huts were all the same.

'*Mon Dieu*,' Malik said. 'The filth.'

'Not like home — eh, Malik?' Tojak retorted.

'You might be used to living in *merde*, Tojak, but I'm not.'

Tojak swung around on him. The two men faced each other angrily.

'Save your fighting for the guerrillas,' Luker sighed. 'It's bad enough in here without making it worse.'

'That is so,' Svenson added in his stilted French accent. 'Let's get some rest.'

Malik lay back. So did Tojak. Malik stared at the filthy wattle above his head, and knew that he would have to watch out for Tojak if there was any shooting.

In Ducan's hut, there was no reference made to their conditions. There was only silence. Ducan and the Sergeant-Chief had nothing to talk about, and Calowski and Baron were never ones for conversation.

They lay on their sleeping bags and felt the perspiration begin to pour out of their bodies as the temperature rose.

The men tried to sleep, but in addition to the stench and the heat, the mud wattle walls and roofs seemed to harbour a host of minute insects that occasionally fell on the men and caused a further irritation. But the burning sun that baked everything bone dry blazed down from a cloudless sky, and they were all glad of the cover.

They eventually slept in their pools of perspiration. Ducan slept fitfully. He was weary, tired, but suddenly conscious of his responsibility. It was a new experience for him. He had always been a loner. Now he had the men to think of. He knew they wouldn't think for themselves. There was also the success of the mission. Lying in the stinking mud hut, it was all in front of him.

'*Mon Lieutenant!*'

The call disturbed Ducan's rest. Ducan was awake instantly. For a second he focused his eyes. His brain told him he was in the native hut. He felt the perspiration roll down his face and caught the sharp stench of the excreta.

'*Mon Lieutenant!*'

It was the Sergeant-Chief. His face was only centimetres away from the Lieutenant's.

'We have a visitor, *mon Lieutenant.*'

Ducan sat upright. He saw Calowski looking through a hole in a side of the wattle wall. Baron, the Belgian, was sitting upright on his sleeping bag with an expressionless look on his face.

'In the distance, *mon Lieutenant*, but coming this way.'

Ducan went to where Calowski was crouched. Calowski handed him the binoculars. Ducan wiped the perspiration from his eyes and studied the foreground.

'Towards the escarpment, *mon Lieutenant*,' Calowski said.

The ground danced in front of Ducan's eyes. There was a heat wave shimmering across the ground. It was all tufted yellow vegetation and small bushes. He saw a small cloud of dust and a dark moving figure. The figure was bent, stooped, and trotting over the ground with a slow, waltzing gait. Ducan lowered his binoculars and handed them back to Calowski.

'He has come from the hills,' he said. 'He could belong to the tribe who left this kraal.'

'Or Azir's camp, *mon Lieutenant*,' Schiller replied. 'He could be one of his scouts. If they heard the aircraft.'

Ducan sat on his sleeping bag. The Sergeant-Chief was waiting for his orders. Ducan was alone, again.

'Warn one man from each hut, Sergeant-Chief. We will let the native come into kraal. I will talk to him. Then we will get our answer.'

'Yes, *mon Lieutenant.*'

Schiller crawled out of the hut on all fours. He returned and took up a position alongside Calowski.

'He's getting close, *mon Lieutenant*,' he warned, 'but his pace is slower.'

Ducan didn't reply.

'They have an uncanny sixth sense, these bastards,' Schiller grunted. 'They can sense our presence.'

He was thinking aloud. 'What do we do if he doesn't enter the village, *mon Lieutenant?*'

Ducan had already been wrestling with that problem. 'If he continues North, we let him go.'

'And if he starts to turn South, *mon Lieutenant?* It would be no good sending anybody after him. They would never catch him.'

Schiller took the binoculars from Calowski.

'Let us wait and see, Sergeant-Chief,' Ducan said. 'You won't have to wait long. He is suspicious.' Ducan still didn't move.

'He is only a few hundred metres away, *mon Lieutenant.*' Ducan felt the perspiration on his body turn cold and shivered.

'*Mon Lieutenant!*' Schiller hissed.

Ducan went to the hole. He saw the stooped figure of the native walking hesitantly towards them. He was a slim, black warrior with a loose fitting brown cloak and a mop of black, curly hair. Suddenly he stopped, studied the ground, and then about turned.

'He's got our scent. He'll warn them,' Schiller growled. 'We must stop him, *mon Lieutenant.*'

'Yes,' Ducan agreed.

Schiller turned to Calowski. 'Get him!' he ordered.

'No!' Ducan intervened.

'But…'

'Give me your rifle, Calowski,' Ducan snapped.

'*Mon Lieutenant!*' Schiller called out.

Ducan took the rifle out of Calowski's hands. He poked the nozzle through the hole in the wattle. He took aim. The poor miserable creature, he thought. Why couldn't he have kept away?

Why…? *Crack!*

The figure lurched forward and fell face down on the ground.

There was a moment's silence in the stinking hut.

Ducan withdrew the rifle and silently handed it back to Calowski.

Schiller took over.

'Calowski, you stay here. Baron, come with me.' Schiller left the hut. Baron followed. Schiller went to the other huts. Svenson joined the party.

Malik suddenly sat upright. He saw the smiling face of the Slav, Tojak, watching him. Tojak was cleaning his machine gun. He grinned.

'Restless, Malik?' he asked, and continued cleaning his machine gun.

'There was a shot,' Malik said.

'It was *Monsieur le Lieutenant*, having some shooting practice.'

Luker had also sat up. 'What happened, Tojak?'

'We had a visitor. He turned and ran away. We couldn't let him leave us, so…'

Malik looked out of the small peep hole and saw Schiller and his party examining the body.

'Poor bastard,' he said.

'It could be you, Malik,' Tojak grinned.

Malik turned on him.

'You like killing, Tojak, don't you? This life suits you.'

'Why else would I join the Legion?'

'I thought you joined to get away from your pigs.' Tojak rubbed the barrel of his machine gun and gave a deep chuckle.

'You don't sleep well, Malik.'

Malik sighed.

'It's the heat,' he said.

'Sure,' Luker agreed. 'The heat makes us all jumpy.' In the other hut, the men also awoke.

'What gives?' Thompson asked.

Verdi explained.

'Who shot him?' Fingers asked.

'*Monsieur le Lieutenant*,' Verdi said. 'He is a first class shot.'

'Bloody insects,' Klaus grumbled, 'and this heat.' He went for his water bottle.

'Take it easy,' Verdi warned. 'It's a long afternoon.'

'Sure, Corporal.'

Klaus lay back in his perspiration.

'I dreamt I was at the Carlton in Cannes,' he said. 'Drinking iced champagne.'

'The Carlton?' Fingers asked. 'You stayed there?'

Klaus frowned. 'Only in my dreams,' he said.

'They must know we are here,' Thompson said, 'if he was one of their scouts.'

'If he was,' Klaus said.

'What do you mean?' Verdi asked.

'He could have belonged to this village, and just come back to collect one of his huts.'

'Yeah! He could,' Fingers agreed. 'Poor bastard.'

'The Sergeant-Chief must have thought otherwise, and the Lieutenant.'

Thompson studied the hills. They looked like a flat topped wall that wove an uneven path across the horizon.

'So that is what we have come to cross,' he sighed, and wiped the sweat from his neck.

'It will be something to tell your kids about,' Klaus said.

'Get some rest,' Verdi ordered. 'All of you. I'm going to see what's going on.'

Schiller and his party silently examined the still black form, and then quickly started to bury him to prevent the birds of prey attacking and attracting attention. The sun blazed down on them as they scratched at the ground with their hand tools.

When he was satisfied, Schiller ordered the men back to their cover. He went to report to Lieutenant Ducan.

Ducan was not in the hut.

'Where is *Monsieur le Lieutenant?*' he asked Calowski. Calowski pointed to one of the empty huts. Schiller frowned. He suddenly expected the worst. He went to the hut and stood in its entrance. Ducan was inside. He was sitting with his body bent and his hands tightly clenched around his knees. There was a smell of vomit.

Schiller's eyes narrowed. He clenched his fists. Ducan looked up at him. His face was pale and tense. Schiller's face hardened and he turned his back on him.

'Sergeant-Chief!' Ducan hissed through clenched teeth.

Schiller stood quite still.

'Sergeant-Chief!' Ducan hissed again.

Schiller turned on him.

'Why did you do it, *mon Lieutenant?*' he demanded. 'Why? The men have been trained to kill.'

Ducan gave a grunt.

'It was my decision,' he said, tight-lipped. 'It was my duty.'

'The mission is also your duty, *mon Lieutenant*. That is more important.'

Ducan gripped his bent knees to stop his body from shaking. Schiller stood watching and waiting.

'Tell me about him,' Ducan hissed.

'He was riddled with disease. He…'

'Never mind that,' Ducan interrupted with difficulty. 'Was he one of them, damn you?'

'Yes, *mon Lieutenant*, he was one of them. He had an automatic rifle and two bandoliers. His rifle was Belgian. He was also wearing some form of uniform.'

Ducan grunted and gripped his knees again. He dropped his head.

'What are your orders, *mon Lieutenant*?' Schiller asked.

Ducan didn't reply.

'Your orders!' Schiller urged. 'Your orders, *mon Lieutenant*.'

Ducan looked up at him. He saw a look of concern on the Sergeant-Chief's face. He had expected to see something else. He dropped his eyes.

'We move out soon,' he said haltingly, as if forcing the words out of his mouth. 'Time is against us. We move in three hours.'

'Yes, *mon Lieutenant*,' Schiller grunted.

He left the hut and stood in the open. His fists were clenched tight and his face looked black. He did not feel the hot sun, or see Verdi standing close by. He was thinking of Ducan and the mission.

'His first kill?' Verdi whispered.

Schiller swung around and saw the cynical smile on the Corporal's face. Schiller pulled him to one side.

'Well?' he growled.

'Perhaps *Monsieur le Lieutenant* will not be as clever as we imagined, Sergeant-Chief,' Verdi said, again with the smile on his lips. 'He doesn't like to kill.'

Schiller's face looked angry. He grabbed Verdi by the jacket and pulled him close.

'I suppose you celebrated your first kill,' he snarled. 'You have seen nothing, Verdi. You remember that, and remember also that the Lieutenant didn't ask anybody else to do his killing. You understand?'

He pushed Verdi away from him. 'I have ways of finding out if you talk out of turn,' he warned. 'Now tell the men we move out in three hours.'

Verdi scowled and quickly went to carry out Schiller's orders.

Svenson had returned to his hut and sat on his sleeping bag. '*Le miserable*,' he said, referring to the native warrior. '*Le miserable*. His eyes were yellow and his body covered with sores. *Mon Dieu*. What a life they live.'

'Malaria,' Luker suggested. 'He must have been riddled with it.'

'He was one of them?' Tojak asked.

'Yes, he was armed.'

'That means they will have a reception committee,' Tojak added.

He continued to clean his machine gun. The men sat in silence. Svenson looked glum.

Verdi entered the hut.

'We move in three hours,' he said, and left them.

'Three hours,' Malik sighed. 'I could sleep all day.'

'You might sleep forever soon,' Tojak suggested with a snigger.

Malik looked up at him. Tojak grinned. The barrel of his machine gun was pointing at Malik.

Malik looked away and lay in his sweat.

Verdi returned to his own hut.

'Three hours,' he grunted. 'Then we move.'

'Was he one of Azir's men?' Thompson asked.

'Yes.'

'Ah well,' Klaus sighed. 'That should give *Monsieur le Lieutenant* something to think about.'

Verdi gave of laugh of derision.

'I don't think *Monsieur Napoleon* is thinking about that at the moment.'

'What do you mean, Corporal?' Fingers asked. He was always quick to learn anything about the other men. His eyes seemed to light up with interest.

'Nothing,' Verdi snapped. 'Forget it.'

Thompson studied the hills thoughtfully.

'Those hills look deserted,' he said. 'It surprises me that anybody can live in them.'

'Underground wells,' Klaus said. 'Something to do with the strata.'

'You know a thing or two, Klaus,' Verdi grunted.

'Not very much, Corporal, or else I wouldn't be here.'

'You have five years of it as well, Klaus,' Fingers pointed out.

Klaus turned on him.

'You are a charming bastard, Fingers.'

'You needn't have five years,' Verdi suggested.

'What do we do?' Klaus sneered. 'Signal the next bus to take us to Nairobi or Cairo?'

'*Le Lieutenant* showed you the route, North into Eritrea. You could get a ship to anywhere.'

'They would ship us back to Djibouti. The Legion would see to that.'

'How can they?' Verdi asked. 'We are not legionnaires. We are all mercenaries. *Monsieur le Lieutenant* told us so. We are legally not in *la Légion*!'

Fingers' eyes lit up.

'Yeah, that is so,' he said. 'That's true, Klaus.'

Klaus made no comment. Thompson silently studied the hills.

'*Monsieur le Lieutenant* did show us the route, Klaus,' Fingers added, breaking the silence.

'It's a long walk,' Klaus grumbled. 'You need supplies. How long do you think it would take?'

'All you need in this country to survive is water,' Verdi said, 'and there is water in the mountains.'

'We could find it, Klaus,' Fingers said. 'I'm sure we could. There is game in the mountains as well as water.'

Klaus looked at him.

'You would come with me, Fingers?' he asked. 'You would come?'

'Yeah, Klaus. I would come. So would some of the others.'

Klaus looked pensive, then suddenly his face clouded over.

'And *Monsieur le Lieutenant*?' he asked, 'and the Sergeant-Chief? What about them?'

Verdi shrugged.

'You make your choice,' he said. 'You are grumbling about having to serve five years. I am telling you of an alternative.'

'Thanks,' Klaus said. 'It's an interesting thought.'

He lay back in his pool of perspiration and kept brushing away the insects that fell onto his body, and wiping the perspiration from his face. The heat and the insects seemed to be bothering him more than the others.

'What do you think, Thompson?' Verdi asked.

'As Klaus has just said, it's an interesting thought.'

A figure appeared in the doorway. They all turned sharply. It was Calowski.

'What do you want?' Verdi snapped.

'Fingers is to take watch in the Sergeant-Chief's hut,' Calowski said.

He came into the middle of the hut. Fingers picked up his rifle. Verdi grabbed him.

'Careful,' he hissed. He brought the barrel of his rifle to point at Fingers' face. 'Be very careful,' he warned.

'Sure, Corporal. Sure.'

Verdi released his hold. Fingers left the hut. Calowski took his place and lay down. He stared at the roof of the hut.

'What do you see, Calowski?' Verdi asked.

'Trouble, Corporal,' Calowski replied, and closed his eyes. 'Lots of trouble,' he sighed.

The others lay down and remained silent. They also sensed trouble.

Chapter Twenty-three

Schiller looked at his watch. Three hours had passed. The sun was still hot, but it had passed its peak. In a few hours, it would be dark. They should be moving out, there was no time to lose, but he did not move. It was up to Ducan to give the order, not him. Ducan was the Lieutenant. He was the officer in charge. Schiller could only make suggestions, but he did not want to go to Ducan again. Not again. He felt his insides go hard. He wanted Ducan to come to him. He had to come. He had to! They needed an officer. They needed someone to lead them. They needed Ducan. Damn him, he thought angrily. Damn him!

'Sergeant-Chief!'

Schiller started. The call had taken him by surprise. It was Ducan. Schiller looked up to see him standing in the entrance to the hut. He looked pale and his eyes were drawn.

Schiller got to his feet immediately.

'We move off, Sergeant-Chief,' Ducan said, and left the hut.

Schiller took a deep breath. 'Move it,' he snapped at the two men in the hut. 'Move it!'

The two legionnaires started collecting their gear together. Schiller went to the other huts and quickly gave the orders. He saw Ducan studying the ground with his binoculars. He went up to him, but he did not speak. He waited and watched.

Ducan felt Schiller's presence and sensed his feelings. Ducan had shown weakness, and Schiller was insensitive to weakness, or gentleness. He was all Legion.

Ducan continued to study the horizon.

'See that the men cover all the exposed parts of their body,' he ordered flatly, 'and check their water canteens. It is going to be a long night.'

'Yes, *mon Lieutenant*,' Schiller replied.

Momentarily, Ducan lowered his binoculars. There hadn't been the expected edge in Schiller's response. His tone had more the sound of relief about it than of contempt. He turned and saw Schiller setting about the men with vigour. He watched him thoughtfully. Perhaps he had got Schiller wrong.

Ducan started the march. He kept a fast pace and a grim face. He rarely looked back. He set his eyes on his target and kept checking his compass. The men followed behind. Schiller brought up the rear. He kept glancing behind him and towards the hills, as if expecting company. But the only company was the sun, the flies and the constant hot breeze that swirled the dust and insects into the men's faces. Soon they became covered with the yellow dust and they stopped trying to keep their faces clean.

Ducan kept to the drill. He stopped on the hour, when he would sit by himself and study his photographs and his maps. Schiller left him alone. He knew that the Lieutenant was still uptight. After three hours' march, the sun began its descent. They were close enough now to the hills to see the huge boulders and sheer face of the rocks that had been eroded by years of the constant wind. They were dirty, white and yellow in colour. A rocky, inert, lifeless barrier that looked more uninviting than the scrub. The ground over which they were marching was still marked with shrubs and tufts of coarse grass, but the bushes were less numerous and did not catch at the men's clothing. But the men had suffered during the three hours in the sun. Their lips and throats were parched, and they felt a physical weariness that they had never felt in Corsica. The terrain was taking its toll on them.

'At this pace, we will all be dead before we get to Azir's camp,' Klaus grumbled at one of their few halts.

'Any man that can't keep up will be left behind,' Schiller warned. They knew that he meant it, and it kept them marching.

Ducan had walked as if oblivious of the men, and he had been oblivious of them. He had been deeply troubled over the killing of the native scout. The thought of it had gone round and round in his mind. It had been his first killing. It had been something that he had never expected. Life was precious to him. To take it made his stomach rebel. His challenge had come unexpectedly. It had been upon him before he had fully realised it. Perhaps they could have captured the warrior, he thought. Perhaps he could have questioned him. Perhaps — there were a lot of perhaps, but the incident had happened. There was no going back. There never was, and he knew that. It had happened and he had to accept it and live with it. It had been Allah's will, he thought sadly, over and over again. It was all Allah's will.

After three hours of marching, he also felt the weariness that the men felt, but he started the march again, hoping to reach the hills before darkness fell. His legs moved automatically and his thoughts of the dead warrior became numbed. His mind seemed to have exhausted itself of its anguish as his body had suffered in the sun and tired itself physically. Instead of the dead warrior, his thought turned to Marcel Poujet in Paris and their talks together. It was all Poujet's doing that he was now on the mission, he thought. It had been Poujet who had sent him to the Legion. It was probably Poujet who had recommended him for the assignment, but the mission had been unexpected. Poujet had made that clear at Ducan's briefing. So just what had Poujet in mind when they talked together in Paris? What had he been planning? Some other wild adventure into the border territories? Or had it been the men that had interested him? Get to know the men and the ways of the Legion, he had said. Ducan wiped the grime from his face and sighed. He had got to know the ways of the Legion, he thought. He was now part of it! And the men? He knew his men, but only superficially. He knew how physically fit they were, and of their military skills, but it was difficult to get beneath the surface with them. The ways of the Legion did not permit it.

A swirling cloud of dust suddenly engulfed him. It got into his nostrils and parched his throat. It irritated him. It was another discomfort to add to the other irritations brought on by his weariness. It made him feel a sudden resentment of Poujet and his shadowy dealings. Poujet was in Paris and in comfort. Ducan was in the scrub and doing the killing. To hell with Poujet, he thought. To hell with them all. He would see this mission through and then they could all go to hell. They could do their own dirty work in future.

He glanced up at the sky and saw the fading ball of fire. He stopped the column. He took a fix with his compass. They were getting close to their objective. Schiller reported to him.

'We take thirty minutes rest, Sergeant-Chief. Let the men drink and eat.'

He spoke crisply, and Schiller noticed that some of the sadness had left his eyes. In its place he saw a look of annoyance.

'Yes, *mon Lieutenant*,' he said with enthusiasm. 'Are we close?'

'We are, Sergeant-Chief. No smoking, no lights.'

Schiller went to the men. He also gave his orders crisply and decisively.

'What's got into the Sergeant-Chief?' Svenson asked. 'He seems to be enjoying himself.'

'He scents the kill,' Tojak said. 'He knows we are getting close.' He leaned over to where Malik was seated. 'We are getting close,' he said. 'You stay with me, Malik. I will look after you.'

Malik looked at him.

'If I stay close to you, Tojak,' he said. 'I'll make sure I don't turn my back on you.'

Tojak chuckled his delight.

'You do that,' he said. 'You do just that.'

'You two still at it?' Klaus said. 'What gives between you and Tojak?'

Malik shrugged. 'Tojak must have his reason, but he is keeping it to himself. It keeps him occupied.' He lay on the ground. 'Otherwise he might have other thoughts.'

Klaus ate his rations.

'Meaning?' he asked.

'I hear Corporal Verdi has become an expert on our legal status.'

Klaus grunted and took a drink from his water bottle.

'It's a strange thing,' he said. 'We have been on the go for four hours. Nobody appears to have talked to anybody, yet suddenly everybody knows everything. I bet even our Sergeant-Chief will have heard about our Corporal's thoughts.'

'He probably heard first.'

Klaus looked at Fingers, who sat opposite them, and scowled. 'Yeah,' he said. 'He'll know.'

'What do you think, Klaus?' Malik whispered.

'The quickest way out of this bloody country for me,' Klaus said. 'I'm beginning to hate this place.' He lay back and closed his eyes, as if the subject was closed.

The others had also heard about Verdi's comments, but nobody discussed them, and when the blanket of darkness fell over them, they were forgotten. The darkness brought the insect noises, and a strange feeling of loneliness. The men sat in silence.

'Check your weapons,' Schiller ordered in a quiet voice. 'We move out.'

The next two hours brought them to the huge boulders that lay at the foot of the steep escarpment. They were large, dark masses of rocks that towered over the men. Ducan had reduced the pace. He was picking his way carefully, as if expecting trouble from every shadow.

Suddenly he halted. They had come to a point where the dark escarpment ran away from them and the open plain faced them again.

The men gripped their weapons and watched their fronts. They waited. For several minutes, Ducan sat as if listening to the night sounds. Schiller went up to him but remained silent. The sky was a navy blue and starry. The warm breeze wafted the roasted air into their faces. Ducan silently drew a half circle in the loose sand. He marked the ground, and in hushed tones, explained their position.

'We are here,' he said, marking the ground on the edge of the semicircle. 'Azir's camp is here.' He marked a point near the top of the half circle. 'About four kilometres.'

Schiller looked across the ground. There was nothing to see except bushes and scrub and the distant blackness.

'No sound,' Ducan said. 'They usually have dogs that bark all night.'

'And animals, *mon Lieutenant.*'

Ducan didn't like it. If the scout had been sent to investigate, it meant that they had got wind of the aircraft.

Suddenly, the silence was shattered by an eerie, baying call. Schiller went back to the men.

'Hyena,' he whispered.

The baying continued. The men gripped their rifles.

'Not the sweetest of love calls,' Klaus muttered.

Schiller went back to Ducan.

'Three parties,' Ducan said. 'You take the outhouse. One party will cover you. I will take the main building.' He paused. 'We shoot to kill — everybody except women and children.'

He had spoken calmly. He showed no embarrassment for his earlier show of feelings. Nor did he feel it any longer. He had accepted the ways of the country. He was accepting his challenge.

'They could be waiting for us in the cover of the escarpment,' he went on. 'We will go in from the front. Away from the rocks. There will still be plenty of cover.'

Schiller grunted his approval.

'And if they are still waiting for us behind their wall, *mon Lieutenant?*' he asked.

'We all veer to the left flank and make for the outhouse. We will hold the outhouse at all costs.'

Schiller returned to the men. They were split into three parties. Corporal Verdi was in charge of one of them, Schiller and Ducan the others. Each party had a machine gun, and each man carried four grenades strapped to his webbing, in addition to their automatic rifles.

Ducan led them away from their cover, across the face of the open ground. He kept low, running from bush to bush. The men followed. Slowly he moved into the inlet, occasionally stopping and listening. He did not like it at all. He had a growing feeling that something had gone wrong. They moved towards the head of the inlet. The cover became sparse. The ground was more fertile and was covered with a layer of wiry grass, but there were fewer bushes. Ducan halted the column again. The men kept close to the ground. Schiller crept up beside Ducan. Ahead of them they could see the silhouette of Azir's stronghold. It was a dark, irregular outline of buildings, palm trees and large bushes. It was the sight of an oasis in a desert. It looked unreal, like an artificial stage setting.

'No animals,' Ducan whispered. He picked up a handful of animal droppings and threw it away. 'Not a sound from their sheep or cattle. I don't like it.'

'Where could they have gone to?' Schiller grunted.

'It's a big country,' Ducan sighed. There was a feeling of despair in his voice.

'It could be a trap.'

'It could. We move closer to the left. There is more cover, but we will keep clear of the escarpment. They could be hiding there.'

They moved quickly now, with heads bent. They were within range of Azir's camp. The men had all seen it on the photographs and they had heard Ducan's suspicions. They were wary. They knew there could be a trap.

As they came closer to the dark mass of bushes and buildings, they came across a broad irrigation ditch that seemed to cross the inlet. They took cover in it. The ground was soft and mushy. There was water about. The men felt a sense of relief at the thought. Water meant life, even to them after such a short time in the territory.

The dark mass of shrubs and bushes were only a few hundred metres away from them. They were behind a small earth wall that enclosed the area and made it like a small estate. The house and estate had belonged to a wealthy tribesman who had got tired of his settled life and returned to his wanderings. Since then it had been allowed to fall into disarray, but it was a popular place for the nomads. It had water and a means of existence for their cattle.

Ducan remembered all this as he lay in the ditch. He remembered, and he knew that he had arrived too late. They had cleared out. Suddenly, a dog started barking. It was a shrill, impatient bark.

Ducan did not delay. 'Quick,' he called out. 'We go in!'

'Move it!' Schiller shouted. 'Move it! Pronto!'

The dog did not give up. Its bark continued. The men reacted according to their training. They ran from cover to cover. Ducan's party went to the front, Schiller's and Verdi's to the left flank.

Ducan came to the small wall. The yapping dog continued to give its signal. Ducan jumped over the wall. Tojak, Svenson and Fingers were with him.

They darted through the bushes. The dog's bark was louder. At the edge of the bushes, they saw the dog and the buildings. The dog was tied to a pole in the centre of a mud baked clearing. It was straining at a lead. It had done its job well. Beyond the clearing was the two storey building with a row of single storey outhouses on either wing. Even in the semi darkness they looked crude and primitive. Ducan saw Schiller's party move to the outhouse. The dog barked aggressively. Ducan moved his party forward. He darted across the open ground expecting a burst of rifle fire to greet them. He heard the dog give a whine, and then become silent. He came to the building. The other three crouched alongside the wall. Ducan turned. He saw Verdi's men move into the bushes. Ducan darted into the open doorway; the others followed. He gripped his rifle, but there was no reaction. There was no one about. He stood quite still. They were in a large square room. It was empty and had a stench of animal and human bodies. In one corner was a staircase to the upper floors. There were a number of openings that once had doors. Now they were just openings.

Ducan stood in the dim light. Tojak came up to him.

'Do we search, *mon Lieutenant*?' he asked.

'Yes, but be careful of booby-traps.'

Tojak and the other two started their search. Ducan felt a surge of anger and frustration. He had got to his goal and the birds had flown. He was too late!

Tojak returned. 'Deserted, *mon Lieutenant*. Completely empty.'

Ducan went to the entrance doorway and stood in the opening. He saw the dog lying flat on the ground. Somebody had quietened it, but it had done its job. It had warned Azir's men of Ducan's arrival. They would know now. That meant that they were not far away, he thought. They had to be close.

'*Mon Lieutenant*!'

It was Thompson. 'Come quickly, *mon Lieutenant*.'

Ducan followed Thompson to the outhouse. Verdi's men were crouched, watching. Thompson took the Lieutenant to one of the rooms.

There was a strong stench of animal manure. On the ground was a layer of stinking grass. Schiller was crouched over a body. Ducan went up to it and shone his torch.

It was a woman. He saw her slim, khaki-clad figure. He bent down. If she was alive, she was just hanging on. He shone his torch on her face. Her hair was long and blonde but matted with dirt, and her face was covered with filth. He felt her brow. It was scorching hot.

'The arms, the legs, *mon Lieutenant*,' Schiller said.

Ducan shone his torch. There were weal marks around the ankles and the arms. The girl's legs and arms had been bound together.

'The bastards,' Ducan hissed. 'Fetch Luker!' he ordered. '*Vite*! Pronto.'

He felt her brow again. It was damp. He felt her pulse. At first he thought that she was dead, and then he felt a faint beat. Luker joined him. Ducan stood up, Luker bent down. He pulled the girl's eyelids open and felt her pulse and her brow.

'She has been left to die, *mon Lieutenant*,' Schiller grunted.

Suddenly, the girl's body moved. It could have been a movement of a nerve, but it gave the impression of pain — a convulsion.

'Can you do anything?' Ducan asked Luker. 'Anything at all?'

Luker shook his head sadly.

'I am not a doctor, *mon Lieutenant*. She could be dying of malaria, typhoid or poison.' He gave Ducan a look of regret.

'Pump anything you have into her — everything you have. She must live! Do you hear me, Luker? She must live.'

Ducan stood up. The girl must live, he thought angrily. She must live. They had to save her. There had to be something worthwhile from their mission.

He left the room. The Sergeant-Chief followed him.

'Who is she?' Schiller asked.

'Not the American girl,' Ducan replied. 'They would not have left her. She must be Mademoiselle Casanou.' He clenched his fist. 'She must live,' he said again.

'They have gone. The dog did its job well. What do we do now, *mon Lieutenant*?'

Angrily, Ducan turned on him. He had taken Schiller's question as being a cynical request for orders, but he saw the grim look on Schiller's face and knew that Schiller was genuinely concerned. Schiller wanted to be told what to do and he expected Ducan to tell him. Ducan immediately calmed down.

'They can't have gone far, Sergeant-Chief,' he said. 'Not if they were relying on their watchdog.' He looked into the blackness thoughtfully. To the South was the way to Azir's forward camp. Somebody would have gone to tell him. The other way led to the hills. But they had taken everything including their cattle, so they could not have gone far.

'Send out a search party, Sergeant-Chief,' he ordered. 'I want to know in which direction they have gone. There will be animal droppings. They will have left a trail.'

'Yes, *mon Lieutenant*.'

Schiller went to give his orders. Ducan went back into the stinking stable. Luker had lifted the body of the girl into his arms.

'It will be better in another place, *mon Lieutenant*.'

'Take her to the main building. Use a sleeping bag.'

'I have given her a stimulant, *mon Lieutenant*. It might help. If only we knew the cause.'

'Whatever it was, they didn't expect her to live.'

Ducan left the building. He walked slowly across the open ground to the area of trees and palms. The ground was soft and there was a trough of water that was used by the cattle. He went up to it and washed the grime from his face. It was dirty, filthy water, but it was water. He saw the crude walls of the well in the moonlight. They had left their lifeline, he thought. That was very strange. Normally they would never leave that. They would defend it to the last man. Why? he wondered. Why had they left it? There had to be a good reason. He turned away from the well. It was probably the only water within a radius of a hundred kilometres, yet they had left it. It bothered him.

He walked slowly away from the area. There was a strong stench in the air. The stench of animal and human filth roasted by the sun. It was a strong, acrid smell. It caught his nostrils. They had not been long gone, he thought, and they would need water for their cattle.

He glanced at the horizon and saw the hills that formed a semicircle around the area. They were a dark ridge on the horizon. Was there also water in the hills? he wondered. Was that why they had fled from their camp?

He returned to the main building. The men were on various duties, either searching the area or acting as *sentinelle*. Only Luker was with the girl. He had taken her to a small room in the main building and laid her on his sleeping bag.

The stimulant had worked, her pulse had increased, but she was in great pain. The perspiration rolled off her brow and her body.

'Perhaps it would have been better to have left her,' Luker said.

'No!' Ducan said. 'No! She must live!'

He got his water bottle and bent down. Gently, he lifted the girl's head. He felt the dampness of her hair.

'Water,' he said. 'You must drink.'

He put the bottle to her mouth. She gave a groan and her head fell away. Her body seemed to convulse with pain.

'Water,' he said. 'You must drink.'

Again the convulsions.

'She is very sick, *mon Lieutenant*.'

Ducan stood up. He felt an anger that he had never felt before towards the natives. That they should have left the girl to die was unforgiveable.

'Sergeant-Chief!' he called out. 'Sergeant-Chief!' He wanted action. Any action.

There was no reply. He stormed out of the room. He saw Verdi on guard.

'Where is the Sergeant-Chief?' he asked.

'With Calowski, *mon Lieutenant.*'

He found them at the rear of the buildings.

'What the devil's keeping the men?' he asked.

'Azir's men have gone that way, *mon Lieutenant,*' Schiller replied. He pointed to the ridge of hills at the head of the inlet. 'I have sent Ferelli and Thompson to follow them.'

So they had gone to the hills, Ducan thought.

'They are watching us,' Schiller warned. 'Calowski can feel them.'

Ducan didn't dispute Schiller's remark, and it did not need Calowski's powers of sensitivity to convince him that Azir's men were watching — but for what? he wondered. What were they waiting for? Was Azir's main force expected back? Were they going to attack?

'What do we do, *mon Lieutenant?*' Schiller asked.

'If they are going to attack, we have more cover in the main building. Get Malik and Klaus to put out some trip flares and get the men ready for an attack.'

'Yes, *mon Lieutenant.*'

As Schiller stood up, two figures emerged from the darkness. It was Thompson and Fingers. They crept up to where Ducan and Schiller were waiting.

'They are in the hills, *mon Lieutenant,* to the North,' Thompson reported. 'That is certain.'

'You saw them?' Ducan asked.

'We heard them. Their sheep.'

'Good. At least we know where they are. I want you to examine the photographs and show me exactly where you think they are.'

'Yes, *mon Lieutenant*.'

'Anything else?' Schiller asked.

'I don't know, Sergeant-Chief,' Thompson said. 'We came across a dead kid.'

'A dead kid?' Ducan asked.

'Yes, *mon Lieutenant*. It must have only been a day or two old.'

'Had it been attacked?' Ducan asked.

'No, *mon Lieutenant*. There was no sign of any marks on it. I wonder why they left it behind?'

'Or how it died,' Ducan said.

Schiller looked at Ducan. 'It troubles you, *mon Lieutenant*?'

'Yes. A dead kid, and they left it behind.'

'Perhaps it had a disease,' Schiller said.

'Disease?' Ducan looked sharply. The girl had a disease, he thought. She was dying. She would soon be dead like the kid. But why? Was it some poison? — Poison! 'Poison!' he exclaimed. That was it, he thought. That was why they had left the well. That was why they had left the girl. They had poisoned the water!

'The well has been poisoned,' he hissed.

'*Mon Dieu*!' Schiller gasped. 'The bastards!'

'The girl was made to take the water,' Ducan said. He saw it clearly. The girl had been made to take the water to see its effects. She was now on death's doorstep. He turned to the Sergeant-Chief.

'Quick! Sergeant-Chief. There is no time to delay. Warn the men. They must not touch the water. And tell Luker.'

The word soon got round. The water had been poisoned! The girl was dying because of the water. The men gritted their

212

teeth and cursed Azir's men. To poison the water seemed an act of treachery against the whole human race. To shoot and kill was one thing, but to poison the water — the water that meant everything to all forms of life — was unforgiveable. The men had felt no particular emotions towards Azir or his men before that moment, but from then on they hated their guts. They would shoot to kill now, without remorse.

Ducan went to an upstairs room in the main building. He stood looking thoughtfully through a window opening across the dark plain. He wanted to think. He wanted to determine their next course of action. Did he go straight after Azir's men, or did he wait? If he waited, it would soon be daylight and they were trapped in the buildings. And how long would it take Azir's main force to arrive? Twenty-four hours? Two days? Probably twenty-four hours, he thought. Azir would know that they had arrived, but he did not have any transport — that meant that they had one further day's grace. What should he do? Attack or rest? The men were weary. They needed rest. So did the girl. He heard Luker and Thompson trying to make her sick. Luker was forcing something down her throat. Thompson was talking to her, urging her to be sick, but the girl was in a daze — barely alive, and barely conscious. Suddenly there was a convulsion. Luker said, 'Good,' and Ducan knew that they were making progress. If they had arrived a few hours later she would have been dead, he thought. If Thompson had not come across the dead kid, they would all have probably died the following day of water poisoning. He clenched his fists. That was what the bastards wanted, he thought. That was what they expected. He heard someone climbing the staircase. It was Luker.

'She is sleeping, *mon Lieutenant*,' he reported.

Ducan turned to face him.

213

'I have given her an injection, *mon Lieutenant*,' Luker added. 'She will sleep. Perhaps after she has slept, she will start to recover.'

'You have done well, Luker.'

'Thank you, *mon Lieutenant*.'

'Where did you learn your medicine, Luker?'

Luker shook his head. 'No, *mon Lieutenant*,' he said. 'I was an ambulance driver. I am not a doctor. Perhaps I would have liked to have been, but I am not.'

Ducan accepted his words and wondered if he had spoken the truth.

In the dim light of the middle night, in the heart of Africa, and with Azir's men surrounding them, lies seemed unnecessary.

'Perhaps you will find a useful service in *la Légion*, Luker.'

'Yes, *mon Lieutenant*.'

'You had better get some rest.'

Luker left the room. The girl would live. Ducan said a silent prayer of thanks. But she would have died and so could all of them. All of them! They would have all taken the water. Then Azir's men would have come back into the camp and found all Ducan's men dead or sick. There would have been no fight left in them. That's what they expected, he thought, and that's what they would have found if it had not been for the dead kid.

He rubbed the grime away from his face thoughtfully. They would be coming back. They would have to come back for their much needed water. If there was no water in the hills, they would come back and purify their well. They would return as soon as they thought Ducan's men were dead. Well, he thought, why shouldn't he encourage them? Why shouldn't he let them think that their scheme was succeeding? He would let

214

the men go to the well and Azir's men would see them drinking. They could even hear them dying. Suddenly he knew that he had an answer to his dilemma, and his spirits soared.

'Sergeant-Chief!' he called out. 'Sergeant-Chief!'

Schiller came up the staircase and into the room.

'Sergeant-Chief,' Ducan said. 'I think we are going to beat these devils after all.'

There was a note of cheerful optimism in Ducan's voice that Schiller had not heard since they had left the Greek island. He saw a smile on the Lieutenant's face and a glint in his dark eyes. In Corsica they had irritated him, but on this occasion they had a different effect. It gave him encouragement. The Lieutenant had something in his mind.

'The men did not touch the water?' Ducan asked.

'Not to drink,' Schiller said. 'They were ordered not to.'

And that was sufficient, Ducan thought. The men were well-disciplined.

'*Bien*. The men have responded well. They have been well trained.' Ducan meant what he had said. Schiller was taken aback. He grunted.

'You have produced a fine bunch of legionnaires, Sergeant-Chief,' Ducan added. 'We shall see how they can die.'

Schiller frowned. He did not understand the Lieutenant.

'Yes,' Ducan said with a glint in his eyes. 'We shall see how well they can die — and how noisily they can do it.'

'I don't understand, *mon Lieutenant?*'

'Let me explain.'

Ducan set about explaining his plan. He was enthusiastic. Schiller listened. They talked about it at length. When they were finished, Schiller said, 'I will see to it, *mon Lieutenant.*'

It was his way of giving his approval. He left Ducan and sought out Verdi.

'Get the men together, Corporal,' he ordered. 'Two men remain on *sentinelle*. The rest in the big room. I want to talk to them.'

'Has *Monsieur le Lieutenant* thought of a way to save the mission, Sergeant-Chief?' Verdi asked.

Schiller's face clouded over. He did not like Verdi's tone of voice, but he controlled his temper. He held back. There was too much at stake.

'Move it, Verdi,' he snapped. 'Pronto!'

Chapter Twenty-four

Ducan stirred and opened his eyes. It was daylight. The sun was streaming through an opening in the wall. In an instant, he was fully awake.

'It is quiet, *mon Lieutenant*,' Schiller said, when he saw the anxious look on Ducan's face. He had been standing close by.

Ducan sat upright. He saw the rough, yellow block walls of the room and the brown earth floor, and he smelt the foul stench. He looked at his watch. It was early morning. Schiller was supposed to have woken him at dawn.

'It has been very quiet,' Schiller explained. 'The men are also sleeping. Trojasky and Thompson are on guard.'

Ducan appreciated the sleep, and he had slept very soundly.

'And Azir's men?'

'They have been watching us, but they are waiting.'

It was as Ducan had anticipated.

'The girl, *mon Lieutenant*.'

Ducan looked at Schiller anxiously. 'She is alive?' he asked.

'She awoke. She is much better.'

Ducan stood up and adjusted his clothing. He left the room that he had been using. In the main central room, the rest of the men lay sleeping. Ducan went to where the girl lay. It was no different from the other rooms — basic, primitive and foul smelling.

The girl lay on a sleeping bag with a small pack under her head. Her eyes were closed. Ducan stood over her. Her face was still dirty and her blonde hair was matted with yellow clay. She had a broad face with a small, pointed nose and a full mouth. She opened her eyes and looked at him. Their eyes met and he felt his insides melt. Her eyes were deep brown, gentle eyes, like the eyes of a young fawn. They were expressive eyes, full of feeling and warmth.

He knelt down beside her. He smiled at her. She smiled back. Her smile was warm like her eyes. Her eyes watched him.

'Mademoiselle Casanou?' he asked.

'Yes, Monsieur,' she whispered.

'I am Simon Ducan,' he said. 'Please call me Simon. We have come to rescue you.'

The gratitude showed in her eyes. She gave a broad white smile. Ducan brought out his water bottle.

'I have had some, Monsieur,' she said.

Ducan looked up at the Sergeant-Chief who was standing behind him, but passed no comment. Instead, he took out his handkerchief and poured some water onto it. Gently, he wiped the dirt away from her face. She was evenly tanned, like Ducan — a brown that came from generations in the sun.

'*Merci*,' she whispered.

'Where are the others?' Ducan asked. 'The American lady?'

'They took them away,' the girl whispered. 'I do not know where. They made me drink the water. I was tied to a post. I do not know where they have gone, but they will not have gone far.'

She closed her eyes as if the long speech had tired her. Ducan gritted his teeth.

'Did they…' He stopped himself from asking what else she had suffered.

'How many men?' he asked instead.

'About twenty, but they will be back.' She opened her eyes and looked at him anxiously. 'Monsieur, they will be back. They will.'

'Yes, I know,' Ducan intervened.

He took her hand and held it. He liked the feel of it. It was soft and gentle, like a child's hand.

'You get some more rest, Mademoiselle,' he said. 'It is important.'

He laid her hand down and stood up.

'Make sure she is not disturbed, Sergeant-Chief.'

'Yes, *mon Lieutenant.*'

They left the room. Some of the men had stirred. Verdi sat propped against the wall watching Ducan and Schiller. So did Fingers. The others were still sleeping.

Ducan went to the first floor. The staircase was formed of stone slabs and the upper floor of rough timber beams and strips of boards. There were no partitions and no windows — only square-shaped openings. Tojak was crouched behind the opening that faced the hills where Azir's men were hiding. Thompson was at another, looking out across the plain.

Ducan went to Tojak first. The Slav handed him the binoculars.

'There has been movement, *mon Lieutenant.* They have been on the escarpment, to the North.'

'The North? What about the South?'

'Nothing, *mon Lieutenant.*'

'Why the North?' Ducan asked, voicing his thoughts aloud.

'They have a better view of the plain, *mon Lieutenant,*' Schiller suggested.

'Looking for Azir's men?' Ducan wondered aloud. The South had more cover and just as good a view of the plain, he thought.

He looked out of the opening. The inlet lay in front of him. It was about four kilometres across and their position was at the centre of the semicircle. The ground was flat, tufted, and a bright yellow in the morning sunshine. It was also marked with bushes and shrubs that were a familiar sight of the plain. The barrier of rocks that formed the hills rose only about two or three hundred metres, but they looked like the faces of a large wall. In their foreground were large boulders the size of one and two-storey buildings that looked as if they had been wedged away from the face of the cliffs. And there were more of them to the South, which would have given Azir's men better cover.

Ducan studied the horizon carefully. He picked out the entrance to the gorge that was their route to safety and the inlet that Thompson had picked out from the photographs, where Azir's men were hiding. Ducan had studied the ground from the aerial photographs. He knew that Azir's men were in an inlet that had no way out except over the hills. But they did have about twenty men, and the American girl.

He handed the binoculars back to the Slav and crossed over to where Thompson sat crouched.

'Nothing, *mon Lieutenant*,' Thompson reported.

Ducan looked at the overgrown shrubs and bushes that had once been a cultivated garden. He saw the yellow, baked ground between the building and the area around the well. It was marked with animal droppings and camel dung. The well had a small earthen wall around it, and close by was a sunken pit that the animals used. Around the area were a number of palm trees and unusually shaped trees.

He turned his attention to the plain. A rough earth track left the camp and disappeared into the distance. A heat wave shimmered across the horizon and his eyes watered. The plain was vast, desolate and it was going to be another blistering hot day.

He looked again at the well.

'This place must seem like paradise to the natives after crossing that plain,' he said to Thompson.

'Yes, *mon Lieutenant.*'

'And yet they poison their own water. Their own lifeline.' He stood up. 'They need water, Sergeant-Chief,' he said to Schiller. 'They can't last long without it. Their animals need it.'

'So they will be back.'

'To a poisoned well?' Ducan shook his head; they would not do that.

'*Mon Lieutenant?*' It was Thompson.

'Yes,' Ducan said.

'The well is very deep. The water is all underground.'

'That is correct, Thompson. There are strata of rocks throughout the territory.'

'So it would be possible to dig another well higher up the strata, *mon Lieutenant.*'

'True,' Ducan said. Suddenly, his eyes sparkled. Schiller had come to recognise the sign. He knew Ducan was onto something.

'They have poisoned this well, Sergeant-Chief,' he said, 'because they have another higher up that leads into it.'

'To the North,' Schiller grunted.

'To the North,' Ducan agreed.

'There is that irrigation ditch to the North, *mon Lieutenant,*' Thompson said.

'And they have been seen to the North — good.'

So there was another well, Ducan thought. They poison the one for Ducan and his men to use, and save the other well for when they return.

He turned away from the window. 'The men know what is expected, Sergeant-Chief?'

'They know, *mon Lieutenant*. They also know that their lives depend upon it.'

'Then the first thing we do is bury the girl.'

'Yes, *mon Lieutenant*.'

Chapter Twenty-five

Verdi wiped the sweat from his face and watched Fingers. Fingers was sitting propped up against the wall of the building, but his eyes seemed to be fixed on the upstairs room where the Slav and Thompson were on *sentinelle* duty.

There was something very suspicious about Fingers, Verdi thought. He was another watcher like Calowski, but the Pole did not try to hide his watching. Fingers watched from behind lowered eyes. And he was a clever bastard, Verdi thought... He was too clever. That was why somebody had fixed him in Corte. Even in Africa, he seemed to have got the best deals. His load was one of the lightest packs. His duties on watch had been at the beginning, or the end of their rest. He never looked particularly weary, or looked as if he was suffering. He was a clever bastard. He was the type that would be at the receiving end when the medals were dished out, but not when the shit started to fly.

Verdi frowned. There were undercurrents amongst the men. He could feel them. He was part of them. The Slav and Malik were sparring. Calowski and Baron were close. Luker was distant and cautious, and Klaus was no longer so sure of himself. Africa did not suit him. He was beginning to lose his cool. Verdi turned and looked at Svenson, the Swede. The Swede was sleeping soundly. Perhaps Svenson was just a big Swede, he thought. He could just be.

'Corporal.'

It was the Sergeant-Chief. Verdi immediately stood up. The Sergeant-Chief never seemed to sleep, and always looked as menacing as he had in Corsica. His features made him look formidable even with his stubby growth and the yellow dust that covered their clothes and faces.

'Wake the men. Eat one pack of rations. Use the second water canteen today.'

'Yes, Sergeant-Chief.'

Schiller did not move away. He held Verdi rigidly with his cold grey eyes.

'Corporal Verdi,' he hissed. 'Today we either live or die. It depends on how well the men behave.'

He brushed some dust from Verdi's shoulder. 'Make sure that they understand that, Verdi.'

'Yes, Sergeant-Chief.'

'And Verdi.' Schiller gave a pained look. 'No more talk about travelling North. Understood?'

'I understand, Sergeant-Chief.'

Schiller gave a snort and went to the staircase. Verdi turned and saw Fingers looking at him. Verdi gave him a look that told the Italian what he thought of his parentage. Fingers turned quickly away.

'*Debout!*' Verdi called out. '*Debout!*'

He woke the men. They stirred and stretched themselves.

'Eat one of your rations,' Verdi ordered, 'and only your second water canteen. You are going to need the others.'

'How is the girl, Corporal?' Luker asked.

'Living, Luker. Go see for yourself.'

'What a place,' Klaus grumbled. 'They must live like bloody pigs.'

'*Sacré bleu,*' Svenson added. 'It's going to be hot.'

'Go take a wash,' Verdi said. 'All of you. Let them see you. They'll be watching. Go to the well. Pretend to drink, and pretend well, but heaven help the man who swallows the water.'

'What about snipers, Corporal?' Fingers asked.

'They intend to let the water kill you off, Fingers,' Verdi replied. He turned to Baron and Svenson. 'Start digging a grave,' he ordered. 'Somewhere where they can see you. Then get something the shape of a body and wrap it in a sleeping bag.'

'We having a burial rehearsal?' Klaus grumbled.

'Yeah, just so that you get the drill correct. Now move it!'

They left the building hesitantly. The escarpment seemed very close — too close for comfort. Gradually they became more confident. Verdi showed them how. He went to the well and drew some water. He poured it over his face and stripped to the waist and washed himself. He took an empty bucket to his mouth and pretended to drink. One by one, the others followed suit. They were eager to rid themselves of the yellow grime that had become ingrained in their skin.

Schiller and Ducan also went through the pantomime. When Svenson and Baron had dug the grave, they had a mock burial. The men lined the two sides of the grave. Ducan bowed his head and mumbled a few words. Schiller and Svenson laid an imaginary body, wrapped in a sleeping bag, into the grave and withdrew the bag. The hole was filled. The men dispersed, but kept a continuous trail back and forward to the well as the temperature rose. Klaus and Malik also made an inspection of the area close to the buildings, and selected suitable places to prepare further booby-traps.

At midday, the furnace doors of the sun were fully open. The heat was tremendous. The men cursed, sweated and felt the irritations that had appeared on their bodies. They took it in turn to give a loud groan, or to appear in the open, gripped in pain. Calowski and Thompson collapsed in the open. Schiller and Baron carried them into the house. The *sentinelles* that had

225

been posted at the corners of the estate did not appear again during the afternoon. All the men were inside, apparently suffering. The groans continued. The men cursed everything and finished off their second water bottle.

'Thompson thinks that he could locate the second well, *mon Lieutenant*,' Schiller reported to Ducan, in the mid-afternoon.

Ducan shook his head. 'It is a great temptation, but it could undo all our good work. The men have two full canteens left.'

'There will be the hostages, *mon Lieutenant*.'

Ducan was insistent.

'We go South when it is dark, not North. Tell Thompson to forget about it, before the men also get the idea.'

'Yes, *mon Lieutenant*.'

Schiller understood. The men were suffering. They were also becoming irritable. There had been flashes of temper between Svenson and Verdi, and Klaus was irritating them with his remarks, which were no longer humorous. The slightest upset was bringing them to flash point. Without Schiller's presence, there could have been serious trouble, but his aggressive pose kept them at bay.

'Forget it, Thompson,' he said. 'We go South.'

'Then what?'

'You do as you are told,' Schiller snapped.

'Yes, Sergeant-Chief.'

Schiller glanced at him. Thompson was thinking too much. He turned to the others.

'Start acting again. Klaus, start groaning. You seem to be able to make a lot of noise.'

Klaus turned his head away and spat.

'Aren't I dead yet?'

Schiller cocked his rifle.

'One more remark like that, Klaus, and you will be.'

The room went quiet. 'Now all of you,' Schiller thundered. 'We are going to get out of this hole alive, but only if you do as you're told. Now start groaning. You die in forty minutes.'

He stormed up the stairs. The men groaned. Ducan watched from an upstairs room. He moved his head thoughtfully and raised his eyebrows. The Sergeant-Chief knew how to get his way, he thought.

He went to see the girl. She was sitting up when he entered the room. She watched him with her large brown eyes. Luker was also in the room.

'How is your patient, Luker?' Ducan asked.

'She is much better, *mon Lieutenant*.'

Ducan turned to the girl. 'This is Luker,' he said. 'He gave you the right injections.'

'I know, Monsieur,' the girl said. 'I have thanked him.'

Ducan turned to Luker.

'You did well, Luker.'

'*Merci, mon Lieutenant*.'

Luker left the room. Ducan sat on the earth floor and faced the girl. She looked at him and then dropped her eyes, as if bashful.

'You should be sleeping,' Ducan said.

'I heard voices — noises.'

'That would be Schiller,' Ducan smiled. 'He is inclined to make himself heard.'

'Are you from *la Légion Étrangère*, Monsieur?' the girl asked. 'Luker called you *mon Lieutenant*.'

Ducan smiled. 'We are here to help you, Michelle,' he said, using her Christian name. 'And please call me Simon.'

He handed her his water canteen. She was perspiring. The air in the room was still and roasted.

'*Merci*,' she said, and took the canteen. Again she dropped her eyes like a timid animal.

'Tell me what happened?' he said.

'We were flying to Eritrea. There were some shots. The pilot had to land. I think the fuel tanks had been punctured. Mohammed Azir's men were waiting for us.'

'And the pilot?'

The girl shook her head. 'I do not know. We heard screams in the night.' She shuddered. 'He is dead.'

'And the American girl?'

'She will be safe. She is valuable to them. She comes from a very influential family.'

'They know?'

'She told them.'

The girl gave a faint smile. 'She has a strong personality,' she said. 'She is a very capable person. She told Mohammed Azir what would happen to him if anything happened to any of the women or children.'

'Which gave Azir the idea of a ransom.'

'Probably.'

'What is Azir like?'

'He is educated, intelligent. He was very respectful. He has his cause.'

'Yet they poisoned you.'

'That was not Azir's doing. He has been away for about a week. He took the Eritreans with him, because of the Princess. He left the camp in charge of a Danakil. Azir would not have poisoned me.' She looked up at him and smiled. It made him feel warm inside. 'He will be back,' she said, with a look of deep concern. 'He will catch up with you.'

'Perhaps,' Ducan replied. 'We leave tonight.'

'What about Carol?' Again she gave a quick look of concern.

'If all goes well, we take her with us, and the Princess.' His face clouded over. 'If it doesn't...' He shrugged. The look lingered on his face.

'It troubles you, Simon?' she asked.

He looked up and said, 'Yes, I want to succeed.'

He did, he thought. He wanted to succeed very much. For once he wanted to come out on top, and it had a lot to do with the girl lying in front of him. He wanted to succeed for her.

'Success is important to you?' she asked.

'I wouldn't know,' he smiled. 'This is the first time that I have really wanted it.'

'I think you will get it.'

She dropped her eyes again.

'And what will you do when you are safely in Djibouti?' she asked. 'Return to France, or go looking for someone else to rescue?'

'I don't mind what I do, so long as I can see you,' he said. He had not thought about it. It had just come out. She made him feel different. He liked being with her. There seemed no problems when he was with her.

She looked up at him. There was surprise in her eyes.

'The sun,' she smiled. 'It has a strange effect on people.' She dropped her eyes again.

'Yes,' he agreed. 'It does, but I still meant what I said.'

She looked up at him again, smiled, and brushed her hair from her face with her hand.

He did not add to his remark. He had said it, and he had meant it, and Michelle seemed to respond to it. They talked freely and there were no barriers and no pretence. He learned about her past. How her father had been a Frenchman and a

Doctor, and her mother a native Algerian. Her father was dead, but her mother was still alive and living in Algiers. Michelle had trained as a nurse in Paris, and then gone to Ethiopia with a French medical team attached to the United Nations. She had met Carol Jackson-Lang at a social function. When the medical team had returned to France, Michelle had remained behind. After the Emperor had been dethroned, the Princess's family had been held at the Prince's estate. The Prince had been taken away, and was still being held in prison. Michelle's passport had been taken from her. So had Carol Jackson-Lang's. That was why they had flown to Eritrea. The Princess had family connections in that territory. They were going to help Michelle and the American girl leave the country.

Ducan was at peace talking to her. The heat and the problems ahead were temporarily forgotten. He liked the way she laughed, and the way she dropped her eyes, or brushed away her hair, whenever he paid her a compliment, or if he caught her watching him.

It was one of Ducan's happiest moments for a long time, but it could not last. Schiller came into the room and the magic ended.

'It will be dark in three hours, *mon Lieutenant*,' he said.

Ducan got to his feet. He looked at Michelle and smiled.

'Excuse me, Mademoiselle,' he said. 'We leave when it is dark. If necessary, I will have you carried.'

'I am sure I shall be able to walk.'

'We will see.'

He left the room. The men lay resting, except Klaus and Malik. They had their explosive equipment laid out and were moulding the plastic explosives into small bombs.

'We will need a lot of trips and booby-traps,' Ducan said to them. 'Also some hand bombs — to make a lot of noise.'

'Yes, *mon Lieutenant.*'

Ducan went up the stairs. Schiller went with him. Calowski was on *sentinelle*, but he kept out of sight.

'Anything?' Schiller asked.

'No, Sergeant-Chief. They are not around.'

'They will be later,' Ducan said. He took Schiller to one side and went over their plan again.

'As soon as it is dark, Klaus and Malik lay out their trips. We move out as soon as possible. We use the ditch for cover and go South. There are a lot of large boulders and plenty of cover. We work our way up the inlet. Unless I am very badly mistaken, Azir's men will come back to their base tonight. They will think that we are either dead or incapable of any resistance. They must move tonight. Their cattle need water. They have collected some from their other well, but they need more. We wait close to the entrance to their valley. When the trips give us the warning, we move, and we move quickly. You will take a small party and set up two machine guns. You will fire at the camp and keep their men occupied. You will block their retreat. I will take a party into the valley. I have studied the photographs. It is not very wide. Luker will stay with you and keep the area lit with star shells. That will show us all the ground. If we find the American girl, we move quickly to the pass and keep moving.'

'And the French girl, *mon Lieutenant?*'

'She remains with your party. One man must be detailed to watch over her, and carry her if necessary.'

'If you don't find the American girl?'

Ducan sighed. 'I will have to think again, Sergeant-Chief,' he said.

'You will find her, *mon Lieutenant*,' Schiller said emphatically.

They were the first words of encouragement that Ducan had ever heard from Schiller. He looked at the Sergeant-Chief's face. It was rough and dirty, and gave no indication whether the remark had been one of fact or encouragement.

'Tell the men, Sergeant-Chief,' Ducan said. 'Tell them what is expected.'

'Yes, *mon Lieutenant*!'

Chapter Twenty-six

As the darkness approached, there was a surge of relief amongst the men. The irritations of the heat, the flies, the stench, and of one another were forgotten. They cleaned their rifles and machine guns with extra vigour. Schiller had briefed them. They were legionnaires now, not actors. They were ready for action.

When the darkness came, Klaus and Malik immediately took their explosive devices and slipped into the open ground at the rear of the building. Calowski went with them and stood guard. Klaus and Malik worked quickly. They pegged the pins to the ground and stretched their wires. The others waited inside the building. Svenson had been detailed to look after Michelle. He was to carry her if necessary, but Michelle was on her feet. She looked frail and delicate, but determined. The minutes passed slowly. The perspiration rolled off the men. The night insects started their incessant clicking, and the hot breeze blew its layer of dust through the openings of the building.

Klaus and his party returned. Schiller checked that every man had their loads and packs fastened, so as not to make a noise. He warned them gruffly what would happen if they mislaid their footing.

'We are ready, *mon Lieutenant*,' he reported.

Ducan nodded his approval and gave the signal. Thompson and Calowski disappeared into the bushes.

Ducan gave them a few minutes, then led the main party out of the building. They darted through the bushes and slithered over the small wall. They came to the broad irrigation ditch and went South. Ducan waited until they were well clear of the buildings before halting. He went back along the line and saw the girl trying hard to catch her breath.

'Carry her,' he said to Svenson.

'No,' the girl whispered, 'I am all right.'

She looked at him. He saw her eyes. Even in the darkness, he saw the appealing look in them.

He nodded in agreement but turned to Svenson and said, 'If she can't keep up — carry her.'

He returned to the head of the line and sat studying the ground. Like the previous night, there was a quarter, Islamic shaped moon. The ground was covered with dark shaped bushes that moved with the warm breeze.

He moved off again and did not stop until they were close to the hills. The men gripped their rifles. There was a faint bird noise. Ducan moved forward into the dark shadows. Thompson and Calowski were waiting. Ducan held up three fingers and nodded his head. Thompson and Calowski moved forward. The men rested, taking protection from the breeze behind a large boulder.

Again Ducan went up to the girl. She was resting on the ground. He bent down beside her. He saw her eyes turn in his direction. He took her hand. It was soft and moist with perspiration. He gripped it tenderly and smiled. She smiled back. He left her and went to Schiller and held up three fingers. Schiller understood. They were moving in three hundred metre advances.

They advanced slowly. There was a lot of cover, but the ground was rocky underfoot and the men had to pick their way carefully. There was also the possibility that Azir's men could be advancing towards them. If that happened, they would have to fight their way into the valley.

The first indication that they were getting close to their destination was the very faint but distant bleating of a stray sheep. Momentarily, Ducan froze. So did the men. When they moved forward again, the atmosphere was tense.

Suddenly, Thompson and Calowski came out of the shadows. They had reached the extent of their cover. Schiller came up to Ducan. Silently, Ducan gave the order for the men to take cover in the shadows. Schiller went along the line. The men melted into the darkness and waited. Ducan glanced at his watch. It had taken them nearly two hours to reach their location. It could take Azir's men the same length of time to reach their base camp. He checked that Michelle was comfortable. She looked more composed than she had done earlier. He returned to his position and waited. The men had all been given strict orders. There was to be no noise until a trip flare, or some other form of trap, went off to indicate that the base was being attacked, and then they were to move quickly.

The minutes passed. The buildings at the base were a dark, undistinguishable, mass in the distance. The bleating of stray sheep became more frequent. It was encouragement to Ducan. It meant that they were not being attended to by the natives.

The minutes became an hour. Ducan's perspiration turned cold, and he knew the uncertainty of doubt. He could be hopelessly wrong, he thought. Azir's men might not be concerned about retaking their base camp. They could be more concerned about their captives. In which case Ducan and his men were going to have to go in and shoot it out. Time was becoming a major factor. They had to get well clear of the area before daybreak. By daybreak, Azir could be back with his main force. He decided to wait another thirty minutes. Another thirty minutes and he would give the order to move into the valley.

He waited anxiously. With each minute, tension increased. He felt as if the outcome of the mission was balanced on a razor's edge, waiting to fall one way or the other. It was either success or failure. His insides felt flat and sickly. A sudden *bang!* made him start. He instantly forgot his concern. There was another *bang!* and a flare burst into the sky, giving a red glow over Azir's base camp. Ducan's relief was enormous. So was the men's. Ducan did not have to give any orders. Schiller took over. He gave a call and Calowski, Svenson and Luker came running out of the shadows. They were his firing party.

Ducan started running to the mouth of the inlet. The others followed him.

He heard a pistol cartridge explode, and the sky was suddenly pierced by a stab of green.

Brrr!... Brrrrr!... Brr!...

Schiller's machine guns were in action. They were spraying the ground in front of the base camp.

The star shell burst, and in a dull green glow, Ducan saw the inlet into the hills. It was U-shaped, about two kilometres deep and only hundreds of metres in width. The sides of the hills rose gradually to a sheer rock face. Sheep and cattle were dotted all over the in-between ground, but there were no native huts.

Another booby-trap exploded at the base camp, and Schiller's guns kept spraying the ground.

Ducan ran forward as another star shell illuminated the sky with its green light. Frantically, he searched the ground looking for some native encampment. Suddenly, there was a loud explosion behind him. One of Klaus' bombs had gone off. Another exploded, and the sound reverberated around the sides of the hills. The sheep and cattle started to panic. They were scattering towards the head of the inlet.

Brrr!... Brrrrr!... Brr!... Brrrrr!...

It was Verdi and Baron firing their machine guns, adding to the noise. Another star shell exploded. Two grenades burst. All hell seemed to be let loose.

Ducan saw something moving along the side of the hill to his right flank. Caves! he thought. They were in caves!

'Caves!' he shouted. 'Caves!'

A further bomb exploded, drowning his voice. Ducan ran forward. There was a series of rifle cracks. The ground was jumping up at him, around his feet. Thompson, Malik and Fingers were following him.

Brrr!... Brrrrr!... Brrrr!...

Verdi fired again. He was spraying the side of the hill to their right flank. He had seen the rifle shots. Ducan saw a dark shape on the hillside fall into the darkness. Again a series of bullets smacked into the ground around his feet. Again Verdi retaliated. So did some of the men. Ducan saw several dark figures on the hillside. They were moving along a ledge. The light faded. Ducan cursed. Another bomb went off. Verdi fired his machine gun. So did Baron. There was a moment's darkness, then another star shell illuminated the area with its hideous, green glow. Ducan saw the natives on the ledge again. One had his arms uplifted. Somebody close to Ducan fired his rifle.

Brrrrr!... Brrrr!...

A series of bursts from their machine guns riddled the figure. It fell from the ledge. Ducan ran towards the forward slope. A sudden explosion ahead of him made him throw himself to the ground. Several bullets smacked into the rocks ahead of him. He went for cover. Verdi and Baron retaliated. Klaus threw some grenades to make more noise. Thompson and Fingers joined Ducan.

'The caves!' Verdi shouted. 'There!'

He fired a burst from his machine gun. Ducan saw his tracer bullets smacking into the rocks on the hillside above them. He saw the cave entrance. He started up the rocks. Bullets were coming both ways. Thompson and Fingers followed Ducan. The green light faded, but another shell burst into the sky. Ducan lost his footing. Thompson went on ahead. A long burst from their two machine guns sprayed the ground ahead of them. There was also some rifle fire from the other men. A figure came alongside Ducan. It was the Slav — Tojak. Behind him came Malik. Malik threw a grenade up the hill. It gave a loud explosion.

Then there was a silence. Ducan and the others rushed quickly up the hillside to the ledge. Thompson got there first.

'Here,' he shouted.

Ducan reached the ledge. Four still bodies lay on the ground. Breathlessly, he went to the dark mouth of the cave, where Thompson was standing. Malik, Klaus and Tojak were close behind him. Another star shell illuminated the sky. Ducan could hear Schiller's gun firing. He saw Verdi and Baron on the ledge. Verdi gave a burst along the hillside. There was a crack from a rifle in response. Ducan moved into the darkness of the cave. Thompson and Malik were with him.

They flung themselves to the ground, expecting a reception committee. It was dark; it was silent.

'If you are in here,' Ducan called out in English. 'Come out at once.'

He held his breath. There could still be some of Azir's men in the cave. They could answer with a bullet.

'Come out!' he shouted, 'or we start shooting.'

There was a faint, childlike whimper from the darkness.

'Who are you?' a woman's voice called out in English.

'Friends.'

A figure emerged. Ducan shone a small pencil torch. He saw a girl in a khaki jacket and slacks, like Michelle was wearing. She was tall, as tall as Ducan. Her face was marked with dirt, and on her head was a bush-hat.

'Miss Jackson-Lang?' he asked.

'Yes. Who are you?'

'We must hurry,' Ducan urged.

'There are others.'

'Get them.'

The girl called out in a native tongue. A slightly built native woman emerged with two small children. The children clung to her robe.

'Princess Towaja?' Ducan asked.

'Yes.'

'Let's go.'

'Where?' the American asked.

'Anywhere, away from here. Klaus, take one of the children. Thompson the other. Hurry.'

He went to the opening. A red star shell pierced the sky. Time was running out on Luker's shells. He was on his last box.

'Hurry!' he urged. 'Hurry!'

The American girl came up to him. She said urgently, 'There is another European girl — a French girl. She —'

'She is with us,' Ducan intervened. 'Now, for God's sake — hurry!'

Brrrrr!... Brrrr!... It was Schiller's guns. They had kept up an intermittent barrage of fire, spraying the ground between themselves and the base camp.

The party scrambled down the side of the rocks. Tojak, Verdi and Ducan brought up the rear. They reached the flat ground as another star shell pierced the sky. It showed them the way. It also made them suitable targets.

Suddenly, Ducan realised they were one short.

'Where is Ferelli?' he shouted.

'Dead!' Tojak shouted back. 'On the rocks!'

Dead! Ducan stopped in his tracks.

'Corporal!' he shouted.

Verdi came to him.

'Get them back to the Sergeant-Chief and make for the pass. I am going back to check on Ferelli. Don't wait for me if I am delayed.'

'Yes, *mon Lieutenant.*'

Ducan saw Malik. 'Malik, you come with me.'

He started back to the side of the hill, as the others made for the mouth of the inlet.

The light faded. It became dark again. One more shell, Luker, Ducan urged, one more — quickly. His prayer was answered. The sky again became a red glow.

Ducan scrambled over the boulders and up the rock face.

'Here!' Malik called out.

Ducan turned and saw the Italian sprawled out, face down, on a vertical face of the rocks. His arms were spread-eagled, and his rifle was still in his hand. Ducan went up to him. There was no doubt that Ferelli was dead. There was nothing they could do for him.

'Take his pack,' Ducan said. 'We need his water.'

Malik unfastened the pack from the dead Italian. Ducan took his rifle. They turned his body over. There was a small, dark patch at his heart. The Italian had died instantly. Ducan turned him over again and hesitated. He did not like the way that the Italian was lying.

Crack! A bullet whined off the rocks above their heads. There was nothing they could do for the Italian, he thought. There was no point inviting trouble.

'Let's go,' he called to Malik.

They scrambled away. Schiller's party was still peppering the base camp with bursts from their machine guns, but Luker had stopped firing his star shells. The sky was in darkness again.

Ducan and Malik reached the outlet. They saw Schiller's party.

Schiller called out, 'Here!' as they approached his position. Ducan went up to him. In the dull light, he could see a smile on the Sergeant-Chief's grubby face.

'You have done well, *mon Lieutenant*,' Schiller said.

'Except for Ferelli,' Ducan replied.

'There are always casualties.'

'There is nothing we can do for him, except save him from the vultures, but there isn't time. We must get away. I will lead the way. Your party bring up the rear.'

'Yes, *mon Lieutenant*.'

Ducan moved along the line to where the American girl was with Michelle.

'We must get clear of the area before daylight,' he said in English.

'You can speak in French, Monsieur,' the American girl replied, with a heavy accent.

'Are you OK?' Ducan asked Michelle.

'Yes,' she replied.

'I will help her,' the American girl added.

'Good.'

Ducan left them and rejoined Schiller.

'Let's get the hell out of here,' he urged.

241

Chapter Twenty-seven

The pass was a narrow gorge between two sheer faces of rocks. It was pitch black, the ground was strewn with loose rocks, and it was bitterly cold. The warm breeze that the men had come to detest had suddenly become an icy blast. The further they went into the gorge, the colder it became. They all began to shiver. Ducan had to stop the column. The men got out their warm clothing.

There was some intermittent firing from Svenson and Calowski, who were protecting their rear. It made them all aware that Azir's men were following them.

Ducan went to the women.

'Here is a pullover,' he said.

He gave it to the American girl. She put it on one of the children. Malik came with two more.

'It belonged to Fingers, *mon Lieutenant*,' he said.

'And the other?' Ducan asked.

'It will soon be warm again, *mon Lieutenant*.'

Malik left them. Schiller joined them. He saw the children wrapped in the pullovers. He gave a grunt and brought out his own, which he gave to Michelle. He left the group and came back with two more for the American woman and the Princess.

'Very gallant,' the American girl said. 'You must all be French.'

'Who did you expect?' Ducan asked.

'With all the noise, I thought it was either the Seventh Cavalry or the Marines.'

Ducan laughed. She had spirit and a sense of humour that appealed to him.

'You know of course, Monsieur, that Mohammed Azir will follow you. He will not give up.'

'So everybody keeps telling me, Mademoiselle. That is why we must hurry.'

He went along the line to Schiller.

'We move,' he said, 'and quickly.'

'I will join Svenson and Calowski,' Schiller said. 'We will be about two hundred metres behind you, *mon Lieutenant*.'

Ducan led the column again. He tried to increase the pace, but the darkness prevented him. It hid the dark boulders that suddenly confronted him, and the cold air seemed to grip his body and urge him to find warmth.

His body became numb. His limbs moved like a rusty machine that was badly in need of oiling. For three hours he suffered — they all suffered, but the intermittent rifle shots and spasmodic bursts from a machine gun to their rear kept them all going.

With the first hint of the approaching dawn, they saw a changing colour of the darkness and they felt the rise in temperature, but a mist started to rise up from the ground and engulf them. Soon the dampness was attacking their bodies. They were approaching the end of the gorge and the start of the open plain that lay between the two barriers of hills. Ducan decided to take advantage of the cover of the mist, and rested the column.

Schiller and his party came out of the mist and joined them. He reported to Ducan.

'There are only a few of them following us, *mon Lieutenant*, but the mist gives them cover as well as us.'

'We must move on,' Ducan agreed, 'but we also need the rest. The open plain is going to be hell, but we must cross it before Azir catches up with us.'

Schiller gave one of his determined grunts.

'We'll cross it, *mon Lieutenant*,' he said.

Ducan gave a smile. He was beginning to appreciate the Sergeant-Chief's confidence.

'Tell the men to eat their rations,' he ordered, 'and give some to the women. We'll rest until the mist lifts.'

Schiller went to the men.

'Give Fingers' rations and water to the American girl,' he ordered Malik. 'Then dispose of his gear.'

He moved away.

Malik unfastened Fingers' pack and removed its contents. He gave the rations and water canteens to the American girl, and put the ammunition in his own pack. As he re-fastened the pack, he noticed two neat holes in the canvas where the bullet had passed through it, after leaving Fingers' body. He fingered the hole thoughtfully.

'Fingers?'

It was Klaus. Malik looked up at him. Klaus had a stark look in his eyes. He had changed, Malik thought. He had changed a lot in the past forty-eight hours. They all had, and now Fingers was dead.

'Yes,' Malik sighed. 'Fingers.'

'How did he get it?'

'In the heart,' Malik said, but it could have been in the back, he thought. Fingers' body had been lying face down on the vertical rock face, but if he had been hit from the front, the force of the bullet would have sent him on his back!

'Something bothering you, Malik?'

Again Malik looked up at Klaus. Klaus' eyes seemed to be trying to penetrate his thoughts.

'Nothing bothering me, Klaus,' he said. 'How about you?'

'Me?'

Klaus' features suddenly relaxed. He started to laugh. He laughed longer than seemed necessary. Then abruptly he stopped.

'He got it through the heart — eh?' he asked, and laughed again.

Malik made no reference to his suspicions.

'Yes,' he said. 'He wasn't a bad guy really.'

Klaus snarled. 'He was a bloody creep. Forget about him.' Malik looked at the rest of the men. They were just distinguishable in the swirling mist. They were all resting. They looked grubby and weary, but they were still alive, he thought, and none of them had mentioned Fingers.

'Everybody else seems to have forgotten about him,' he said, and stood up and threw the pack behind some rocks.

'We're all going to die in this stinking country,' Klaus growled.

'Not if we can get across the plain before Azir catches up with us.'

'You're a clever bastard, Malik,' Klaus said.

'Not really, Klaus, or I would still be driving my truck.'

Klaus liked the remark. He gave a chuckle that turned into a laugh, and again his laugh seemed to be tinged with a release of emotion.

'How about you, Klaus?' Malik asked. 'How clever are you? Why are you really here?'

Klaus looked at him with a puzzled look on his face, as if trying to figure out Malik's angle. A faint smile gradually came to his lips, and his eyes seemed to light up. But he did not answer Malik's question. He slowly got to his feet and said, 'Don't try to be too clever, Malik,' and walked away.

Malik watched him return to where he had left his pack, and then forgot about him. But he did not forget about Fingers. Either the Italian had been shot in the back by a stray bullet, or he had been murdered.

Ducan was having similar thoughts. Either Ferelli had been stuck by a stray bullet, or somebody had purposely shot him in the back, and if he had been purposely shot in the back, there was a killer amongst them. It was not a pleasant thought. It made him feel uneasy. It made him think again of Marcel Poujet, but he quickly dismissed the thought. If Poujet had known, he would have warned him. There was too much at stake on the mission. He wondered if he should tell Schiller of his doubts. He saw the Sergeant-Chief checking some of the men's weapons. The Sergeant-Chief was doing the job that he had been trained to do, and he was doing it well. Ducan decided not to burden him with his suspicions.

'You are tired, Simon?'

Ducan looked up. It was Michelle. She had come alongside him and was sitting on the ground. The pullover that she was wearing was too big for her, but she still managed to look very feminine in it. Her face was smiling, and the smile made him put his problems to one side. The smile seemed to melt his insides.

'You are all right?' he asked, and resisted the temptation to run his hand gently over her long, soft hair.

'I will not let you down.'

'No.'

He rubbed the tiredness out of his eyes and felt the stubble on his chin.

'I must look a terrible sight,' he said.

She laughed. 'That does not matter,' she said. 'We all look terrible.'

'Not you.'

She dropped her eyes. He liked to see her do that. It was delicate; it was feminine.

'You are very complimentary.'

'My mother told me that it would get me everywhere.'

'It will.'

Again she dropped her eyes.

'You do not look terrible,' she said, and added, 'Have you eaten?'

'Yes.'

He saw the mist beginning to lift. The pass would soon become clear again, he thought. It was time to move out.

'I could sit here and talk to you all day,' he sighed, 'but unfortunately we must march again.'

'There will be other times.'

'I hope so.'

'So do I.'

Again the smile and the drop of the eyes that meant so much, then she left him. He watched her join the American girl and the Princess. She was tired and bedraggled, but she was also warm and tender.

He stood up and called the Sergeant-Chief.

'Now for the heat, Sergeant-Chief,' he said. 'We must cross the plain and get cover in the hills.'

'Yes, *mon Lieutenant*,' Schiller replied. 'I understand. I'll get the men together.'

'I'll tell the women,' Ducan said.

He left Schiller and went to where Michelle and the American girl were resting with the Princess and her children. It was the first time that Ducan had seen the children. It was the first time that Ducan and the American girl had seen each other in daylight. She was older than Michelle and much taller. She had a friendly, freckled face that had a quick smile. The Princess, by contrast, was small, slim and very dark skinned. Her eyes were bright and clear and showed no sign of tiredness. Her two children were asleep in her arms.

Ducan crouched down in front of them.

'We are doing fine,' he said in English, 'but we must cross the plain before Azir catches up with us. It is going to be hard going, but after the plain we have a chance.'

'You call the shots, Lootenant,' the American girl said, 'and we will just play along with you.'

Ducan smiled at her turn of phrase.

'What about the children?' he asked. 'I will get somebody to carry them.'

The Princess spoke in her native tongue. Ducan understood. She was telling the American girl that the children would be all right. That they were used to the sun. Ducan replied, also in her native tongue, before the American girl had time to translate her remarks.

'If they need any help, Princess, please let me know. My men will help them.'

A look of gratitude appeared in the Princess's eyes.

'They certainly picked the right guy, Lootenant,' the American girl drawled. 'You are sure doing a great job. John Wayne couldn't have said that.'

Ducan smiled again. So did Michelle.

'But he could walk differently,' Ducan said, and left them.

He rejoined Schiller. Schiller had got the men ready to move out. He was telling them the importance of crossing the plain.

'If any man falls, we leave him behind for Azir's men to collect, and you know what they will do to you.'

The men knew. They did not have to be reminded. They were as eager as Ducan to get some distance between themselves and Azir's men.

Ducan spoke to Schiller about the children. Schiller detailed Tojak and Svenson to watch them and carry them if necessary.

Ducan took a compass bearing on a distant peak and started the march. The flaming red ball of fire was poking its head over the horizon again. It looked fierce and angry, but as he started the march, Ducan's thoughts were not of the sun. He was thinking again of Ferelli.

Chapter Twenty-eight

When he awoke, Poujet immediately felt that it was going to be a significant day. It was warm and sultry, and the dark sky was charged with a pending storm. The atmosphere struck a sensitive chord in Poujet's makeup. He felt a tingling excitement.

An early call from his office did not surprise him. It was as if he had been expecting it.

'*Monsieur le Director* wishes to see you at ten o'clock,' his assistant explained. 'He has a meeting at nine at the U.S. Embassy. Also, *Monsieur le Chief Inspector* Renau, of Interpol, wishes to talk to you. I arranged for him to come to your office at eleven.'

'Good.'

'We have received two reports, Monsieur,' his assistant added. 'One from Marseilles about the unidentified body they found in the harbour.'

'And the other?'

'From Stockholm.'

'Svenson?'

'Yes, Monsieur.'

'I will come at once.'

Poujet arrived at his office as the storm was breaking. His assistant commented about the sultry heat, which seemed to trouble him, and the storm. The rest of the staff appeared as gloomy as the dark sky, but not so Poujet. He accepted the files and read the reports eagerly. When he had finished, he called in his assistant.

'So,' he said. 'Svenson is one of Carson's men.'

He returned the file to his assistant.

'What do we know about Chief Inspector Renau?'

'He specialises in narcotics, Monsieur.'

'Narcotics? *Mon Dieu*! What next?'

He did not want an answer. He dismissed his assistant by leaning back in his chair and closing his eyes. There was a faint smile on his lips. His assistant knew that his thoughts were elsewhere. Even the thunder would not disturb him.

At ten o'clock, Poujet reported to the Director. The Director looked solemn.

'They have heard from Addis Ababa,' the Director said. 'The negotiations have abruptly ceased.'

'Ducan has arrived.'

'And made his move.'

'And how is Carson?'

'On edge.'

'He worries too much.'

'Not like you, Marcel, eh? You seem in good spirits today.'

'My intuition, Monsieur. I have a good feeling.'

'About Ducan?'

About Ducan? Poujet wondered. Yes, he thought. He felt good about Ducan.

'Yes, Monsieur, about Ducan and about our problems.'

'You also have some facts.'

'A report from Stockholm and Marseilles. Stockholm has made an interesting discovery.'

'Svenson?'

'Alias, Johanson, Lieffer, and Carlson. The Svenson background is authentic, except that the real Svenson died about six months ago.'

'Just before Svenson left Gothenburg.'

'Our Svenson was born in Detroit, twenty-eight years ago. He arrived in Stockholm five years ago as a representative for an American Automobile Company.'

'C.I.A.?'

'So it would appear.'

'Go on.'

'The unidentified body in Marseilles harbour, Monsieur, has now been identified as Carl Lassenan. He was known for his underground activities for the C.I.A.'

'So Svenson went to Marseilles to see Lassenan?'

'Yes. He flew to Marseilles to link up with Lassenan, only to find that Lassenan was missing. Lassenan was a shipping agent for the C.I.A. Svenson was presumably taking a package to the States.'

'And the package was the Fox?'

'Yes, Monsieur.'

'But the Fox wasn't interested.'

'The K.G.B. could have got to Lassenan before the Fox had time to contact him, or the Fox might have become suspicious.'

'And Svenson arrives in Marseilles to find no Lassenan and no package. He makes enquiries and suspects that his package has joined the Legion.'

'That would appear to be so, Monsieur.'

The Director sat back in his chair and threw up his hands.

'And does Carson know where this Svenson is?' he asked.

Poujet shrugged.

'I don't think so, Monsieur. He certainly does not know that he is now with Ducan in Africa.'

'Carson doesn't know that he has a representative on the mission?' the Director asked.

'I don't think so, Monsieur.'

'*Bon*,' the Director chuckled. 'If there should be any embarrassing outcomes to Ducan's mission, Marcel, we have a trump card to force the Americans' hand. Yes?'

'We have, Monsieur. I think we might also be able to get all of American Electrics for France.'

The Director was pleased with the turn of events. So was Poujet. He knew that he was not directly helping Ducan and Pascal, but he was getting a clearer picture of their situation.

He returned to his office and waited patiently for Chief Inspector Renau to arrive.

The Chief Inspector arrived promptly. As they were introduced, Poujet immediately realised that Renau was the prompt, precise type of policeman. Everything about him was neat and correct. His hair was straight and neatly trimmed. So was his moustache. His suit was dark, his shirt white, and both fitted his portly figure without a crease. He looked the type of man who was disciplined in all ways, and rarely bent the rules.

The two men shook hands. Poujet offered coffee. Renau accepted.

'I have been directed to you, Monsieur, by Inspector Gaston of the Marseilles Sûreté,' Renau explained. 'I have also been informed that you are interested in the enquiries of the Italian Inspector Paledo.'

Poujet handed the Chief Inspector his cup of coffee.

'That is so,' Poujet agreed. 'Perhaps we can help each other.'

'We shall see,' Renau said. He was not a man for unnecessary platitudes or general conversation. He handed two files to Poujet.

'I wish to interview these two men.'

Poujet opened the files. He did not read the typed details. He glanced at the photographs of the two men. They were faces from a police library. They were the faces of Ferelli and Baron. Poujet closed the files.

'I understand that both these men joined *la Légion Étrangère*,' Renau added. 'However, the Legion is being uncooperative.'

'The Legion protects its own, Monsieur.'

'They do not protect men wanted for a serious crime,' Renau retorted.

'Are these men wanted for some particular crime, Monsieur?'

'They can be of assistance to my enquiries.'

'Which is not quite the same thing, Monsieur.'

'I could find a charge if necessary, Monsieur.'

'It would have to be a very serious one. The Legion does protect its own.'

'This is no game with me, Monsieur,' the Chief Inspector snapped.

'Nor with me,' Poujet replied.

'We understand each other, Monsieur.'

'We do,' Poujet agreed. 'Perhaps you could tell me more. Before I can tell you about the whereabouts of these men, I must be taken into your confidence.'

Renau frowned. He looked momentarily uncertain.

'I have also spoken to Inspector Gaston,' Poujet added, 'and anything you tell me will be in the strictest confidence. Come, Monsieur.'

Renau made a quick decision that he was going to have to take Poujet into his confidence, or he would leave the office empty-handed.

'My department is concerned with apprehending those who are responsible for the traffic of narcotics,' he said. 'There is a steady flow of drugs of all types. It comes via Africa and is distributed around Europe, or shipped to the U.S.A. Most of it comes into Europe by ship. To the ports of Marseilles,

Barcelona, Naples and Ajaccio. It is smuggled ashore and moved inland. It is a well organised operation. It is as effective as some of the organisations in your business, Monsieur.'

'I can appreciate that, Monsieur.'

'Lately we have been successful. We have reduced the flow of supplies considerably, and we have made many arrests. However,' the Chief Inspector shrugged, 'it will start up again. The main operators are lying low, waiting for the opportunity to resume business again. Some of them, Monsieur, turned their interests to other outlets. They temporarily diversified their operations. They took to smuggling other valuables. Some went into the jewellery business.'

'Ah!' Poujet exclaimed. 'I am beginning to see some connection. Inspector Rossini and Inspector Paledo of the Naples Police Department.'

'Naples has been for some time a storing and holding port. Many tourist ships call at Naples and many of them take away packages of narcotics. An organisation exists in Naples that has a link with a syndicate in the States.'

'Mafia, Monsieur?' Poujet asked.

'Perhaps, Monsieur. So Inspector Paledo believes, but that is incidental. As you are aware, there was a jewel robbery of some note earlier this year. Contessa Vallego, a distant relative of the Alfonso family of Austria, had her jewellery stolen whilst on holiday at her villa on Lake Maggiore. They were valued at about six million francs. As a result of a break-in at a warehouse in Naples belonging to a Signor Bassito, we now believe that we have found a link between this jewel robbery and the organisation that operates in narcotics.'

'So Inspector Gaston informed me,' Poujet remarked. 'He is also of the opinion that the men responsible for the robbery were, for a time, in Marseilles, and possibly joined *la Légion*!'

'On the night of the break-in into Signor Bassito's warehouse, two men were smuggled onto a Liberian freighter, the *Hellanca*. It is owned by a Greek shipping company in Naples. The *Hellanca* sailed to Marseilles and then to London. Two of its crew went missing as soon as the ship docked in London. One was the second mate, the other was a deck hand. Nobody else on board the ship could describe the two men who took passage to Marseilles. The Captain swears that he knew nothing about it. It is possible that he is telling the truth.'

'And in Marseilles, Monsieur?'

'They were two wanted men. Wanted by the Italian police, by the people they robbed, and by us.'

'By you?'

'Some of the Contessa's jewellery had already turned up in the U.S.A. To get there, it had used the narcotic route. If we can establish the source of the jewellery, we can establish the narcotic connection.'

'But you know where the jewellery was stolen from in Naples, Monsieur?'

'There are powerful, influential interests at stake, Monsieur. We must have proof. The jewellery could have been planted at Signor Bassito's warehouse. I do not think so, but to support our case, we want the two men who have them — alive.'

'And the shippers will want them dead.'

'Yes, Monsieur — dead.'

'They could have left Marseilles — for South America, for instance.'

'Inspector Gaston does not think so, and neither do I.'

'Why, Monsieur?'

The Chief Inspector laid his hands on the two files he had offered to Poujet.

'Because of these two men, Monsieur,' he said.

Poujet raised his bushy eyebrows questioningly.

'The Italian is known to us as Focelli,' Renau explained. 'He has many names. To the Legion he is, I understand, Ferelli. He has a criminal record. He has been part of the underworld that operates from Marseilles to Milan, for some time.' The Chief Inspector lowered his eyes. 'He has also been one of our informers for some time, Monsieur,' he added secretively. 'He has been well paid for his services.'

Poujet nodded his head understandingly.

'He would not join the Legion for a change of scenery,' Renau said.

'Nor for your favours, Monsieur,' Poujet added.

'No, I agree, but he would for the sum of six hundred thousand francs.'

Poujet looked impressed. 'You mean the insurance reward?'

'Perhaps,' Renau shrugged. 'The Austrian Insurance Company are offering a ten per cent reward.' The Chief Inspector looked serious. 'The Insurance Company want to recover the jewellery, but it is well known, Monsieur, that Bassito was prepared to outmatch the reward if the men responsible for the robbery were eliminated, and the jewels recovered. This man you call Ferelli is a greedy man. He is also unscrupulous. He would not be averse to using a knife.'

'So you think that the robbers took to the Legion for protection and Ferelli followed them.'

'I do, Monsieur. Ferelli would live in comfort, and with protection, for the rest of his days if he could please Signor Bassito. It is a great temptation for a man like Ferelli.'

'But the Legion,' Poujet said. 'Surely there are other safer hideaways.'

'A prison, Monsieur?' Renau shook his head. 'A small hotel? A cruise ship? A safari?' Again Renau shook his head. 'The Legion was a safe gamble if they had not been spotted.'

'By Ferelli?'

'And perhaps by the man who now calls himself Baron. Who knows?'

'Another informer?'

'No, but a dangerous man, Baron — or as we know him, Beauchamp. He has been a link man for the Marseilles operation for a number of years. Occasionally, he makes trips to Africa, and keeps the links going. It is worldwide, Monsieur. The packages find the most devious routes. You would be surprised. Beauchamp is an organisation man.'

'Has he fallen out of favour?'

Renau shrugged. 'That is always a possibility. He might have other reasons for joining the Legion. That is why we would like to talk to him, and Ferelli — and time is running out.'

'Running out?'

'We believe that the key to the whole operation is Signor Bassito. We need evidence to make him talk. Signor Bassito is a very troubled man. He fears for his own safety and that of his family. Inspector Rossini is of the opinion that the American syndicate are bringing pressure to bear, and that they will try and stop Bassito giving any testimony. Bassito has also lost his mistress, Gena. She has disappeared.'

'Disappeared? Is that significant?'

The Chief Inspector gave a faint smile.

'She thought it advisable to seek protection, but she will not talk. She is too afraid. With the right encouragement, I am sure she will talk.'

'You think she is involved?'

Again the Chief Inspector smiled. Poujet understood.

'And the men who broke into the warehouse?' Poujet asked. 'Can you pick them out?'

'Inspector Gaston has been very cooperative. I have my suspicions. I am waiting for Gena to talk. Perhaps you can help me persuade her, Monsieur. We could arrange for her to be confronted…'

'Ah! Monsieur,' Poujet said, and held up his hands in protest. 'Monsieur, you have been very honest with me.' He shook his head sadly. The Chief Inspector frowned. Poujet leaned on the table and put his hands together. 'I shall try to be as honest with you as my authority permits,' he said. 'The men that you seek are not officially members of the Legion. They are, at the present, independent mercenaries on a mission for another power.'

The Chief Inspector looked perplexed. Poujet helped him as much as he thought advisable. He gave the Chief Inspector enough information to make him realise that it was all a matter of top level security. A matter at Presidential level.

The Chief Inspector sat frowning when Poujet had finished. Before he had entered Poujet's office, the situation had seemed very straightforward to him. Now it was all rather vague.

Poujet took pity on him.

'Monsieur, I am flying to Djibouti for a few days sightseeing,' he said. 'I am leaving at eight p.m. this evening from Charles de Gaulle Airport. Perhaps you would care to join me?'

Again the Chief Inspector made a quick decision.

'It would seem a wise move, Monsieur,' he said. 'I will make the necessary arrangements.'

'Good,' Poujet said. 'I look forward to your company.'

He stood up. So did the Chief Inspector. They shook hands.

'*Au revoir,*' they said.

The Chief Inspector left the room. Poujet went to his window and watched the rain cascading out of the rainwater pipe onto the cobbled courtyard. It was indeed a significant day, he thought. It was indeed.

His assistant came into the room.

'*Sacré bleu*,' he grumbled. 'The rain. First the heat and now the rain, and tonight we had a barbecue arranged.'

Poujet thought of Ducan and his men, and looked at the rain. He liked the rain. He was glad it was raining.

Chapter Twenty-nine

Ducan took another compass fix on the distant hills and wiped the dirt away from his parched lips. The next few hours were going to be hell, he thought, but it was make or break for them. Ahead lay a desolate, open plain, with rivulets of rocks like waves of sand dunes. There were no bushes, no scrub, no sharp features. The small hills, like the dunes, were rounded and bare. Everything had been eroded by the hot, scorching breeze.

Ducan started the march again. The ground was rock hard under a layer of sand, but the sand hid crevices and depressions in the rock formation, and suddenly they would encounter a deep layer of soft sand that made going difficult. The breeze whipped up the fine particles of sandy dust and carried it with it. They covered their faces, except their eyes, and all parts of their bodies, but still the fine sand got into their clothing and irritated their bodies. The men had all developed some form of rash or irritation. Thompson's neck was red. Malik's arm was troubling him from a scratch from a thorn bush. Klaus's irritation was more personal, and his annoyance showed on his face. But they all suffered, nobody escaped, and it made them irritable and quick tempered whenever they rested. Schiller kept a close watch. He knew that they were beginning to feel the strain. He also knew that they still had to face Azir's men.

'Save your bickering and fighting for Azir,' he snarled at Tojak, who had flared up at Luker. 'They aren't through with us. If you want to live, save your fighting.'

He gave Tojak a kick on his boot. 'Understand?' he growled.

'Yes, Sergeant-Chief,' Tojak grumbled.

The march continued. The men had no stomach for it. They were tired and exhausted with the heat, but suddenly their attitude changed.

Calowski called out. 'Sergeant-Chief!'

Schiller turned; so did the men. Calowski had been watching their rear. They saw the reason for his cry. At the end of the pass that they had just left stood a group of figures, and three riders on camels. They stood immobile on the fringe of the plain. Azir's advance party had arrived!

Ducan joined the Sergeant-Chief and studied them with his binoculars.

'They will not come after us,' he said.

'They will keep out of rifle range, *mon Lieutenant.*'

'Once we get to the pass, we have a chance.'

He replaced his binoculars in their case.

'We march, Sergeant-Chief.'

He trudged forward again. The column followed him, eager to get away from Azir's men.

Ducan tripped and fell. He heard a sharp cry. A hand helped him to his feet. It was Malik. Ducan set off again. He was feeling the strain, but it was not all physical. He knew that they were poised for success. He did not want anything to foil him. Not again. The thought seemed rivetted to his brain. It kept him going.

The temperature began to rise sharply. First it was only the dusty breeze that tortured them, but then it became, also, the fierce heat. Ducan kept them going until there was a cry that someone had stumbled, when he would rest the column. They would gather in small groups and sit with their heads bent. Some would glance anxiously to their rear, but there was no sign of Azir's scouts. As the morning passed, the heat began to burn the ground, making it unbearable to sit on. They became a column of stooped plodders. No one spoke. They all remained silent, but they all thought. Ducan thought about the protection they would get in the distant pass. Schiller thought about Azir's men and kept glancing behind him. Malik thought about Fingers' body lying face down with a bullet through his back, and had a shrewd idea who had killed him. What the others thought about was a secret that they kept to themselves, but occasionally Klaus would give an audible grunt, or a wild laugh.

The women also suffered, Michelle more than the others. She had not fully recovered from her sickness. She became dizzy and fell. The American girl dragged her to her feet. Svenson picked her up and carried her. Tojak relieved him after the first half hour, and they took it in turns. The dark skinned Princess and her children suffered the least. They kept close together and never complained.

After several hours of march, they came to a ridge of sand that ran directly across their path. On the other side, the ground fell away sharply, like the sides of a sand dune. The men slithered down the slope and lay at its base, where they were protected from the breeze. They were in a state of collapse. Ducan went to the women. The American girl was trying to give Michelle some water, but the canteen was empty. Ducan gave her his.

'Give her as much as she needs,' he said, 'and yourself and the children.' The American girl smiled her gratitude.

Schiller came up to him. 'We can't delay, *mon Lieutenant*,' he whispered, 'or the men will never move.'

Ducan looked at the hills. They were within their grasp.

'Tell them that it is only one further effort, Sergeant-Chief.'

'Yes, *mon Lieutenant*.'

'Sergeant-Chief!'

Ducan had raised his voice. Schiller saw the hazy look in his eyes.

'We must make the hills,' Ducan said. 'We must!'

'We will, *mon Lieutenant*. We will.'

Ducan's body sagged. Schiller started shouting.

'On your feet! On your feet! Pronto!'

Nobody moved. The men lay still. Some looked up, and there was rebellion in their eyes.

'If you want to stay here and die, that is your choice,' Schiller snarled. 'Azir's scouts will soon be along to pick you up and cut off your testicles. We are marching to the hills. There we will survive. Now get on your feet!'

Still nobody moved. Schiller had his rifle in his hands. He pointed it at Thompson. 'On your feet, Thompson, or I shoot.'

There was a pause, then Thompson obeyed. Verdi followed suit, and so did Malik.

'Tojak!'

Tojak swore. '*Cochon*,' he grunted, but got to his feet. So did the others, except Klaus. He lay still. He looked all in.

'Klaus!'

'*Au Diable*,' Klaus grunted.

'OK, Klaus, you die now.'

Schiller took aim.

Malik intervened. He grabbed at Klaus. Klaus brushed him angrily aside.

'The bastard wouldn't shoot,' he snarled, and struggled to his feet. His eyes looked wild, and his hands gripped the butt of his rifle menacingly.

'Don't you ever bet on it, Klaus,' Schiller warned. 'Don't ever do that again.'

Klaus scowled at him, still with a wild look in his eyes.

Michelle had also got to her feet. Ducan had helped her. Schiller went up to them.

'I will help her,' he said. 'You lead the way.'

Ducan looked at Michelle. She gave him an encouraging smile.

He started the march. The column followed behind. He kept looking at the hills. If Azir's men had got there first, they were finished. It would be the end. The men could not fight. They needed rest.

Azir's men had not got to the hills, but Ducan had stopped thinking about them when he staggered into the rocky pass. He collapsed in the shade of the first boulder. The others followed suit. Schiller, Tojak and Svenson had helped the girl. Even Schiller was lost for words. He joined the Lieutenant, and lay exhausted.

Ducan was the first to revive. He put his hand affectionately on the Sergeant-Chief's shoulder and said, 'We made it. Now we have a good chance.'

He drank some water and went to the women. The Princess looked at him with her dark eyes.

'The children?' he asked.

'They are tired, Monsieur. They will sleep.'

She gave a smile of gratitude. The American girl looked up at him appealingly. She was all in.

'We aren't moving off again?' she asked.

'No, we wait until the sun has lost its fire. How is Michelle?' She was lying quite still. 'She is all right?' he asked anxiously.

'She will be,' the American girl said. 'I am sure.'

Ducan returned to the Sergeant-Chief.

'We need two *sentinelles*, Sergeant-Chief. Any sign of visitors and we must be ready to fight.'

'I will see to it, *mon Lieutenant*.'

Schiller was his old self again. Ducan heard him give his orders couched in veiled threats of reprisals, and he lay back and smiled. There was something very comforting about the Sergeant-Chief, he thought, and fell asleep.

Ducan was woken by the Sergeant-Chief. He opened his eyes, and at the same moment felt the aches of his body. It was as if every joint had seized up. He looked into Schiller's rough face that was covered with a yellow beard.

'Trouble?' he asked, fully alert.

'No, but it is time to move.'

Ducan struggled to his feet. The sun was still bright and hot, but it was on the decline. He saw Baron on top of a huge boulder on *sentinelle*. The others were all resting. He looked along the pass. The sides were several hundred metres in height, and a sheer face of rock. The ground between was much wider than the previous pass — about a hundred metres wide. It was flat, rocky and there were a number of bushes. He studied his photographs. The pass was about nine kilometres deep. It made a wavering line through the hills. At its head was the fork that led to the French territory.

'No sign of Azir's men,' Ducan stated.

'No, *mon Lieutenant*,' Schiller agreed, 'but the native woman thinks that they are getting close.'

'She will be right,' Ducan sighed. He frowned. His limbs still felt seized.

'You all right, *mon Lieutenant?*' Schiller asked.

'Yes. It is the sun. It affects people differently. I will be OK. Get the men ready.'

The men had also suffered from the sun. Some had burns, others had their irritations. Some were like Ducan and found it difficult to move their limbs. All of them were very tired and weary.

Schiller ordered them to eat their rations. He checked their water and reported to Ducan.

'They are all down to their last canteen. Some have broken into it.'

'Let us move as soon as possible.'

Ducan led the way. His pace was slow. His limbs wouldn't respond any quicker. Schiller kept watching the hills and their rear. He was in sympathy with the Princess. Azir's men were getting close.

It soon became obvious to Ducan that they were going to have to rest, and not just for a few minutes. They walked with difficulty and without spirit. They needed a long rest, otherwise they would never reach the French border. He kept looking at the pass as he turned each bend, hoping to find some suitable ground to order a resting place. Finally, he found what he was hoping for. The pass did two sharp turns. The first entered into a narrow gorge about fifty metres wide. The ground was strewn with large boulders, but the cliff walls were high and smooth. The second bend was about three hundred metres further into the pass, where it turned and broadened out again. At the end of the narrow part were several very big boulders that had at some time been part of the rock face.

Ducan stopped the column at the second bend in the pass. He waved Schiller to join him.

'We are about three kilometres from the fork junction,' he explained. 'Unless Azir has gone over the top, and that will take a lot of time, he will have to come through that narrow pass.'

'It is a good place to make a stand, *mon Lieutenant*.'

'If necessary. Check with Klaus and Malik, Sergeant-Chief. They might have some trip flares left. If they have, set one or two where the pass narrows. If they haven't, we need some form of warning. We are going to rest here until dawn.'

Schiller didn't question the decision. He knew that the men were all in, and the Lieutenant also.

'If Azir doesn't come during the night, Sergeant-Chief, he will certainly be here in the early morning.'

'Yes, *mon Lieutenant*.'

'Make the women comfortable. Get the men resting. I am going ahead to see if there are any obstacles that could cause a problem.'

'Yes, *mon Lieutenant*.'

Ducan was away two hours. When he returned, it was dusk. He saw the men in small groups, resting. Some were sleeping. Malik was about fifty metres down the pass on higher ground, on *sentinelle* duty.

'They had a few trips left,' Schiller reported. 'They have laid them out. They also have some explosives.'

'That is good. It will be useful.'

He left Schiller and went to the women. The Princess was asleep with her two small children nestling in her arms. The American girl and Michelle were also sleeping. Ducan turned to leave.

'Simon!'

Ducan turned. Michelle was awake. She sat upright.

'You are back,' she whispered. 'I am glad.'

Even in the dusk, he could tell that she meant what she was saying. It was in her eyes. There was warmth and feeling.

'How are you?' he asked.

He took her hand and felt its soft, gentle, velvet touch.

'Have we far to go?' she asked, evading his question.

'One good day's march and you should reach the border.'

She looked at him anxiously. 'You will be with us?'

It was his turn to be evasive.

'That depends on Mohammed Azir,' he said. He gave a sigh. 'I think I could sleep for a week,' he smiled.

'Tell me what will you do when we are back in French territory?' she asked.

He saw her drop her eyes when he looked at her.

'I shall take a long, cool bath, and have a bottle of iced champagne. Then I shall take you out for dinner to a very quiet restaurant, where we will be able to sit all night and not be disturbed.'

She smiled. Her eyes sparkled. He put his hand tenderly on her face.

'I will enjoy that,' she said.

So would he, Ducan thought, but there was Azir and his men to contend with first.

'Simon.'

Again she dropped her eyes.

'Yes?'

'They didn't…' She hesitated. 'They didn't touch me like you might have thought.'

'I am glad,' he said, 'but it would not have changed my feelings.'

'Your feelings might change when you are back in Paris.'

'They will change about many things,' he said, 'but not about you.' He looked wistful and remained silent.

It was dark now. The blanket had suddenly fallen. The twilight was only a short time of the day. Now it had gone.

'I think we will all have changed after this,' he added. 'I once met a man; my father introduced me to him. He was an eccentric, bearded Englishman. He had travelled from Tripoli to Djibouti by camel and on foot. It had taken him a year. I thought he was mad. When I asked him why he had done it, he said that he had been wanting to find his soul, and it is only in Africa that you can find it.' He looked at her. 'I still thought he was mad, but I don't any longer. You have to suffer the harshness of all this to get a true sense of values, and to find oneself. People live and die in their little boxes and never know each other, or themselves. They worry about so many things that are trivia. Yes, I will have changed. I was brash, cocky, cynical. I even thought I could improve *La Légion*. I was against everybody and everything. I thought the colour of my skin was to blame. It had made me different to other people. Now I know it wasn't that. It was just me — my inner self. Well, that will have changed now.' He looked at her and smiled. 'But never my feelings for you.'

She did not answer him. She lay down and closed her eyes. There was a smile on her lips as she fell asleep.

Ducan sighed. He was becoming quite the philosopher, he thought. He left the women and joined Schiller.

The men were resting, but not sleeping. They were in small groups. Corporal Verdi was with Thompson and Luker. The others were close by. Only Klaus sat by himself. He looked as if he hadn't fully recovered from the effects of the sun. He sat staring at the ground.

Ducan opened his rucksack.

'I know that this was not permitted, Sergeant-Chief,' he said, 'but I brought these along with me for such a night as this.'

He withdrew two half bottles of brandy.

'There are times, *mon Lieutenant*, when officers are allowed to bend the rules,' Schiller said solemnly.

Ducan poured some into a mug.

'Take the bottles,' he said. 'I will give some to Verdi, Thompson and Luker.'

He was grateful to Thompson and Luker. Without Thompson's observations and Luker's medical knowledge, Michelle would have died. They would have all died of poisoning. He went over to them. Schiller went around the others.

'Some brandy,' Ducan said. 'You have earned it.'

'Brandy!' Verdi exclaimed.

The three men sat up eagerly. They got their mugs. Ducan rationed out the brandy. There was an instant air of excitement. Brandy! It was like finding gold. Verdi's eyes lit up. He gave an eager laugh. He looked at his brandy and laughed again.

'*Na zdrovye!*' he called out.

Thompson raised his mug and hesitated. 'Cheers!' he said.

Ducan also hesitated. Verdi had given the Russian toast!

Luker said, '*Sante*!'

Verdi raised his mug. So did Ducan.

'*Na zdrovye!*' Ducan said.

The brandy tasted good. It was like a charge of fresh energy to their bodies.

'So you speak Russian, Corporal,' Ducan said.

Corporal Verdi smiled.

'A little, *mon Lieutenant*,' he said. 'I worked on a lumber camp in Canada for some time. There was a commune of Russian emigres. We used to drink together. They were some drinkers. And you, *mon Lieutenant*, you also speak Russian?'

'Yes, I do. My ancestors were Russian. I speak it as well as I do other languages.'

Corporal Verdi smiled.

'*Na zdrovye*,' he said again, and finished off his drink.

Thompson and Luker both remained silent. They looked all in.

'Sleep well,' Ducan said.

He walked away from them. He had learned a lot about his men on the mission, and now he had learned some more. He had learned that Verdi spoke Russian! But that was not all that troubled him. Verdi had given the Russian toast without thinking. He had given it instinctively. Ducan lay down on the ground and stared long and hard into the darkness. He was thinking of Poujet again.

Malik also stared at the darkness. He did not feel Azir's men like Schiller, but he listened carefully. A sudden noise made him fully alert. It had come from his rear. He swung around.

'Who is it?' he hissed.

'Me — Calowski.'

'Calowski?'

'I have brought some brandy for you, from *Monsieur le Lieutenant.*'

'Brandy! That will be very welcome.'

Calowski sat down beside Malik. He gave him his mug of brandy. Malik took a sip. Calowski sat staring into the darkness.

'You feel them close?' Malik asked.

Calowski shook his head. 'No, but they will come.'

'Logic or intuition?'

'Both.'

Calowski was a strange man, Malik thought. He was deep, sensitive and an unknown factor. Malik had rarely spoken to him. Calowski had kept close to Baron and had been a silent member of their group. This was the first occasion that Malik had ever been alone with him, and he sensed that it had a purpose.

'How did Fingers get it?' Calowski asked.

'You're the second person to ask,' Malik said. 'The others have not breathed his name. It was as if he never existed.'

'He was a grass,' Calowski said. 'They all knew that.'

'A grass? An informer?'

Calowski nodded his head in agreement.

'They can be sniffed out. A con can smell them, just like he can a pig.'

They lapsed into silence. So Fingers had been an informer, Malik thought. He was beginning to understand why he had been shot in the back.

'We seem a very strange group,' Calowski said.

'It is *la Légion*.'

'Do you think so? Or was it planned that we should be kept together?'

'Planned? Why?'

Calowski shook his head and did not reply. Malik knew that he was not going to expand upon his remark, but it had not been spoken lightly. Calowski was deep, and he was suspicious. Malik had even wondered about it himself. Had they been purposely kept together?

'I can't see any logic in why we should be selected to remain together,' he said.

'Can't you?' Calowski asked.

'No.'

Calowski shrugged. 'Perhaps I feel too much,' he said.

'How did you develop your sensitivity? Was your mother a clairvoyant?'

'No. She was a Jewess in the Warsaw Ghetto. That was where I was born. Perhaps it is a natural trait.'

Malik looked at him but did not say anything. He looked away.

'Yes, I am Jewish,' Calowski said.

'It doesn't matter.'

Malik finished his brandy. He gave the mug back to Calowski, but Calowski did not leave.

'Your parents still in Warsaw?' Malik asked.

'Yes, I have not seen them for eight years.'

'Tell me what happened?'

Calowski stared into space. 'I jumped a ship and went to Israel. I tried to arrange for my parents to join me. There were a lot of negotiations. Official negotiations. They came to nothing. I tried the unofficial way. It could have been arranged, but I needed money, more money than I could raise.'

'The underground?'

Calowski gave a half laugh.

'The Communist officials,' he said. 'The people in power can be bought.'

'So you left Israel?'

'I left Israel to try and get some money. Now I am in *la Légion*.'

'What did you do? Where did you work?'

Calowski shook his head. He was not talking.

'Why have you told me this?' Malik asked.

Calowski replied with a question. 'You didn't tell me how Fingers died?'

'He got a bullet in the…' Malik hesitated. 'There was a neat hole in his heart, and in his rucksack.'

'In the back?'

Malik shrugged. 'There was a lot of shooting. A lot of bullets flying about.'

Calowski stood up.

'Take care, Malik,' he warned, and returned to the men.

Malik watched him. He sat so that he could watch both fronts of the pass. Calowski had given him enough warning.

Chapter Thirty

Schiller's hand gently shook Ducan.

Ducan awoke and immediately went for his rifle. It was still dark.

'They are here?' he asked.

'No, *mon Lieutenant.*'

'What is it?'

Schiller gave a sign for the Lieutenant to be silent. He led him away from the party.

'Thompson is missing. He has gone.'

Thompson gone! Ducan was wide awake instantly.

'How? Where?'

'A short while ago. Verdi heard him leave the area. He thought he was going on *sentinelle.*'

Thompson gone! Deserted! My God! Ducan thought. He must have been desperate.

'He can't get away, *mon Lieutenant.*'

'Can't get away?' Ducan asked.

'He'll be making for the old North pass, *mon Lieutenant.*'

'The old North pass,' Ducan whispered, and realised what Thompson had been thinking.

'The North pass is not a pass, Sergeant-Chief,' he said. 'It is a dead end. That is why I referred to it as the old pass.'

'I know that, *mon Lieutenant,* but no one else.'

'You knew?'

'I studied your photographs whilst you slept. On the Greek Island.'

Ducan relaxed his body. 'If he goes South, he will be picked up by our patrols. He will go North, hoping to make for the mountains. *Mon Dieu*! He must be desperate. It is a long way that he hopes to travel.'

'He has a full canteen. He has some rations. He has disciplined himself.'

'He has prepared for the emergency.'

Thompson had prepared for the emergency. Ducan frowned. Thompson had intelligence. He would know what he was up against. Even if the North pass had not been blocked, Thompson's chances of surviving in that territory were slim. There had to be a very strong reason for him to take such a step. There was something going on amongst the men that Ducan did not understand, but he was beginning to suspect that he had inherited one of Poujet's nightmares. Only Thompson could give him any answers. He wanted him brought back. He wanted him brought back — alive.

'I want him brought back, Sergeant-Chief.'

'Verdi has volunteered to go after him.'

'Verdi!' Ducan was suspicious of Verdi, and Thompson had been with Verdi when he had given the Russian toast. Thompson had even responded to it. That could be significant. There could be a connection.

'Send two men, Sergeant-Chief,' he ordered.

'But the mission, *mon Lieutenant*?'

'Thompson won't have got very far. We are close to our goal. There is no sign of Azir's men?'

'No, *mon Lieutenant*, but there is another matter.'

Ducan looked at him. 'Another?'

'Baron, *mon Lieutenant*. He is dead.'

'Dead!' Ducan gasped. 'How?'

'Somebody slit his throat when he was on *sentinelle*.'

'*Mon Dieu*.'

'We have strange company.'

'We certainly have,' Ducan hissed. 'I didn't like the way Ferelli died, Sergeant-Chief. I believe he was shot in the back.'

'Ferelli was an informer, *mon Lieutenant*. The men knew that.'

'And Baron?'

'There is a private score that is being settled on this mission, *mon Lieutenant*.'

Ducan clenched his fist. There certainly was. He felt a surge of anger. If it was Poujet's doing, he had lot to answer for.

'*Mon Lieutenant*. I suggest we let the men settle their own differences. We bring Thompson back.'

'And Baron?'

'We blame Azir's men.'

'They will not believe us.'

'But they will not dispute us. Time is running out. It is almost daylight.'

Ducan glanced at the sky. Time was running out, and Schiller was talking sense — a lot of sense.

'So be it, Sergeant-Chief.' He gripped Schiller's arm. 'I want Thompson back, Sergeant-Chief.'

'I understand, *mon Lieutenant*.'

They rejoined the party.

Quickly Schiller woke the men and warned them to be silent.

'Azir,' he said in a whisper. 'They have killed Baron — *Aux armes*.'

The men awoke instantly and grabbed their weapons. They slipped behind the rocks and quickly prepared themselves. Malik found his hand shaking. Baron was dead!

Ducan woke the women. He told them that they had to move out. That Azir's men were about. The Princess took his arm. He shook his head, telling her to remain silent.

Schiller went amongst the men. He talked quietly, but they all heard him. '*Monsieur le Lieutenant* will lead the way, with the women. We will follow. Malik and Tojak bring up the rear.'

'What about Baron?' Calowski asked.

'We can do nothing for him.'

'Where is Thompson?' Svenson asked.

'He has gone,' Schiller growled.

Gone! The word spread around the men like an electric charge. Thompson had gone! Deserted! Klaus gave a cynical laugh. Schiller scowled at him angrily.

'Gone!' Svenson exclaimed. 'The bastard has deserted. The *cochon*.'

'The North pass?' Luker asked.

'Nobody travels,' Schiller hissed. 'Nobody gets away. We bring him back.'

'Let me get the *cochon*,' Svenson snarled.

'No, we need you here for the women.'

'I'll go after him, Sergeant-Chief,' Verdi said.

Schiller grunted his agreement, but he needed somebody to go with him. He looked around the group. Luker stood up. It was as if he had been reading Schiller's mind.

'Take Luker with you,' Schiller ordered. 'Thompson won't have got far. The North pass is blocked. It is a dead end.'

'Dead end!' Verdi said, and smiled.

'Here is your rifle, Corporal,' Luker called out.

'Leave your machine gun,' Schiller ordered.

Verdi exchanged his machine gun for his rifle.

'You know the route to join us?'

'Yes, Sergeant-Chief.'

Schiller turned to Luker.

'Leave your pistol and your cartridges.'

Luker removed them from his pack. There were only two red cartridges left. He gave them to Schiller.

'On your way,' Schiller growled.

The two men hurried away. They overtook Ducan, who was leading the women and children. Ducan saw them and frowned. He was equally suspicious of Luker as he was of Verdi. He was now suspicious of them all.

'Now we move out,' Schiller ordered the men.

They came out from their cover and slipped down the side of the rocks. Calowski hesitated and suddenly scurried back up the pass. Schiller saw him and went after him. The others hesitated. Svenson said, 'Come. We go this way.' He led the way.

Calowski moved quickly. He climbed over the rocks and ran up the pass. He came to the large boulder that had been their lookout position. In the early light, a mist hung over the ground, but he did not have to look for Baron. The vultures were already there. They flapped away as Calowski stopped in his tracks. He came to Baron's body. The birds had torn at his guts and his eyes.

Calowski stood breathing heavily. Schiller caught up with him. Calowski's face looked black with anger.

'The bastard!' he spat.

'It was Azir's men,' Schiller snarled.

Calowski swung around. Schiller cracked the butt of his machine gun into Calowski's head. Calowski crumpled to the ground. Schiller grabbed him and pulled him to his feet.

'When we get to Djibouti,' he hissed, 'you can talk as much as you like. Until then, it was Azir's men — understand?'

Calowski caught up with his breathing.

'And if you ever run the wrong way again, Calowski, I will kill you. Understand that also?'

'He was *mon ami*,' Calowski stammered.

'You have no friends, Calowski. Remember that. You have only enemies. Now move it.'

A dull bang made them both start. A trip had gone off up the pass. Schiller's eyes tried to pierce the swirling ground mist. They saw nothing, but he knew that Azir had arrived.

'Move it!' he hissed.

They hurried back to the column. The mist was lifting. They were in a narrow, rocky pass, but ahead they could see the broad, open basin that marked the beginning of the South pass that led to French territory.

That moved quickly. They heard another trip go off and they all knew what it meant.

Ducan in particular knew what it meant, and he knew that at their present speed they would not cross the basin into the South pass before Azir overtook them. Something had to be done. He had been thinking about it as he had been walking. He studied the rocks at the sides of the pass. They were loose and numerous. There was also a lot of cover where the pass met the basin. He made his decision. He dropped back and walked alongside the American girl. Michelle was behind them with the Princess. Svenson and Malik were carrying the two children.

'You can see the South pass,' Ducan said to the American girl. He pointed across the open ground that lay ahead. About two kilometres away was the start of the pass.

'Keep going South,' he said. 'You should be safe in that pass. You will meet some friends.'

'And you?' she asked.

'I have something to do,' he said.

He looked back and saw Michelle looking at him. He smiled at her. She returned the smile. He stood to one side. She trudged past. Their eyes met. She did not have to say anything. He saw it all in her eyes. Her concern and her feelings for him. It was all there, and his heart warmed. He turned quickly and went back along the column to where Schiller was bringing up the rear.

'We move quickly, Sergeant-Chief,' he said. 'Listen and...' He hesitated.

'And — *mon Lieutenant?*'

'Do as I say without question,' Ducan said.

'*Mon Lieutenant?*'

'I want two machine guns and ammunition. I will take one of them. I want the other loaded and placed at that pile of rocks at the head of the pass with some ammunition.'

He pointed to the position.

'I want Klaus to place the rest of his explosives in two piles. One up the slope alongside the rock at the spur.' Again he indicated the position. 'The other by that bush.' There was a single thorn bush in the middle of the pass. 'I want the explosives prepared so that they will go off when I fire at them.'

'You, *mon Lieutenant?*'

'Yes, Sergeant-Chief — me. I am going to hold off Azir's men. You are going to take this party to the South pass. Four kilometres along that pass, you should find a forward patrol of *la Légion*. If Azir gets past this position, you will be able to hold him in that pass.'

'But...'

'Sergeant-Chief. There is no time to delay. I give the orders. Above all else, I want these women to get to safety. Azir might have outdone us. We will not know until you reach the South pass. If he is there, I want somebody I can trust to look after the women. If he is not there, you do whatever is necessary.'

'I will come back, *mon Lieutenant*,' Schiller said with feeling.

Ducan looked at him and smiled. 'Let's move it,' he said.

Schiller gave him his gun and some ammunition. Ducan left him and started climbing the side of the pass. Schiller watched him and scowled. He shouted for Klaus. Klaus came up to him. Schiller saw Ducan taking up a position behind some rocks. His face looked black when he turned to Klaus.

'Get the rest of the explosives from Malik,' he ordered. 'Set them at that rock and that bush.' He indicated the positions. 'And Klaus, make sure they will go off when they are fired at. Understand?'

'Yes, Sergeant-Chief.'

Schiller left him and hurried along the column. They were approaching the end of the pass. There was no ground mist now. It was all clear, and it was going to be hot again. He went up to Tojak. 'Leave your machine gun and ammunition behind that large boulder. Take the spare rifle from Malik.'

'Why, Sergeant-Chief?' Tojak asked.

'Do as you are told,' Schiller snapped. He caught up with Svenson, who was leading the column, carrying one of the children.

'You see the South pass, Svenson?'

'Yes, Sergeant-Chief.'

'I am going to put Luker's pistol and two cartridges in your pack. The pass leads to French territory. Azir's men should not be there. If they are, fire two cartridges. If not, fire only one. Leave the other for emergency. One of our patrols should be looking for you. Whatever happens, Svenson, get these women and children to safety.'

Svenson grunted his agreement. 'And you, Sergeant-Chief?'

'I am going to stay and help the Lieutenant stop Azir.'

'The others?'

Schiller spat his disgust, but he knew Svenson was not Fingers' killer.

'They are a murderous lot of scum. Listen, Svenson. Ferelli was shot in the back and Baron was murdered. One of these four scum is a murderer. You will find out which one, and you know what to do when you get to Djibouti.'

'How will I find out?'

'When you get to the pass. If there is no reception committee, send the men back. Our murdering friend will want to stay. Tell the authorities in Djibouti what I have told you.'

'What about Thompson, Sergeant-Chief?'

'He will be back. He will help. Now hurry!'

Schiller stood to one side. Calowski and Tojak came alongside him.

'If there is no reception committee when you get to the South pass,' Schiller growled, 'you come back and help. Tell Malik and Klaus.'

Malik had given Klaus the explosives and was hurrying to catch up with the column. Schiller had lost sight of Ducan. He went to where Tojak had placed the second machine gun and watched Klaus preparing the charges. Klaus was working as if Azir's men were already on top of him. Schiller scowled. He did not trust Klaus any longer.

Brrr!… Brrrrr!… Brrrr! Schiller looked up. Ducan had had his first sighting, he thought. Azir's advance party had arrived.

Klaus finished preparing the charges up the slope. He ran to the bush and started preparing his second set. Schiller watched him through his sights. He had the positions pin pointed. He removed his pack and took out his water bottle and his treasured *kepi*. He laid his *kepi* alongside his pack. It reminded him that he was a *sous-officier* in the Legion again, and he felt better.

Chapter Thirty-one

Verdi moved quickly. The white ground mist swirled around his feet, and the dampness dried on his face. He knew what was at stake. He had to get to Thompson. He gave a faint smile as he thought of the pass being blocked. The Lieutenant had been very clever, he thought. He had tempted them with a route to freedom, knowing that the pass was blocked. Yes, the Lieutenant had been very clever, or very stupid. He looked over his shoulder and saw Luker behind him. He had not had much to say or do with Luker, he thought. Luker was all right as a medical orderly, but not as a legionnaire. So why was he there at all? Verdi frowned. Was Luker really the quiet Swiss? Or was Luker… Verdi shook his head. No, he thought, not Luker. Klaus, Malik, Tojak, perhaps, but not Luker. He looked up. They were in the North pass now. The scenery did not change much. It was the same yellow and dirty white rocks. The same large boulders and thorny bushes. '*Mon Dieu!*' he thought. What a country. He glanced up at the sky. It was a clear blue, not a cloud to be seen, and the sun was beginning to make itself felt.

Luker missed his footing and went crashing to the ground. Verdi stopped, cursed him and went back to him.

'You hurt?'

'Just a bruise, Corporal,' Luker said. 'Why did Thompson have to decide to travel?'

He groaned as he got to his feet.

Verdi shook his head. 'Why did Schiller send you? Have you ever fired that rifle?'

'On the range, Corporal.'

'Come on.'

Verdi started off again. His eyes kept scanning the rocks, and at each bend, he looked hopefully for an end to the pass.

Crack! A bullet whined off the rocks close to his head. He stopped dead in his tracks.

Crack! Another bullet smacked into the rocks. Luker had taken cover behind a boulder. Verdi joined him.

'Is it Thompson?' Luker asked.

'Yes,' Verdi said. 'He must have found the pass blocked and made his way back.'

He moved to the edge of the boulder.

'Thompson!' he shouted. He heard his voice echo along the pass. 'This is Verdi. I have Luker with me. The pass is blocked. There is no way out.' Again the words echoed along the pass.

Crack! Another bullet whined off the rocks.

'Thompson, I am a friend. I am not going to shoot back.' *Shoot back! Shoot back!* The words trailed away and faded into silence.

The silence settled over the valley. No further shots came from Thompson.

'I am sorry about last night,' Verdi shouted. 'I had to make sure that it was you. I am a friend. I had to make sure before I made my move.'

Again his voice echoed along the pass. He turned and saw Luker crouched beside him. But the look on Luker's face suddenly made him suspicious. Luker was listening very carefully, and he did not quite look the innocent that he had always appeared. And his hands held his rifle tightly, and it was pointed in Verdi's direction! Verdi did not take any chances. He half stood up and suddenly swung the butt of his rifle in a scything action. It caught Luker unexpectedly on the side of his skull. Luker grunted and fell forward. Blood trickled down his face. He groaned and lay still.

Verdi turned away. He took a deep breath.

'Visinsky,' he called out. 'I am authorised by the French Government to offer you full protection. Not even Luker will know. Luker has had an accident. He is resting. You must be quick before he recovers.'

Verdi waited tensely. 'Come on, Thompson,' he called out. 'Come on.'

He looked at Luker. His rifle was still in his hands, but his head lay still against the rock face.

'Who do you work for?' Thompson called out.

Verdi gave a sigh of relief.

'I work for *Le Service de Documentation et de Contre-Espionnage*,' he shouted back. 'I was sent to help you when we heard of Madame Zena's murder.'

'Where did you go?' Thompson shouted.

'To Vienna, then to Zurich. Carl Russo had transferred you to Marseilles instead of into hiding. He had sold us out to the Americans. You knew that in Marseilles. He sent you to Lassenan who was meant to ship you to the States. The K.G.B. got to him first. I picked up your trail at *Le Chien Noir* — I saw Picasso. He is also dead. I followed you into *la Légion*, but I was not sure of your identity until last night.'

Verdi paused. 'I am going to stand up. You can shoot me if you wish, or you can come and join me. My Government will help you.'

He stood up. His waist was the height of the boulder. His head and chest were exposed. He felt the sun on his body, and his eyes watered as he studied the sunlit walls of the pass. There was no shot. Then he saw Thompson emerge, and he gave a broad smile.

'Come Thompson — *mon ami*,' he called out.

He glanced down at Luker. Luker had stirred. Thompson slid down the rocks into the valley. He came towards Verdi, a little hesitant in his step.

Verdi stood in the open. Thompson approached.

'Where is Luker?' Thompson called out.

'He is here. He has been sleeping.'

Luker groaned as he came to.

'The K.G.B.,' Thompson called out. 'They are after me. I know.' There was a quiver of fear in his voice.

'We will protect you,' Verdi called back. 'You are safe now.'

'Safe! Can you really protect me?'

His voice quivered again as he spoke the words.

'Yes, we can protect you. You need fear no more.'

Thompson climbed over the rocks to where Verdi was standing.

'Thank goodness it is all over,' he said.

'Yes,' Verdi replied. 'It has been a long trail from the Rostov Academy.'

Thompson froze. He was only about two metres away from Verdi.

'What was my code name, Verdi?' he asked.

Verdi shook his head.

'It doesn't matter now,' he replied. 'Drop your rifle, Comrade Visinsky. You didn't think we would let you get away from us?'

Thompson's body sagged. Verdi's rifle was pointed at his chest.

'Drop it,' Verdi said in Russian.

He put the first pressure on his trigger and took aim. Thompson dropped his rifle.

'Put your hands on your head,' Verdi ordered. 'Move to one side.'

Again Verdi had spoken in Russian. Thompson lifted his hands and moved away from his rifle.

'What about Luker?' he asked, playing for time.

'Luker!' Verdi scoffed. He turned to Luker. Luker lay on the ground. His eyes were open, but dazed. They were watching Verdi.

'Luker is going to die,' Verdi said. 'Then you, Visinsky, but first you are going to tell me everything.'

He pointed his rifle at Luker's head and squeezed the trigger. There was a metallic *click*. A look of horror came to Verdi's face as he quickly re-loaded and squeezed the trigger again. Again there was a metallic *click*. He looked at Luker. 'You…!' he gasped. Luker squeezed his trigger. There was a sharp *crack!* and Verdi was dead.

Chapter Thirty-two

'OK, Sergeant-Chief?' Klaus asked, eager to be away. 'I have prepared them well.'

'You had better, Klaus. Or I'll have your guts.' Schiller looked into Klaus's wild looking face and purposely spat. He had Klaus marked as a coward. He spat again.

Brrrr!… Brrr!… Brrrrrrr!…

More spasmodic firing from Ducan. It was answered by a series of rifle cracks.

Klaus looked at the Sergeant-Chief.

'OK?' he asked again.

'Point them out to me,' Schiller ordered.

Klaus pointed out the two positions. He knew that the Sergeant-Chief was purposely making him wait.

'When you get to the South pass,' Schiller said, 'you will either find it peaceful or busy. One flare means that it is peaceful. Two that there is trouble. If it is peaceful, Klaus, you come back.'

'Sure, Sergeant-Chief.'

Schiller spat again.

'And when you do,' he snarled, 'you fight like a legionnaire.'

Again Ducan opened up. Again there was a spasmodic reply of rifle fire.

'OK Klaus. You can go.'

Klaus did not delay. He moved off at the double. Schiller gave a scowl of disgust and followed him with the barrel of his machine gun, and an itchy finger on the trigger. He had a strong desire to squeeze the trigger. He did not trust Klaus any longer.

He heard rifle shots from the North pass. Either Thompson was being difficult or Azir's men were in the pass. He turned away from the figure of Klaus running away.

Brrr!... Brrrrr!... Brrrr!...

Schiller rubbed his beard. The Lieutenant would soon be out of ammunition at the speed that he was firing his machine gun.

There was another burst of rifle fire. Another long burst from Ducan. Schiller fingered his trigger anxiously. Ducan would not be able to hold them, he thought, and neither would Ducan and Schiller together. They would need help.

'Miserable scum,' he muttered, as he thought of Klaus and the others.

A red flare suddenly pierced the sky in the South pass. Schiller waited. There was no second flare. He gave a grunt of relief. The pass was trouble-free.

Svenson would get the women and children to safety. His face clouded over. He wondered how many of the bastards would come back and help.

Klaus had no intention of returning. He saw the single red flare, and he started to laugh. The South pass was trouble free. He was going to make the border. He was going to survive. He unfastened his water canteen and took a long drink. He wiped his mouth. Just one little job first, he thought, and then he would be home safe and dry. His eyes caught the sun's glare, and it made them smart. He would never return to Africa again, he thought. Nothing would induce him back. He had had enough of the sun and the dust. He would spend the rest of his life in a more temperate climate, and in more luxurious surroundings. He laughed again. It was a wild, hysterical laugh. The sound of Ducan firing his guns made him stop abruptly. He started for the pass at a trot. He met the others before he reached it. He saw them coming towards him. He recognised

Calowski, Tojak and Malik. He stopped in his tracks and glanced about him. He was in a small depression. The pass with Ducan and Schiller was hidden from his view. It was the ideal place, he thought. He let them come to him.

'*Vive la Légion*,' he called out, as they approached. '*Vive la Légion*,' he mocked.

'The pass is clear, Klaus,' Malik shouted. 'We have to return and help *Monsieur le Lieutenant* and Schiller.'

'And Svenson?' Klaus asked.

'He is remaining with the women and children.'

'Come,' Malik said.

He had only taken one step when Klaus shouted, 'Hold it!'

Malik turned in his tracks. Klaus had his rifle pointing at him. He also had a mocking smile on his grubby, bearded face.

'Hold it!' Klaus shouted again. He stood back. 'You also, Tojak!'

He waved his rifle from Malik to Tojak and back to Malik again.

Malik looked at him with disbelief.

'What's this all about?' he demanded.

Klaus waved his rifle at him menacingly. The sun burned down on them. They were standing in the open ground. A small group of bearded and tired men, but Klaus had his rifle in his hands, and a wild look in his eyes.

'For God's sake, Klaus,' Malik shouted. 'They need help.'

He turned away from Klaus.

'Don't move!' Klaus shouted wildly, and then added, 'You're going to help nobody.'

Malik looked at him defiantly.

'What the hell are you up to?' he shouted. He looked at Calowski, who stood watching with his machine gun in his hands. 'What's happening, Calowski?'

Calowski did not answer him. He stood quite still, as if his hands were frozen to the trigger of his machine gun.

'As if you don't know,' Klaus sneered.

'No, I don't!' Malik returned. 'But I know that they need help. What the hell has got into you Klaus? What's it all about?'

'Six million francs,' Klaus laughed out. 'That is what it is all about. Six million francs' worth of jewellery, and Fingers.'

'Fingers?' Malik asked.

'Yes, Fingers,' Klaus said, and suddenly swung his rifle to point at Tojak, who had moved. 'Don't Tojak,' he warned, 'or you're dead. Throw your rifle away — and you Malik.' His face hardened. 'I mean it!'

The two men hesitated, then threw their rifles to the ground. They saw the look of madness in Klaus's eyes. He was in a dangerous mood. He laughed out loud.

'What about Fingers?' Tojak growled.

'Ask him,' Klaus said, pointing his rifle at Malik. He did not wait for Malik to answer. He turned to Calowski. 'Get their rifles,' he ordered. Calowski hesitated.

'Get them,' Klaus snapped.

Calowski collected the rifles and threw them to one side. He still had his own machine gun in his hands. He was watching Klaus.

'You know who killed Fingers,' Klaus said. 'Don't you, Malik? Don't you, *Monsieur le Policeman*?'

'Policeman!' Tojak snarled.

'Don't play the innocent, Tojak,' Klaus mocked.

Malik knew the score now. Klaus and Calowski had pulled off a big jewel robbery and had taken refuge in the Legion — and they thought that Malik was after them. He gave a mocking laugh.

'So that's what it's all about. You think that I am a pig. Well, you are wrong, Klaus. You are wrong! I am not a pig!'

'Aren't you?' Klaus snarled. 'You ask Tojak. He had you marked for a pig from the beginning. Just like the rest of us. You stink like a pig.'

Malik controlled his anger. They were standing in the blazing sun playing games with a madman when they should be fighting for their lives. It was unbelievable. He looked at Calowski appealingly. Calowski's features did not relax. Malik turned to Klaus in desperation.

'All right, Klaus, I was a policeman before I joined the Legion. But why do you think I joined the Legion? I had to, Klaus. I had to. I am on the run like you.'

Klaus laughed again.

'You still stink, Malik. A pig always stinks.'

His plea had not worked. Malik knew that Klaus was insane. Their only hope was to play for time.

'And informers?' he asked.

'And informers,' Klaus agreed. His eyes lit up. 'You knew, Malik. You knew who shot him.'

'I knew it had to be you, or Tojak,' Malik said. 'Verdi and Baron had the machine-guns. But why Klaus? Why?'

'Why?' Klaus's face clouded over.

'Don't come that, Malik,' he scoffed. 'You knew what Fingers was after.'

'And Tojak? What about him?'

'Tojak?' Klaus laughed again. 'Tojak is as much a Slav as Fingers. Who sent you Tojak? Bassito?'

Tojak made a move, but Klaus brought his gun to point at him. 'Another of Bassito's hired killers?'

'*Merde* to you, Klaus,' Tojak spat. 'I don't know what you are screaming about, but if I had my rifle I would willingly kill you.'

'I saw you and Ferelli together,' Klaus snapped. 'Did you agree to work together?'

'He told me nothing,' Tojak growled. 'You're mad. I was on the run like I told you.'

Malik looked at Calowski again. Calowski's face was still expressionless, and he held his machine-gun pointing in their direction.

In the distance, there was a burst of machine-gun fire. It was followed by a series of rifle fire, then another burst from a machine-gun.

'For God's sake, Klaus,' Malik urged. 'They need us. I don't know what the hell you have in mind, but we are all suffering. Forget all this.'

'Forget!' Klaus hissed. 'No, Malik, this is the end.'

'You aren't going to get away with it. Schiller and…'

'Azir's men will get them,' Klaus mocked. 'Two men can't stop Azir's men.'

'The authorities in Djibouti will get to know,' Malik said hastily. 'Don't be a fool, Klaus. They will get you.'

'It will have been Azir's doing,' Klaus sneered. 'Azir will have got you along with the rest of them.'

He laughed and raised his gun. Malik desperately played for time.

'What about Baron?' he asked. 'Did you kill him as well?'

'He knew too much. Calowski made a mistake bringing him along. He was dangerous to us. He was too well-known.'

'And Calowski? Will you kill him also?'

Klaus's face clouded over. Malik knew that he was insane.

'Don't try that tack,' Klaus said.

Tojak gave a yell and went for his gun.

Malik jumped to one side as Klaus squeezed his trigger. The bullets shot past Malik's head.

Brrrr!... A burst of fire came from Calowski's machine-gun. The bullets ripped into Klaus's body. Klaus died instantly with blood splattered all over his chest. He fell to the ground. There was a moment's silence. Tojak picked up the rifles. He hesitated, then handed one to Malik. Calowski stood quite still.

'It was Azir's men,' Tojak said. 'Now we go and fight.' He headed for the sound of fighting at the double. Malik looked at Calowski.

'Come on,' he said. 'Let's go.'

They followed the bulky Slav, increasing their speed as the sound of shooting became more rapid.

Chapter Thirty-three

Ducan nestled behind his boulder and kept his eyes fixed on the bend in the pass. He saw a dark shape dart from one pile of rocks to another. He did not think; he gave it a burst.

Brrr!… Brrrrr!… Brr!… He saw the tracers spatter the distant rocks. Damn the tracers, he thought. They would give away his position. He stopped firing. Then more figures moved in his line of fire. *Brrrr!… Brr!… Brrrrr!…* Again he sprayed the ground. He kept firing until his gun was empty. Calmly, he reloaded.

Crack! Crack! Crack! A series of bullets ricocheted off the side of the rocks above his head. He kept his head low. When they stopped firing, he quickly opened up again. He finished off another magazine. He removed it. The gun was hot to touch. He quickly reloaded and slithered away to another boulder, lower down the slope. He peered around his cover and felt a tremor pass through his body. There seemed to be about three dozen figures running into position. Wildly, he fired and kept on firing. The figures disappeared, but they returned his fire. Bullets were coming both ways. He ceased firing. He was wasting precious ammunition. He had to make it last. He lay still, then moved his body so he could see the ground in front of him.

The seconds ticked by. Every second was important. Every second that he held them would help Michelle. The thought encouraged him. Then they moved. A wave of khaki-clad figures with burned faces darted towards him. He fired his gun. He kept on firing. He was vaguely aware of a loud explosion and a cloud of dust, and a burning sensation in his shoulder.

He fired until the gun had no more ammunition. Instinct told him to get out of his position. He picked up the two remaining magazines and his gun. There was a *crack! crack! crack!* and the bullets smacked into his cover. He slithered down the slope and darted along the pass… Something hit his leg and sent him to the ground…

Brrrrr!… Brrr!… Brrrr!… A machine gun blazed away. It was Schiller. He was standing beside Ducan firing from his hip. Ducan struggled to his feet.

'Get going!' Schiller yelled, and fired again. Ducan moved, but there was a sharp pain in his left leg. He kept going. Schiller kept firing. Ducan saw the pile of rocks that he had planned to make for, and stumbled behind it. He lay on the ground, the perspiration rolling off his face. Schiller jumped in beside him.

'The women?' Ducan asked.

'Svenson will look after them,' Schiller said. He removed his bush hat and placed his treasured *kepi* on his head.

'You hit, *mon Lieutenant*?'

Ducan took stock of himself. His shoulder was bleeding, but that was only a superficial would. But a bullet had ripped through his calf muscle. He looked up at Schiller. Schiller was watching the pass. Ducan saw his *kepi*.

'*Le kepi!* Sergeant-Chief!' he exclaimed. His eyes danced mischievously.

Schiller's face looked serious.

'If I am going to die for France, *mon Lieutenant*,' he said, 'I am wearing this *kepi*. I am a legionnaire. To hell with anything else.'

'Sergeant-Chief,' Ducan said with a chuckle, 'you have bent the rules. We are invaders!'

'No, *mon Lieutenant*. I have served in this territory before. This is no-man's land. It is in dispute. It is not Ethiopian territory.'

Ducan gave a loud laugh, and then coughed. Schiller looked at him anxiously. Ducan got his breath back.

'You really do amaze me, Sergeant-Chief,' he said. 'This is the second time that you have amazed me.'

'The second time, *mon Lieutenant*?'

'In the hut,' Ducan said, but said no more. Schiller could have acted differently then, he thought. He could have been all contempt, but he had not been.

'We needed you, *mon Lieutenant*,' Schiller said. 'Besides, I was the same after my first kill.'

He saw some movement. He fired a burst from his machine gun.

'Where is my *kepi*?' Ducan called out.

Schiller looked at him. His features relaxed into a rough smile.

'You don't need one, *mon Lieutenant*,' he said, and turned away. 'Klaus laid out the explosives. You OK?'

'Yes.'

Ducan reloaded his gun.

'Take the rock, *mon Lieutenant*,' Schiller said. 'I will take the bush. When the bastards come, we'll give them a surprise.'

'There are a lot of them, and they have grenades.'

'So have we.'

Ducan did not answer. He suddenly felt very tired.

'Here they come, *mon Lieutenant*.'

Schiller gave a short burst. Ducan moved into a firing position. Schiller gave another burst. Ducan could not see what he was firing at.

'They are on the spur,' Schiller shouted. 'We'll keep them there as long as we can. Verdi and Thompson will be back soon.'

'Thompson!'

Ducan had forgotten about him. He saw a figure move. He fired a short burst. The figure disappeared into the rocks.

'Here they come!' Schiller shouted.

Ducan saw them darting forward. An army of brown figures. Something exploded in front of him. It was a long way in front. They were throwing grenades, he thought, but they were out of range.

Schiller fired his gun. Suddenly a stream of lead ricocheted off the rocks above their position.

'Machine gun,' Schiller shouted, and fired his gun. So did Ducan. He kept it blazing up the pass. He saw a figure fall, and another, but they were getting closer. Another grenade exploded in front of them. This time, it was close enough to shower them with fragments of rocks.

Brrr!... A burst of lead hit their position again. It made them both take cover.

'Get the explosives!' Schiller shouted. He slipped back into a lower position.

The machine-gun ceased firing. Ducan edged around his cover. He saw the advancing figures. They would soon be in range with their grenades, he thought. He saw the position where Klaus had laid his explosives. He fired at it. Nothing happened. He fired again. The bullets smashed into the rocks.

There was a loud explosion in the middle of the pass. Schiller had set off the other explosives. Ducan fired again. There was a flash and a roar as the boulder disintegrated. The shockwaves hit Ducan and sent him on his back. As he took cover, he saw the rocks tumbling down the side of the pass. A heavy dust cloud engulfed the pass. Schiller fired his gun. Ducan fired into the dust cloud. Then they waited.

The dust settled. The pass was strewn with small rocks. There were several still figures.

'They'll not give up,' Ducan called out.

Schiller was on his side. He pointed to their rear and held up his thumb in an encouraging gesture. Ducan turned and saw three figures approaching. It was Tojak, Malik and Calowski.

Crack! Crack! Crack!

Ducan went flat on his back. A bullet had torn into his side. Schiller fired his machine gun. He kept firing angrily. Ducan tried to get up from the ground, but he could not move himself. Schiller ceased firing. He scrambled over to Ducan and lifted him into a safe position. Ducan felt hazy.

'You will be OK *mon Lieutenant*,' Schiller assured him. 'The bullet has missed the vital parts.'

Ducan tried to say something, but the words would not come out.

'Sure,' he muttered eventually. 'It is hot.'

Schiller tore Ducan's shirt open and got a bandage ready.

'Move it!' he shouted to Tojak and the others. 'Move it!'

There was an urgency in his voice. He turned and fired a burst from his machine gun up the pass.

Malik, Calowski and Tojak rushed into a position close to Schiller.

'Bandage *le Lieutenant*,' Schiller shouted to Malik. 'Take his machine gun. Leave him your rifle. The rest of you — spread out!'

Malik saw the hazy look in Ducan's eyes. He tied a bandage carefully around his side. There was also blood on Ducan's face.

Brr!... Brrrr!... Brrrrrr!...

Schiller was firing his gun. So were Azir's men. Their bullets were hitting the rocks close to where Schiller and the others were crouched.

'Give Tojak all your grenades,' Schiller shouted to Malik. 'Tell him to move forward. We cover him.'

Malik took another look at Ducan. Ducan gave a faint smile. Malik darted across the ground to where Tojak was firing his rifle.

'Take the grenades and go forward,' he said. 'We cover you.'

Tojak stopped firing his rifle. He accepted the grenades from Malik and Calowski. He hesitated. Calowski and Schiller fired their machine guns. Tojak darted forward to some large boulders. Malik joined in the covering fire. Tojak threw his grenades. They went far up the pass. They exploded one after another.

Tojak remained behind his cover. There was a lot of movement in the pass, and a lot of shooting.

Calowski kept firing his gun. Malik saw his bullets smacking into the rocks. A burst of machine gun fire came back at them. They took cover.

Tojak started to move back again. Suddenly he fell. He scrambled behind a rock, dragging a leg.

Calowski called to Malik, 'I'll cover you.'

Malik darted forward across the rock strewn ground. Something spurted up at him from his feet. He rushed into Tojak's cover. Tojak gave a big grin.

'It's nothing,' he said.

The bullet had torn through his thigh. Malik ripped away the trousers and got out a bandage from his pocket. A bullet smacked against the rock, and made him duck his head.

'They are a lot of bastards,' Tojak grinned.

Malik tied a temporary bandage to stop the bleeding.

'You'll live, Tojak.'

Malik kept low. Calowski and Schiller were firing steady bursts from their machine guns, but so were Azir's men. Malik looked through a slit in his cover. He could see rocks and more rocks, but he saw a long burst of fire from one of the rocks. It was their machine gun. He had their position.

'Any grenades left?' he asked Tojak.

'Sure, two. I was saving them. You going after them?'

'Yeah!'

Tojak grinned. 'OK, Policeman.'

'It had you worried, Tojak?'

'What Klaus said,' Tojak grinned. 'You can smell them. I had you figured.'

'You on the run?' Malik asked, and studied the pass.

'Don't you know?'

Yes, Malik thought, he knew. He had seen the reports in the police files. He knew a lot about Tojak.

He turned and waved to Calowski, bringing him forward.

'Klaus was wrong about me. How about you, Tojak? Were you after him and Calowski?'

Tojak grinned, and said, 'It's time to start shooting again.' He moved to the side of his cover. 'Klaus had too much sun,' he said as he fired his rifle. 'Too much sun.'

Calowski scrambled into their position.

'I've fixed one of their machine guns,' Malik said. 'Cover me.' He gave Tojak his machine gun, and took Tojak's rifle.

Calowski moved to a position where he could fire his own gun. Tojak sat back.

'*Bonne chance!*' he called out.

Malik darted forward and went flat. Above his head, Calowski's bullets peppered the air. Schiller also started firing, but the bullets were still coming both ways. Malik moved on all fours. The ground bruised his hands and body, but he scrambled forward. Two bullets smacked into the ground in front of him. Another grazed his boot. He rolled to one side. Calowski fired again, and so did Schiller.

Malik saw the small row of rocks ahead that was his target.

There was another burst of covering fire. Malik made the rocks and threw the grenades. He scrambled back. There was an explosion, and another. He moved quickly. He got to his feet and started to run. A bullet winged him in the shoulder and sent him crashing to the ground. A hand grabbed him. It was Calowski firing from the hip. He dragged him into their cover again.

Tojak grinned.

'You got them good,' he said.

It was Malik's left shoulder. It burned like hell, but he could still fire a gun. He took the machine gun from Tojak.

'What now?' he asked.

'They'll make a big attack,' Calowski said. 'I wonder if the Sergeant-Chief has anything in mind.'

Schiller had watched Malik. Malik had done his job well, but time and ammunition were running out. And time was also running out for Ducan. The sun was now burning their bodies. Ducan's eyes were hazy. He had lost blood. He was in pain. Schiller suddenly felt a great wave of anger. He did not want Ducan to die. He wanted him to live. He fired his gun in anger and sprayed the rocks.

There was a return of rifle fire. The pass was being peppered with cracks, like a Chinese firework display.

But some of the cracks were coming from higher ground. Schiller saw a figure collapse behind a rock. He had been hit from behind! Schiller looked up to the sky. He saw two puffs of smoke from the top of the rock face. He turned to Ducan.

'Verdi is back,' he said. 'Verdi is back.'

'Verdi,' Ducan muttered. 'Verdi!' The thought took time to penetrate his brain. 'Back! And Thompson?'

Schiller gave a burst from his gun.

'We shall see, *mon Lieutenant*. We shall see.'

Again there were a series of rifle shots from the high ground. Schiller decided it was time to make their move.

'I will be back,' he said.

He picked up his gun and crawled across the pass to where he could see Calowski's position. He waved and signalled. Calowski got the message. He had also seen the shooting from the high ground. He turned to Malik.

'We advance,' he said.

'I go with you,' Tojak called out. 'Get me to my feet.'

Calowski got him into a standing position and leant him against the side of the boulder. He struggled to a position where he could fire his gun. Malik had his machine gun in his right hand. Calowski went first, firing from the hip. Schiller and Malik followed suit. From the higher ground, the legionnaires joined in the shooting. Tojak fired from his half standing position.

They had advanced about thirty metres, when suddenly Schiller yelled, 'Stop! *Cessez le feu!*' His raucous voice was loud and clear. '*Cessez le feu!*' he shouted again.

Malik stopped shooting. Calowski gave one further burst and also stopped.

They all stood still. They could see Azir's men. They were retreating. They were darting back up the pass.

Schiller could have gone for the kill. They could have picked off Azir's men, but he stood still. Calowski and Malik looked at him.

'They won't bother us any more,' he growled. 'We have more important things to do.'

He waved his arm to the legionnaires on the high ground, telling them to join him, and turned to the others.

'Let's go,' he shouted. 'We must hurry. Calowski, cover us.'

They hurried back to where Ducan lay with his eyes closed. Calowski kept a watch up the pass, but Azir's men had gone.

'Get a sleeping bag and rifles,' Schiller ordered.

Schiller got his water bottle and gently wiped Ducan's brow. He tore a strip from his shirt and soaked it in water and laid it over Ducan's mouth.

They quickly made a stretcher and laid Ducan on it. They shielded his face from the fierce rays of the sun that were burning down on them.

'Luker! Sergeant-Chief,' Calowski suddenly called out. 'Here comes Luker!'

They all looked up to see Luker coming down the rock face. Schiller frowned. Luker was alone!

Luker hurried to their position. His face was matted with dust and congealed blood.

'Verdi?' Schiller growled, 'and Thompson?'

Luker caught up with his breathing.

'Azir's men were in the North pass. They got Verdi. A stray bullet got Thompson.'

Schiller glanced up at the high ground where he had seen and heard rifle fire from two positions, and then at Luker. His eyes narrowed. He did not believe Luker, and it showed on his face.

'When we meet the patrol, Luker, you will give a full report, and it better be good. Understand?'

'Yes, Sergeant-Chief.'

Schiller grunted and glowered at the others, who were gathered around him.

'Klaus?' he asked.

There was no immediate reply.

'He is dead, Sergeant-Chief,' Malik said. 'Azir's men.' Schiller looked at him. He had had a shrewd idea who had murdered Baron and Ferelli. Now he knew he had been correct. A private score had been settled. This he understood, and agreed with.

'A stray bullet?' he asked.

'A stray bullet,' Malik agreed.

Between them, they had put the official seal on the matter. Klaus had been killed by a stray bullet.

'Go and bury him,' Schiller ordered. 'Take Calowski and Tojak.'

'Yes, Sergeant-Chief.'

'Malik!'

Malik hesitated.

'You be quick. We need help to carry the Lieutenant. We move fast, even in the sun.'

'Yes, Sergeant-Chief.'

Malik hurried away, accompanied by Calowski. Tojak limped behind them. His thigh was bandaged and he trailed his leg, but he moved quickly. The others set off for the pass, carrying Ducan.

Malik's party found Klaus's body. The vultures were there, but they kept their distance. Silently, Malik and Calowski scratched a hole in the sand with their hand tools. They worked quickly and silently. Even the sun was forgotten. They had only one object in mind: to get the hell away from the place as soon as possible.

It was only a shallow grave, and the cover would soon be eroded by the constant breeze, but Klaus would rot away in peace. The vultures would not get at him.

'He was a cheerful bastard,' Calowski said, more to himself than to the others, 'but deep inside he was too greedy, and too impatient.'

'Too much sun,' Malik added, 'and too much suspicion.'

He wiped the grime and sweat from his grubby face, and looked at Tojak. Tojak had also been full of suspicion, he thought. There had been feeling between him and Tojak.

'Still suspicious of me, Tojak?'

'You're sure you know nothing about me?' Tojak asked.

'Nothing,' Malik said. 'I've never seen your ugly face before.'

Tojak's face lit up.

'You must have been a lousy pig,' he said.

There was the sound of relief in his voice. Malik turned to Calowski.

'What now?' he asked. 'Stay on the run?'

Calowski looked at him with uncertainty in his eyes.

'There will be a reward for the recovery of the jewellery,' Malik pointed out.

Tojak gave a laugh. 'They would let Calowski get the reward?'

'Sure,' Malik said. 'If he helps them get what they want, and they will want to recover the jewellery. He'll come to no harm from anybody else.' He looked pointedly at Tojak. 'Will he, Tojak?'

'He'll come to no harm,' Tojak agreed. 'You sure know a thing or two, Malik.' Again he laughed.

Calowski looked at the grave where Klaus lay. For the first time, Malik could read his thoughts. He could see him going back over the past months. He could see Calowski and Klaus making their plans. He could see them scheming together. Klaus eager, laughing, confident. Calowski cautious, uncertain. He could see them in the Legion, and he could see Klaus becoming sullen, depressed and finally suspicious and unbalanced. It had all gone wrong for Klaus. It was all over.

Calowski turned away from the shallow grave.

'We hurry,' he said. 'We must help the others.' He looked at Tojak. 'You need help, Tojak?'

'Not me,' Tojak said, 'but if I do I'll come to you, Calowski.'

They moved off. Tojak trailing his left leg; Malik with his shoulder bandaged and Calowski with an easy confident gait. He was no longer the watcher — the thinker. He had become another Calowski. He even turned to Malik and smiled. Malik smiled back at him. And so did Tojak.

Chapter Thirty-four

A reconnaissance unit of the French Foreign Legion had extended the limits of its patrol, when they had heard the sound of rifle fire, and entered the South pass. They had met Svenson with the women and children and been able to help them. They had gone to the assistance of Ducan and his men, but the fighting was over before they had cleared the pass. However, they were able to help bring Ducan and his men quickly into French territory, where two troop-carrying helicopters and one small reconnaissance helicopter were waiting to transport them to Djibouti, the capital of the territory.

The two troop-carrying helicopters quickly flew away with Ducan's party. Only Luker remained behind. He had been ordered, by the Legion officer in charge of the reconnaissance operation, to speak to a senior Government official over the radio. The official was Marcel Poujet. Luker's conversation with him was in private, but as a result of their talk, the Legion officer was given orders that Luker was to return with the pilot of the reconnaissance helicopter to where the Legionnaires Thompson and Verdi had been killed and bury them. The pilot of the helicopter had been previously briefed by Poujet to accept, without question, any mission that might be ordered of him. Poujet had prepared for any eventuality.

It was much later in the day when Luker arrived at the Legion's Garrison Camp in Djibouti. If the other members of the party had any curiosity about his actions, they made no reference to it. Malik and Tojak were in the hospital being treated for their wounds; Svenson was content to rest and recuperate; Calowski had agreed to join the company of Chief Inspector Renau and was not seen again by the other members of the party, and the Sergeant-Chief's concern was not with Luker's actions, but with the welfare of Lieutenant Ducan, whose condition had deteriorated with the effects of the blazing sun.

Ducan had drifted into a state of semi-unconsciousness before the fighting had finished. The move into the South pass and the flight to Djibouti were part of a series of blurred visions that kept appearing and disappearing before his eyes like a recurring nightmare. He also saw the faces of Michelle with her deep, brown eyes filled with concern; the rough, sandy bearded face of the Sergeant-Chief and other strange white masked faces. They all came and went in a parade of visions that had no meaning and seemed to be endless. But they had an ending, and he finally awoke to the smell of anaesthetic and the feeling of being rigidly fastened to a bed. He opened his eyes and saw a white ceiling. At the same instant, he felt the touch of soft flesh in his left hand. He turned his eyes away from the ceiling. They saw a glass screen, a white coated doctor — and Michelle. His eyes met Michelle's and he gripped her hand. She smiled and her eyes became moist and full of tenderness. He felt a flood of emotions and a surge of relief.

'I thought I might not see you again,' he whispered.

'I will not leave you, Simon,' she said.

He closed his eyes. 'Now I will get well, very quickly.'

He opened his eyes again. Michelle was sitting on the edge of the bed, watching him and smiling. She moved her eyes fractionally. He followed their movement and saw the Sergeant-Chief standing at the other side of his bed. The Chief was a *sous-officier* of the Legion again — clean shaven, smart and formidable. His features cracked into a smile. Ducan moved to lift his right arm to shake the Sergeant-Chief's hand, but he was too weak to lift his arm. He could only move his hand. The Sergeant-Chief saw the action and moved to the bed and placed the Lieutenant's hand in his own. Their handshake was firm and friendly.

In the corridor, outside the Lieutenant's bedroom, Poujet wiped the perspiration from his brow and turned away from watching the tender scene. He was joined by the doctor who had thought that his presence in the room had become unnecessary.

'Would you like to talk to the Lieutenant, Monsieur?' the doctor asked.

Poujet shook his head and walked away from the room. 'Perhaps some other time,' he said. 'I do not think my presence would be appreciated at the moment. Besides, I have a plane to catch.'

The doctor smiled. 'I understand.'

He walked with Poujet to the hospital exit where a military car and driver was waiting to take Poujet to the French Air Force Base. Several hours later, Poujet arrived at another Air Force Base close to Paris. Raphael was waiting for him. Poujet looked tired and weary from his flight, and his suit was more crumpled than usual, but Raphael quickly sensed a feeling of contentment in Poujet's manner. He sat alongside Raphael in the car, as Raphael drove him away from the base without talking and noticed the faintest of smiles remaining on Poujet's lips.

But there were matters that had to be talked about, and once on the open road Poujet asked about their Fox.

'He is safely in our lair, I presume?'

'He is, Monsieur. He is safely in our lair and very relieved indeed to be there — and very grateful.'

'You have spoken to him?'

'I have, Monsieur, and he has told me what took place.'

Poujet nodded his head in approval. '*Bien*,' he said. 'Pascal did well — very well.'

Raphael looked at him. 'I thought, perhaps, Monsieur, that Pascal would have returned to France with you.'

Poujet quickly scotched the very idea of such a move.

'Pascal is Legionnaire Luker,' he said, 'and as such he must play out the charade to the very end.'

'But I thought, Monsieur, that they were not legionnaires any longer.'

'Technically that is so,' Poujet agreed, 'but the formalities and the honours must be respected.'

'So when will he return, Monsieur?'

'First the Legion will honour the men who were killed in action, as well as those who survived, in a public ceremony in Djibouti. After that, the party will return to the Legion's Headquarters in Aubagne — both the fit and the wounded. In Aubagne, they will be invited to re-enlist and sign their papers again. Those that do not wish to do so will be quickly and secretly transported elsewhere and allowed to slip into the shadows.'

'Will any of them re-enlist, Monsieur?'

'Oh, yes. Two of them — Malik and Tojak — have already stated that it is their intention to do so. They have both found something that fulfils them in the Legion. And, of course, there is the Sergeant-Chief.'

'But not Svenson, Calowski or Luker.'

Poujet smiled. 'Svenson will return to his controllers a much fitter and wiser man. Calowski has already returned to France, and Pascal will slip back into the bedchamber of his lover.'

Raphael sighed and shook his head sadly.

'I fear not, Monsieur,' he said. 'I am told that Madame Cantois has found a new lover. A rather handsome and successful tennis player.'

'Bah!' Poujet dismissed the remark. 'A tennis player will be no match for Pascal. Pascal is so fit and virile. He is a Legionnaire. He has endured many perils. A tennis player will be no match for Pascal. You will see. He will get what he wants.'

'And what about Lieutenant Ducan, Monsieur? What of him?'

'Ah! Lieutenant Ducan.'

Poujet's smile broadened and he turned his lazy eye towards his companion.

'I think the Lieutenant has found what he has been looking for, for a long time. He has found a very beautiful and warm hearted woman who truly loves him, and also he has earned the respect of a very good friend. There is a good career for the Lieutenant in the Army, a very good career. He is a very fortunate young man, but he has earned his rewards.' Poujet nodded his head. 'Yes, he has earned them.'

'Is it the French girl, Monsieur?'

'Yes, the French girl. She is very beautiful. She reminds me of…' Poujet shook his head and let the matter drop.

'Perhaps of Madame Poujet when she was younger?' Raphael suggested.

Poujet turned to face Raphael again. The suggestion appeared to have pleased him.

'Thank you, Raphael, it was very nice of you to make the suggestion.'

Poujet looked away. Raphael thought that they might lapse into silence again so quickly asked, 'And everyone believes that Thompson is dead, Monsieur?'

'Yes,' Poujet said. 'Yes. Those that know otherwise, and there are very few, are well aware of the consequences if they ever talk out of turn. The officers who flew him to France were handpicked because they could be trusted.'

'Also the helicopter pilot?'

'Especially the helicopter pilot! I did not know what had taken place, or what would be needed, until I had spoken to Luker, but I reasoned that if Luker had uncovered the identity of our Fox I might have to bring the Fox out alone. I had to be very selective with the helicopter pilot. However, the pilot can certainly be trusted. He is a distant relative of mine.'

Raphael looked at him in surprise. 'A distant relative, Monsieur?'

Poujet was looking out of his window.

'Well, very distant,' he said, 'but there is a connection.'

Raphael thought that it would be diplomatic not to pursue the connection.

'And the Russians will now release our man, Bichante?'

Poujet looked thoughtful and then solemnly nodded his head.

'In time,' he said, 'in time. They will play it their way. They will ask questions about how Visinsky was killed and they will make their own enquiries. They will also try to make political advantage out of the release, but eventually our man will be returned to us. I fear that there will be no publicity — nothing that *Monsieur le Président* will be able to make capital gain out of, but it will take place.'

'Pascal did well to outsmart their man, Verdi. I cannot understand why Verdi had not made a move sooner.'

'Ah, yes, but Visinsky put on a very convincing act during his days at Corte. He had also managed to partially change his facial appearance in Marseilles before joining the Legion. His training all those years at the Rostov Academy paid off. He really did become Thompson, the brash, cheeky, young Englishman. Perhaps even Verdi was in doubt about him. Perhaps that is why he delayed. He had to be certain.'

'It was very close for Visinsky.'

'Too close,' Poujet agreed. 'When Visinsky realised that he had given himself away, he took fright for the first time since his defection. Verdi had tricked him into making a slip.'

'So I understand from my conversation with our Fox. Fortunately, Pascal was able to outsmart Verdi.'

'Yes he did,' Poujet agreed, with a look of satisfaction on his face. 'Of course, I was able to pass a coded message to Pascal through the good offices of my relative.'

'Captain Moutoner?'

'Yes. Through the Captain, I was able to tell Pascal about Verdi.'

'And did you also ask the Captain to send the Sergeant-Chief to assist Lieutenant Ducan?' Raphael asked.

Poujet shook his head. 'Good gracious me! No!' Again he shook his head. 'That was out of my province. I do believe that the Sergeant-Chief volunteered because of his regard for *Monsieur Le Lieutenant.*'

'But I understood, Monsieur, that the two men did not exactly see eye to eye.'

Poujet gave a shrug of his shoulders and made a facial gesture that could mean anything. Raphael took it to mean that Poujet didn't know the full facts about the affair.

'That might have been so, but I believe that there was, nevertheless, respect for each other.' Poujet didn't wish to pursue the matter. He changed the subject. 'You also talked with Chief Inspector Renau when he returned with Calowski. Was he pleased with the outcome of his trip?'

'Very pleased, Monsieur. I do believe that Calowski has been very cooperative, to such an extent that the Chief Inspector intends to forget Calowski's past record and even help him obtain some of the reward money.'

Poujet looked surprised.

'He must have been very pleased indeed,' he mumbled.

'Yes,' Raphael went on. 'He told me about the case.'

Poujet was not particularly interested in police matters, but out of politeness to his assistant he raised an enquiring eyebrow.

'It appears that Klaus was not the original ring leader,' Raphael explained. 'Klaus was a small time confidence trickster looking for a big break. He teamed up with Calowski on the Riviera. Calowski was operating a small smuggling ring with a contact in North Africa. He was friendly with Beauchamp — or Baron as he became known in the Legion. Baron was employed by the drugs syndicate as a courier. He and Calowski were close friends and had worked together, although Calowski had never become involved with drugs. Calowski and Klaus met an Italian called Garcini. This was not by chance. Garcini had been on the lookout for somebody to help him relieve his employer, Signor Bassito, of some very valuable jewellery. Klaus and Calowski were the ideal partners for Garcini. Klaus had the good looks and charm to work on Signor Bassito's mistress — a girl called Gena — who knew all about her lover's business and secrets, and Calowski had the contacts for disposing of the jewellery, and Baron was prepared to help them. The three men went into business immediately. Gena fell for Klaus' charms and was able to find out all that they wanted to know about the location of the jewellery. It was to be a big catch, so they agreed to hide the jewellery and remain undercover for at least six months before making any move.'

Poujet knew what had occurred through his own talks with the Chief Inspector.

'I understand that Garcini was shot dead by one of the guards,' he said, 'and Calowski and Klaus came to Marseilles by boat.'

'Correct, Monsieur,' Raphael agreed. 'Baron gave them cover and protection, but the syndicate who were behind Signor Bassito put the pressure on their contacts in Marseilles and offered big money for the identity and whereabouts of Garcini's accomplices. Signor Bassito also offered his own reward. Baron could not protect them any longer, and his own position had become dangerous as he had been operating against the syndicate. So they all took refuge in the Legion, and the legionnaire called Ferelli, who was after any reward that was available, followed suit. He had picked up their trail in Marseilles and followed it into the Legion.'

'I suppose Gena lost her nerve and contacted the police,' Poujet suggested.

'The police made the first move, Monsieur, but she had become very nervous. The syndicate were threatening Signor Bassito and they had also visited Gena on several occasions. When the police offered her protection, she became cooperative.'

Poujet shook his head sadly.

'It would appear, Raphael, that we picked some very strange companions for Pascal to travel with.'

'We did indeed, Monsieur. I do believe that Tojak and Malik, for instance…'

Poujet held up his hand and shook his head. 'Please,' he said. 'No more. They are not our concern.' He sat back in his seat in a relaxed pose and closed his eyes. Robbery, smuggling and drug syndicates were unsavoury matters that soon tired him.

'What about the American girl, Mademoiselle Jackson-Lang?' Raphael asked.

Poujet opened his eyes. 'Ah!' he said. 'Mademoiselle Jackson-Lang.' She was somebody who didn't tire him. She was somebody he was prepared to talk about. 'A most remarkable woman,' he said. 'Mademoiselle Jackson-Lang is a very strong-willed and determined person. She had gone to Ethiopia to help the Princess and her children, and that is what she still intends to do. She would not be deterred. She has made up her mind. She intends to travel with the Princess and her children into Eritrea.'

'But, Monsieur! There could be another incident. There could be trouble.'

Poujet cast his lazy eye in Raphael's direction. 'There will always be trouble,' he said. 'Always incidents. That is why *Monsieur le Director* employs us.'

'Oh! *Monsieur le Director!*'

'He wishes to see me to discuss our success with the Fox?' Poujet asked.

'He wishes to see you, Monsieur, but not to discuss the Fox. He has another problem.'

'Another problem! There, what did I tell you? Always trouble, always problems.'

'Do you wish to return to your office tonight, Monsieur, and speak to *Monsieur le Director?*'

Poujet again cast his lazy eye in Raphael's direction and gave him a long, patient, paternal look.

'Not tonight, Raphael,' he said, 'not tonight. I think *Monsieur le Director* and his problem can wait until the morning.'

And tonight, Raphael thought, Poujet was going to enjoy his own thoughts about their Fox, and the company of Madame Poujet. Perhaps the French girl did remind Poujet of his wife when she had been younger. Perhaps she did.

A NOTE TO THE READER

If you have enjoyed the novel enough to leave a review on **Amazon** and **Goodreads**, then we would be truly grateful.

Sapere Books is an exciting new publisher of brilliant fiction and popular history.

To find out more about our latest releases and our monthly bargain books visit our website: **saperebooks.com**

Printed in Great Britain
by Amazon